UMBERLAND

Also by
WENDY SPINALE

EVERLAND

UMBERLAND

OZLAND

LOST BOY
(a prequel novella to *Everland*)

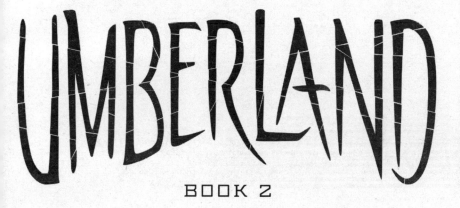

UMBERLAND

BOOK 2

WENDY SPINALE

SCHOLASTIC INC.

ISBN 978-0-545-95319-1

10 9 8 7 6 5 4 3 2 1   18 19 20 21 22

Printed in the U.S.A.   40
This edition first printing 2018

Book design by Christopher Stengel

To Gavin, Keaton, and Riley.

My life would be complete madness,

absolutely bonkers without you.

Thanks for being my favorite

Lost Boys.

· ALYSSA ·

The rancid scent of rotting flesh and the sound of distraught whimpers make my stomach turn. Controlling the urge to retch, I hum a lullaby as I sit near Bella's bed, made up of hay and old blankets, and administer another dose of painkillers. Her eyes flutter as she drifts into a haze. When the pixie-faced girl finally relaxes, I stand and stretch, working out the ache in my muscles. Gwen sits three beds over, her siblings, Mikey and Joanna, lying between us. They look so tiny tucked beneath their blankets. Having cried herself to sleep, Gwen's head rests on her forearm as she holds her mother's frail hand. The Professor, like Bella, is far worse than the others. Doc predicts it will be only a matter of days, if not hours, before we lose her to the disease. I feel a pang of sympathy as I think of watching my own parents die.

Daring a reluctant glance, my eyes scan the sea of people. Rows and rows of sick lie wailing on their beds, each in excruciating pain, their battle crueler than the day Captain Hanz Otto Oswald Kretschmer bombed London. There are so many, I'm not even sure where they've all come from. Alnwick Castle has become home for hundreds of refugees, some so sick they are beyond help. All I can do is keep them comfortable as their bodies blister and scab over . . . or die.

Bella, Gwen, and the Lost Boys arrived here only a few

months ago after narrowly escaping Captain Hook. With Hook dead, the Marauders no longer chase them, but I am not at all sure Alnwick Castle is any more of an improvement. Although the antidote has staved off death in some, the side effects are horrific. Guilt settles like a broken, jagged brick in my chest.

It was my decision to have those seeking refuge be treated with what I thought—what we all thought—was the cure. The temporary relief it brought was only an illusion.

Unable to look at the bedridden exiles any longer, I retreat to the doorway of the stables, our temporary infirmary, welcoming the chill of the early evening air. Horses no longer reside here. Instead the hay stalls have become beds to those who are sick. Others lie outside, bundled up in blankets between the guest hall and the clock tower.

I take a deep breath of fresh air as my eyes roam over the makeshift shanty homes that cover the outer courtyard of the castle grounds. What once were vibrant green grounds have become the foundation of a filthy refugee encampment. Fire pits built in old rubbish bins flicker, casting eerie shadows on the worn faces of those who gather around them. Though none are older than eighteen, nineteen at the most, the toll of death and disease has aged them years beyond their youth.

Shouts erupt, drawing my attention. A scrawny boy darts from a crowd and chases some sort of critter. Probably a rat since they outnumber us by the thousands, feasting on corpses that have yet to be disposed of far beyond the castle walls. The boy stumbles, regains his balance, and throws his coat over the rodent, successfully capturing it. It takes only moments before he is surrounded by the others and a fight ensues, fists and boots leaving their marks on the boy's emaciated body. Drunk on fermented grains and potatoes, it is only the first of many brawls that will erupt this cool evening. With food scarce, the meager morsel would satisfy someone's hunger, at least for tonight. But in the melee, the rat manages to escape, dashing into the white rose bushes that line the castle walls. Somehow the rodents still flourish while we wither and rot. With a final kick to the boy's gut, the others leave and return to their fire pits. Wincing, I turn away. I know how this will end. Only the biggest and strongest survive.

Bella cries out. Rushing back to her side, I whisper soothing words in her ear until she quiets. Even in sleep, her face is etched with pain. It's the same expression I've seen time and time again, urging me to do something more than just sit idly by and watch those who have come to me for aid suffer. With so many dead or missing, the Queen of England has executive decree, but even she is too sick to rule. She's barely conscious these days. And with her younger sister not interested in stepping up, there's just me.

The rumble of disgruntled voices rises from outside, only this time my name is tossed about in harsh, angry tones. My guards, most of whom are former Lost Boys, shout warnings to stand down. Although they are skilled fighters, having battled the Bloodred Queen's men, they are young nonetheless, and the refugees outnumber them ten to one. I snatch my sword and sheathe it in the scabbard on my hip. Wrapping my cerulean cloak around me, I pull up the hood over my head and race through the shadows of the shantytown's outskirts toward the castle, careful not to be seen. With guards busy quelling the commotion, I slip through the castle doors.

Just inside, I am greeted by Pete and Lily. They are armed and their expressions filled with worry.

"I've never seen them this hostile," Lily says.

"Me either. I need to get this under control now, before someone gets killed," I say.

"With all due respect, Your Grace, I think you should let the Lost Boys handle this," Pete says.

"I appreciate your concern, but this crowd is too much for them to handle on their own."

Pete's mouth opens as if he wants to protest, but instead he simply nods.

The hint of burning oak fills the air, casting a ghostly haze over the inner bailey. I try to calm my nerves before stepping back through the doors into the courtyard. When I do, all I can see are homes built of cardboard, scrap wood, and rusted metal stretching from within the inner castle grounds to beyond the stone walls. The structures threaten to topple the first time a severe storm hits. Scuffles have ensued between the rioters and the Lost Kids.

"Your attention," I say, projecting my voice as much as possible.

It takes a few moments, but soon the fights have died out and all eyes are on me.

"Your anger and frustration are warranted, that much I won't deny. You were promised refuge here, and instead you continue to suffer from hunger and illness. But, as in the past, I implore to you to remain calm and peaceful while we figure out ways to help you."

Rage-filled eyes glare at me. Armed with torches, sticks, and fistfuls of stones, the gathering of refugees holler obscenities. I will myself not to flee into the safety of the castle.

Out of the corner of my eye, I see that Lily and Pete now flank either side of me, their shoulders rolled back and weapons in hand—a reminder that there are those who will still fight for England's royal family. Lily's black-and-gold sari and Pete's dark green coattails whip in the wind as they stand their ground. Many have stepped up, filling in the vacancies the Queen's guard left behind as they succumbed to the Horologia virus. The sight of the exiles' gaunt faces weighs heavy on me. The all-too-familiar sunken cheeks and hollow eyes don't look too different from those who bravely try to maintain peace in spite of their growing hunger and weakening conditions.

As the crowd continues to shout, I hold up my white-gloved hands, which hide evidence of my own sickness. I try to quell the air of frustration, but any attempt to assure them that I'm doing everything within my power to help falls on deaf ears.

"What kind of duchess are you that you do nothing while your people die?" yells a boy, gripping a fiery torch. "You have failed us. You have failed those who have come to Alnwick seeking your help. You ought to be held responsible for your crimes."

"We need a cure!" screams another boy, shaking a blistered and bloody fist in the air.

"There is no cure. I assure you I have people working around the clock seeking a new solution. Until then, we will continue to treat the symptoms as best we can. I ask for your continued patience."

The irate throng erupts in allegations, accusing me of atrocious crimes.

"Lies!" a boy yells. A rock flies by my head and strikes the stone wall behind me. I'm shaken but unharmed.

Pete steps in front of me, pointing his daggers at the crowd. "Enough!"

Lily stands shoulder to shoulder with him, her sword drawn as a hushed murmur falls over the group. "Duchess Alyssa is doing everything she can to find you, to find all of us, the cure," she says. "So unless you are here to offer your assistance, go back to your shelters or you will be arrested."

The shouting of discontentment begins again. Lily takes me by the elbow and is leading me away when someone shouts, "Duchess Alyssa, just where do you think you're going?"

The outskirts of the horde part as someone trudges forward with an air of boldness. Katt, the Queen of England's kid sister, holds an ungloved hand up, quelling the grumbling boys. As if under her spell, the refugees grow quiet. Finally, she grins with perfectly painted lips, a stark contrast to her white corset, lacy skirts, fishnet leggings, and white boots. Just a year younger than her sister, she is now as opposite from the Queen as night is from day. Even sick, the Queen possesses a grace and kindness that Katt once had. But with all that has happened to their former home of London, Katt's charming demeanor has bloomed into an icy bitterness.

She glares at me. I'm certain it is because, although she is the princess and rightful heir to the crown, she will never take the throne as long as I can help it. With the United Kingdom in chaos, very few trust those in power and I trust her even less. By aligning with the Poison Garden's caretaker and condoning his offer for assisted suicide of the sick, she has forfeited her right to the crown, not by law but by sheer betrayal.

I step forward, ready to face whatever Katt has to hurl at me, whether it be stones or harsh words. Lily flashes me a worried glance, but I give her a nod, letting her know that I can hold my own.

"Princess Katt, you look well. Have you come back to denounce your alliance with Maddox Hadder?" I ask.

"Hardly," she sneers.

Taking a breath in, I stand a little taller. "Unless you cut your ties with him you are no longer welcome here."

"Turn on the only person, the only means that has helped these people? No thank you. These people don't want to be placated with false hopes and promises of a future that will never exist. They are dying! *We* are dying. What is needed is someone to stand by them while they take their last breath, hold their hand when the pain is too much. I am where I need to be, with and among my people. Not holed up in some castle, pretending to know what I'm doing," Katt says, gesturing to the crowd. "*This* is where I belong. This is what a real queen does."

The group with her roars in solidarity.

Katt points a clawlike finger at Pete. "And you, Pete, this is equally your fault. No, perhaps it's actually *all* your fault. You brought us the antidote. We were coping just fine here in Northumberland. Then you showed up with your miracle cure, and now we're all as good as dead."

Pete frowns. Her accusations are unfair and I know they slice him to bits, each allegation like a newly sharpened knife to his heart. He already blames himself for the predicament we're in. It's a burden too large for any one person to bear. The added accusation must devastate him.

With the help of medications being sent by the Professor, Northumberland and its residents were managing, but when Pete arrived with a cure, the Queen jumped on the opportunity to help everyone in spite of the Professor's warning that it needed further testing. We had no idea that the positive results would only be a temporary relief of what was yet to come.

"But since you haven't found the cure, as rightful heir to the crown I have no other choice but to find it elsewhere," Katt declares in a singsong voice.

"Between the Professor's research and Doc's knowledge of the virus, *we* have the best chance of creating the cure. Who else could possibly help you?" I demand. And even though I don't trust her, my heart beats wildly at the small hope that Katt might actually know of an antidote, or at least someone who can create it. However, if she truly did, she would have saved herself months ago.

"I have my resources," she says airily. "You've had plenty of time to fix this and still, kids are dying daily. Since you can't save us, I've found someone else who can."

"Who?" I ask.

As if on cue, music booms in the distance on the southeastern horizon. Beyond the shantytown, torchlight flickers like fireflies. Of the many gardens that once adorned Alnwick's grounds, the only one to survive is the Poison Garden.

With a wave of her hand and a swish of her skirt, Katt turns toward the music. "Come. Maddox calls," she says. "I'll be back, Duchess Alyssa, and next time I won't be kind. So figure something out."

Katt leads the group down a cobblestone walkway and through the southern gates of the stone barbican. A few, too intoxicated to notice the group's departure, linger, continuing to cast insults at me. I can hardly breathe knowing that I have lost the trust of Princess Katt and someone else has gained it. Someone who may not have the survivors' best interests in mind.

· PETE ·

As we return to Duchess Alyssa's sleeping quarters, I study her, knowing she is fiercely loyal and protective of her people. To be accused of anything otherwise must cut deep. Worry glazes her bright blue eyes.

Lily stands by protectively, exhibiting the same fierceness she has for those she rescued from Everland. She gives me a quick glance, but her eyes lack the spark they had when I first met her. The hint of hope we held on to when we left the ruins of London has diminished. Safety, family, home—promises neither of us could keep.

"Any news from Germany?" Lily asks.

"No, and it isn't like the Bloodred Queen not to gloat about her triumphs," the duchess says, going back into the castle and heading up the stairs to her chambers.

"Perhaps she doesn't know yet," I say, following, Lily on my heels. "With Hook and Jack dead and the Marauders' fleet of zeppelins destroyed, it's possible she doesn't have all the details about what happened in Everland."

Inside her chambers, Alyssa removes her cloak and tosses it on the bed with a defeated sigh. Just as Lily steps into the room, there's a loud crash, and stones hit two of the windows. We shield our faces as one shatters the pane, raining shards on us.

Gabs, one of the youngest Lost Boys, peeks through a crack

inside the duchess's wardrobe. He must have taken shelter in there when the mob became hostile. "Oh boy. Oh boy. Oh boy. Are they ever mad at you guys. I've never seen anyone so angry. Well, except for that one time when Snot saved up two months' worth of his boogers, dyed the whole thing red with beet juice, and offered it up as bubble gum. Those Lost Boys were so angry then. I thought Pyro was going to blow a gasket and . . ."

His lip quivers and silence hangs heavy in the room. It's been two months since Pyro was lost to Hook's crocodiles in Everland's sewers. The deep bruise left on my heart, on all of our hearts, has yet to heal. I lost a friend, a brother, that day and since then, I've lost many more to the virus.

Trying to lighten up the mood, I ruffle his fine, dark hair. "That booger gum would've been better if he'd mixed it with earthworm guts, right?"

He gives me a crooked grin that quickly disappears as another stone flies into the room. Gabs squeals, yanking shut the wardrobe door.

"They're becoming more hostile by the day," Duchess Alyssa says, peering through the broken window. "I don't know how much longer we can appease them with promises. At some point it won't be enough."

My stomach knots as I recognize fear in her expression. She's a symbol of strength and solidarity for her people, unwavering in the face of trouble, even as they revolt. Yet now, although she tries to hide it, she trembles. None of the others notice, but it's the first sign of weakness I've seen in her. If she's worried, we should be terrified.

"I can't say I blame them," Lily says, joining her at the window. She flinches as something foul splatters on the frame. "Things are no better here than where they came from. It's everyone for themselves."

Shouts continue to erupt from outside the castle walls, many of them the very same kids Lily rescued from the streets of Everland, kids that Alyssa took in. A few are the very Lost Boys I saved as London burned.

"This is your fault, Pete," someone screams from the courtyard. Something else explodes on a window frame. "Come face us, you coward!"

I wince.

Coward. The word encompasses everything I am not, or at least what I've fought so hard not to be. But there is truth in their accusation. Maybe I still am the frightened orphan child who couldn't save his parents. The one who couldn't help his sister when she succumbed to the virus. Fear is a weakness, a costly one, and there's no place for that in this new world we live in.

The room grows quiet as all their eyes fall on me. They long for assurances that things will work out, promises that we will survive these troubled times. Promises I can't make. I tried once before. I thought I had found a way to help the orphaned and sick, the way I couldn't help Gabrielle. I became a leader, but here I am nothing more than a survivor myself. Suddenly, I miss the Lost City and what we built there.

Placing a hand on Alyssa's shoulder, I feel her shake beneath my touch.

The lies are bitter even before I say them. "Everything will be okay, Your Grace. Doc will fix this. If anyone can find a new cure, it's him. It's only a matter of time," I assure her, attempting to sound confident, but I have my own doubts. Because the clock is ticking and we're running out of time.

Although Doc is one of the smartest Lost Boys I know, odds are, even he can't perform this miracle. He was a prodigy child interning at the local hospital at the age of sixteen, and I always seem to expect more from him. Solutions. Answers. A cure. But he's disappointed me in the past—my sister's death, Bella's condition—so I don't know why I assure anyone that he'll be of help. And with the Professor getting worse, she's unable to help either.

"We can't just stand by and do nothing," Alyssa says sternly. "They're becoming sicker every day. These symptoms are entirely different since we've administered the antidote."

"Yeah, like they're becoming wild beasties or something with those crazy hands and feet, and all that growling they do. Well, not they, just that Katt girl, but then again she's always been kind of on the grumpy side since I've known her, so maybe that's not a new thing," Gabs's muffled voice says from inside the wardrobe. "Hard to believe she's a princess of any sort. But this sure is way different from the other sickness they had."

"Not entirely different," Doc says, storming into the room. The sight of him makes my blood crash in my ears. Each lifeless body is a reminder that our days are numbered and there is nothing I can do about it. But Doc can. However, time and time again, he's let me down, and seeing him makes the frustration almost too much.

Lily, on the other hand, gives him a weak smile. The virus has taken its toll on her as well. Before, her flirtatious demeanor and vibrant energy were infectious. Enough so that even Doc, whose nose was always in a medical textbook, took notice. Since then, they've grown close over the last few months. How close, I'm not sure. Doc, having once courted my sister, is careful not to show any public displays of affection in front of me.

Doc opens a spiral notebook on the table and thumbs through the worn pages. He stops on one filled with crude annotations, drawings, and graphs. "I was going over the Professor's notes again and found some things I missed in my initial studies.

"We're not getting anywhere with the antidote I created. And I can't figure out how it changed. So I decided to go back to the original disease, thinking that maybe there's something I missed. The Professor identified all the same components of the illness that I did, most of which are easily attainable. However, there is one component she's notated only as pwazon pòm. It's taken me nearly a week, but I think I figured out what that is," Doc says, breathless. He looks up from the notebook.

"What is it?" I ask, the tone of my voice hard. Bella would be by my side, not lying sick in the infirmary, had Doc figured this out long ago. Her absence feels as if I'm missing something important.

Doc shakes his head, and despair etches his expression. "The base property is, believe or not, an apple."

"An apple?" It sounds so stupid, so trivial. An apple is what's ending the world? "You're telling me all this time . . . all this time the missing component to the cure was a simple apple?"

Alyssa touches my arm, her stare warning me to control my anger. I swallow my frustration and combat my short fuse the only way I know how—by throwing barbs at Doc.

"The missing ingredient isn't some cosmic mineral or the saliva of a rare insect or something else obscure? An apple is what eluded the smartest Lost Boy we have?" I ask sarcastically.

"I'm afraid so," Doc says, dropping his gaze.

Lily's eyes meet mine, and she frowns disapprovingly.

The wardrobe door bursts open, and Gabs leaps out, bouncing on his tiny toes. "Oh! I like apples! Red ones and yellow ones and green ones and purple ones and blue ones . . ."

"Gabs, you hate apples," I say, eager to stop the lengthy discussion before it starts.

His nose wrinkles. "Oh, that's right! Apples are icky! Blah! Thanks for the reminder."

I turn my attention back to Doc. "Tell me about this apple."

"The pwazon pòm loosely translated means 'poison apple.' It was a tree indigenous to the tropics, but because of how toxic the fruit was to humans, it was destroyed. Completely eradicated," Doc says.

"Toxic?" the duchess asks.

"The juice alone can leave scalding burns," Doc says.

"That explains the blisters," Lily says, rubbing two gloved fingers together.

"One bite of the apple and you'll be unconscious within minutes. Turning it into an inhalant, like what was done with the Horologia virus when it went airborne, is more lethal than eating it because it paralyzes the lungs, killing the victims almost instantly. It's especially deadly in high doses. That's why so many died quickly when the virus was released. Without the apple, I don't think I can create the antidote."

Gabs's face pales, and he scoots back inside the wardrobe. "Now I know I wouldn't like those kind of apples, not one bit. I might even be deathly 'llergic to them. In fact, I'm sure of it."

"How can a poisonous apple help create a cure?" I ask.

"Think of it like a vaccine. Usually the solution contains a weakened or killed form of the microbe. The body recognizes the organism as a threat and destroys it, but creates antibodies in the event that it encounters the same disease. Vaccines are given to prevent illness. Antidotes work the same way only *after* the patient has been infected, particularly when dealing with poisons. When I created the cure for the Horologia outbreak, I treated it as just that: a disease. But what I missed was that it wasn't a disease at all. We were poisoned," Doc says.

"Poisoned?" Lily says, peering at her gloved hands.

Duchess Alyssa's face pales beneath the fading sunlight. "So the cure was not a cure at all? Just something to help relieve the symptoms?" she asks.

"More like a paper bandage on a lopped-off limb," I say bitterly.

Doc's expression darkens as he narrows his eyes at me. Ignoring my remark, he continues, "I believe the lizard protein helped stanch the effects for a short time, but ultimately, we're not dealing with a virus or bacteria at all. What we have here is mass poisoning. Imagine an airborne arsenic created to target the adults, but that inadvertently leaves the children with a slower die-off."

"So you think this apple is the key to the cure?" Lily asks.

Thoughts spin wildly in my mind. *Poisoned?*

Doc grimaces and nods. "Yes. We need the original ingredient to create the antidote. But, unfortunately, the tree no longer exists. I'm afraid there isn't much more I can do." He slams a fist on the table. "What I wouldn't give to get my hands on the doses that the Professor made!"

"Please don't do that," Gabs whimpers from behind the rattling wardrobe doors. "I'm scared enough as it is. Everyone is always so angry. Those kids outside are angry, Pete's angry, Doc's angry. If growing up means yelling and pounding on stuff and throwing stuff, I think I'll just stay a Little forever and ever and ever."

Doc opens the wardrobe door enough to peer inside. "Sorry, Gabs."

"It's all right," Gabs whispers. "Although you might want to practice some deep breathing or counting backward from ten or something. My mum used to say that I was going to give myself a cornenary when I threw a temper tantrum when I was littler than a Little. And I don't know what a cornenary is, but it sounds pretty bad and I don't like corn all that much. It might have even been worse than those apples you were talking about."

"Wait, I thought you said the injections Gwen's mother gave were vaccines?" I ask.

"When she described them as injections given over a period of time, I had assumed they were vaccines. The reality is that the Professor was giving Gwen and her siblings small doses of the poison in order to make them immune in the event that Germany ever attacked. Smart woman," Doc says. A look of admiration crosses his face for a second before it slips away. "The bad news is that Gwen and her siblings have developed some resistance to the poison, but total immunity comes with continuous exposure over years. And Gwen's antibodies were helpful to those who were given the cure in the short term, but the only real solution is the antidote itself. I still need the apple"—he presses his lips together—"to fix what I did."

Poisons. Antidotes. The cure. Thoughts scramble in my head.

Another stone sails through the window, knocking more glass from the frame. Gabs pulls the wardrobe door shut again. "Son of a pollywog, what's wrong with those crazies?!" he says.

Fed up with the violence and betrayal of the refugees, fury courses through me. I pick up the rock, ready to hurl it back out the window, when Lily lightly touches my arm. "Let it go, Pete."

"What's wrong, Lost Boy? You letting a girl tell you how to be a man?" a boy shouts up at me.

Lily's face flushes. She pushes me aside and leans out the window. "This girl is just about done with you bloody nitwits. If the bunch of you keep it up, I'll have no other choice but to come down there and show you how much of a girl I really am when I kick you in your trousers."

The boys erupt in a cacophony of cackles and insults, fueling my growing anger. Sometimes you just want to fight back, even if these boys aren't actually the enemy. Driven to rage, Lily snatches the rock from my hand, takes aim at my ridiculers, but I grip her wrist tightly.

"Don't bother," I say quietly.

Her breath is quick as shock brings her back to reality.

Neither of us has ever intentionally hurt anyone, not unless we were fighting for our lives or the life of another. But simple mockery from a few inebriated kids has reduced us both to the uncontrollable need to retaliate.

"Thank you," she whispers, dropping the stone. "Are you okay?" she asks, giving my hand a squeeze.

Pain shoots up my fingers, and I wrench my hand back. Through my leather gloves I feel two small blisters on my finger burst and blood gush from the wounds. Lily frowns. Although my symptoms are not new, I've done my best to hide them from everyone else, but not well enough.

I ball my hand into a fist, despite the pain. "Gwen doesn't know. She can't know. Do you all understand me?"

Alyssa, Lily, and Doc exchange apprehensive glances but nod.

Furious, I kick the stone, sending it sliding across the floor, and scream, angry at the world we live in.

"I don't know about you all, but I'm scardier than a big ol' fraidycat. You all can come join me in here if you want," Gabs says, peeking from the cracked door. The bottom of an ivory lace petticoat cloaks his head of dark hair. "I'll make room if you want, but you ought to leave those outside. You're liable to poke an eye out or something," he says, gesturing toward Lily's and Alyssa's swords.

"I think we'll be okay, but thank you," Lily says, smiling sadly. I'm sure she's thinking what I'm thinking: Gabs reminds us all of the innocent kids we've lost. Her gold chain belt jingles as she shifts, turning her attention back toward the crowd outside the window. Her mood has grown darker since we arrived in Northumberland. She's always given off an air of fierceness, but this is different. Hostile. Some days, more often than not, I can relate, especially when I visit Bella.

I bite the inside of my cheek, to keep from showing any hint of the anger bubbling within me. Bella. My Bella, who was alone and frightened when I found her after the bombs. I took care of her as if she were my own sister. She was cured when we arrived here. Better than she had been in over a year, and now . . . My jaw clenches, the muscles in my neck tightening like thick ropes.

"What about the lizard protein?" Duchess Alyssa asks to break the tension. "How does that come into play?"

Doc shuts the notebook and sighs. "What these people are suffering from is no longer the Horologia. By adding the lizard protein it's become an entirely different beast and is even more contagious. Their only hope is that apple and an antidote."

"This is your fault!" I shout as I lunge toward Doc, but Lily stands between us, her hand gripping tightly on the hilt of her sword as if warning me to stand down. I don't let it stop me. "Now not only are they poisoned, but they're also suffering from what you said was the cure."

"Pete!" Alyssa says with warning.

Reluctantly, I stand down.

Again the wardrobe rattles. "Okay, now you guys are really, really, really scaring me. Stop with the shouting and slamming and banging or I'm never gonna come out," Gabs says.

"So what is the solution?" Lily asks impatiently.

Doc sighs. "I've created a binding agent that will attach to the lizard protein. If I could re-create the original toxin with this nonexistent apple and the binding agent, I could develop a true antidote. As of now, no one is safe from this new illness, and judging by how rapidly it's accelerating, we'll all be infected soon."

My pulse races. His news isn't good.

"Are you saying everyone is going to die?" Duchess Alyssa asks, panic evident in her voice. Her face pales.

Doc drops his head but doesn't answer.

"What about Gwen?" I ask. "She was immune to the Horologia virus or disease or whatever it was . . . is. She must be immune to this one, too."

Not meeting my gaze, Doc shakes his head.

Fury pulses inside, thrumming in my veins. Close behind it, I feel desperation. I grab Doc by the shirt and shake him. "How could you let this happen? What have you done? And now Gwen, too?"

Gabs whimpers within the wardrobe.

"Pete, stop it!" Lily says, trying to pry my hands from Doc. Finally, he shoves me hard. I nearly stumble over a chair.

Doc's blue eyes are daggers, ready to skewer me, but I don't care.

"Do you think I did this on purpose? Everyone, every single person, has been exposed, myself included, and I'm spending each blasted waking moment trying to find a way to fix it," he shouts defensively. "What more do you want from me?"

"Nothing! Nothing at all! You've made it worse!" I shout.

"Enough!" Alyssa says with an air of authority.

Doc and I exchange murderous glares.

Outside the music ratchets up a notch. Alyssa turns to the window, gazing far into the distance, seeming lost in thought. "If you had the apple, could you create the cure?" Alyssa asks.

"I could try," Doc says, running his hand through his hair. "At this point, it would be our only hope. But, like I said, the tree doesn't exist anymore."

The rhythmic sound of drums calls from the distance, and the duchess catches my gaze with a glint in her eye like none I've seen before. With each percussive beat my thoughts sift, until finally something, one single answer makes sense. I make the same connection that I believe the duchess has made. If by chance that apple does exist, there is only one person who would know where it can be found. I rush out the door, heading toward my quarters.

"Wait! Pete, where are you going?" Lily asks, chasing after me.

Inside my room, I start sorting through my weapons. Turning, I notice that everyone has followed me, including Gabs. They stare at me with curious expressions. Everyone except Alyssa.

"The Poison Garden," I say. "If anyone knows where to get this toxic apple, it's Maddox."

Duchess Alyssa's eyes narrow. "You do realize that those who enter the garden never return. Caretaker Maddox is not only the proprietor of the garden, but also a mercenary of death. You have no business going in there. None!" she says fiercely.

"That boy is bonkers," Gabs agrees, twirling a finger at the temple of his head. "He's totally lost his marbles, or at least what few he had to begin with. This one time I was peeking through the garden fence even though I knew I wasn't supposed to be over there because you told me to stay away from there, but I just told you the truth, so you can't give me latrine duty. Anyway, he was tossing tea saucers like they were flying disks and that's no joke. Cross my heart, pinkie swear that I'm telling the truth, the whole truth, so help me. And besides, I wouldn't lie about anything anyway because Yosef, the woodworker on my block, told me my nose would grow if I lied and that birds would use it as a perch and we all know what happens when birds perch." Gabs pokes his tongue and gives a raspberry.

"Duchess Alyssa is right," Lily says. "I'll go with you."

"Me too," Gabs says, rolling up his sleeves and making fists. "I'll give him a big old smack in his snot locker if he tries anything."

"Can you even reach his snot locker?" I say.

"You bet! I've been practicing my ninja moves." Gabs leaps in the air, swings a fist, and kicks wildly, knocking over an iron fire poker.

"No, I will go alone," Alyssa says sternly. "As I'm the duchess, Maddox might listen to me, but he won't take orders from a newly arrived stranger."

I'm about to retort with a snarky remark when a shrill scream slices through the dull rumble of the refugees outside the castle. I know that scream. Panicked, I race down the grand staircase. Two Lost Boys guard the castle doors. Pushing past them, I spin the wheeled lock, forcing the chain to grind against the gears. I shove the doors open and sprint out into the courtyard. From the makeshift infirmary in the stables, another scream pierces the chilly evening air. My face flushes, my heart skipping several beats. I bolt toward the rising wails of sorrow, pushing people out of my way, their faces blurring as I race past them.

Bursting through the stable doors, I find Gwen, the girl who stole my heart, sitting on the Professor's bed, her body laid across her mother's. The Professor's lips have a blue hue, and blood spills from the corner of her mouth. There is no rise or fall of the woman's chest. "Mum, don't leave me," Gwen cries. "Please come back. I need you."

In a nearby bed, Bella lies still, undisturbed by the commotion. Close by, Gwen's siblings, Joanna and Mikey, weep holding on to each other. Although extremely weak, they still manage to have enough energy to cry for their only parent. Their father was called to protect the Queen of England on the day the bombs dropped and never returned. Their mother was all they had left.

My legs fail me, and I collapse near Joanna and Mikey. I have no words of comfort. Joanna and Mikey crawl to me and bury their heads in my lap. As natural as it is to breathe, I pull them close, feeling as if I'm lost in a dream I'll never wake from. The Professor wasn't only a mother to Gwen, her sister, and her brother, but also to so many others: the children abducted by Hook and his Marauders, the Lost Boys, and in some ways—in every way—she's the only mother I've had since I lost my parents when I was just a kid. A hot tear slips down my cheek as I lose a mother for the second time.

· A L Y S S A ·

Drums beat wildly in the distance, the nightly party in the Poison Garden summoning those who wish to end their lives. They answer Maddox Hadder's call to spend one last evening giving in to indulgences before letting death take them.

After the Professor died, I insisted on seeking Maddox's help on my own. Leaving Pete in charge of the castle, I follow the rhythmic call. With Pete comforting Gwen, Lily looking after Joanna and Mikey, and Pickpocket and the rest of the Lost Boys standing guard, I know that those within the castle walls are in good hands. Gwen's obvious grief over the death of her mother makes me think of my own pain at discovering my parents' bodies. I try hard to push those thoughts away. I need to be strong now. Silently, I pass through the slums. Cries ring through the rickety city, mingling with the evening songs of bullfrogs and crickets. Zigzagging, I duck under clotheslines draped with dirty sheets, trip over garbage and broken bottles, and pass people sleeping in huts made of scraps. Many call after me, begging for water, food, and help as I pass by them, but I don't meet their gazes. Each glance into the pleading faces, eyes that reflect my failure as duchess, makes me feel as if I've fallen down a rabbit hole. Instead, I keep my face hidden beneath the hood of my cloak as I race into the night, chasing the beat of the booming drums.

Following the cobblestone walkway past the Alnwick Garden gates, I veer left, making my way to the only part of the grounds' gardens that are still being maintained by Caretaker Maddox. He seized control of the Poison Garden when the Horologia sickness spread, locking everyone out to create his own version of a sanctuary for only those who were the sickest. Not that there was anything in there at the time that anyone would want. Now they all beg for entrance, for relief of their symptoms . . . for a merciful death.

As I draw closer, the entrance buzzes with activity. Torches illuminate a dirt pathway, leading to a wrought-iron fence. Kerosene lanterns hooded by copper cylinders with odd shapes cut from them spin wildly, casting peculiar pictures in every direction: mushrooms, teapots, cakes, and bottles.

The skulls of those who have died in the garden hang like ornaments along the length of the enclosure. Adorned with machinery parts, the glitter of the torchlight reflects off their metallic grins. The entrance gate is marked with a skull-and-crossbones symbol and a dire warning: THESE PLANTS CAN KILL. Music rises into the evening sky, pulsing from somewhere in the middle of the garden. The bass rattles my bones. Above the entrance, Chester, a smiling copper cat, bobs his head to the tempo of the music. Hordes of people gather at the gate protected by a single guard.

Koh, one of the few left from the royal military and Katt's personal guard, watches over the surging pool of refugees. Armed with a scythe, he glowers at them, as if challenging them to give him a reason to take off their heads. The lamplight gives his thick leather-and-chain-mail armor a burnished glow. If the rumors are true, its red tint is not from rust, but rather the blood of those who have crossed him.

A boy in a dark cloak dashes from behind a shrub and toward the fence. He scales the elaborate loops and swirls of the black metal. But as his left hand grips the top, his scream is so fierce that I cover my ears. Flailing, he falls, striking the ground with a sickening thud. Others rush to his aid, but it's too late. There is very little left of his hand. Bloodied bones shrouded by hunks of burned flesh hang from the end of his arm. Koh shakes his head and snorts but doesn't bother to offer assistance. Even I knew of the acidic poisons glazed along the top of the fence.

This is not the first time I've watched someone attempt to climb the poisoned fence and seen their limbs become nothing but scraps of skin and bone. It won't be the last, at least not anytime soon. Still, my stomach turns. No one enters the garden without invitation and even then, it is no ordinary garden. Every single plant, shrub, tree, and flower in there will either make one as mad as a hatter or dead as a dormouse. Once you go through the gates, you don't come back.

The others now ignore the boy writhing on the ground, and fists start to fly as Koh grants someone else admission. Another boy rushes the entrance, but he is struck across the back of the head with the shaft of Koh's scythe. The boy crumples to the ground like a marionette. Partygoers swarm him, stealing everything they can get their hands on. Soon enough, his unconscious body lies in nothing but his ragged drawers. For as many times as I've seen this same scenario, I'm left horrified and sick to my stomach.

I scoot through the crowd, overwhelmed by the flashing lights and music. The salty smells of sweat and liquor sting my nose. Bodies press against one another, making it difficult to walk. Each person is in varying stages of the disease. Some still only have blisters on their fingers, while the limbs of others are covered in scaly-looking scabs.

A boy grabs my hand and pulls me into him. He stares at me with yellow irises set within crusty eyelids. Like a maniac, he twirls me, releasing me back into the mob of kids. I stumble, falling into the arms of a girl, one of the very few left and just a few years older than me. She licks her dark, scabbed lips. Repulsed, I pull away, bumping into another girl, who hisses. Hands paw me, tugging at my cloak. A scream catches in my throat. I pull my sword from its sheath. With wide-eyed alarm, the crowd backs up from me in a synchronized hush, but hooded as I am beneath my cloak, none seem to recognize me. By the disdain that flashes over their faces, I feel as if I've broken some unspoken rule.

"Duchess Alyssa, miss me already?" someone growls behind me.

Spinning, I turn toward the voice. As the crowd parts, Katt pushes open the iron gates. Koh steps to her side. Through his shaded aviator goggles I sense his glare.

"I'm here to see Maddox," I say, my voice rising above the music. My knuckles ache as I tighten my grip on my sword.

Katt leans up against the gate and crosses her arms, smiling at me smugly. Koh draws closer, his sharp scythe glowing in the torchlight. My breath quickens as I take a step back, keeping my sword between me and the hulking boy in front of me. Dozens of eyes bore into me.

"You ought to know by now that no one enters the garden unless Maddox Hadder says so," Katt says with a tilt of her head and a wide smile.

"As the Duchess of Northumberland it's my right to access the garden." I try to keep my tone reasonable, although I'm sure the effort is wasted on Katt.

"Unless you've come to tell us you've miraculously developed the cure, you aren't welcome here. Go back to the castle, Alyssa," Katt sneers.

"Alnwick is my jurisdiction, this garden included. You will grant me entrance or . . . "

"Or what? You'll infect me like you've done to my sister? Too late. Let me remind you, Duchess Alyssa, I am the next in line to take up the royal crown. I may not sleep in a castle, but it's still my kingdom. At any given point, all this power, this authority you seem to think you possess, can be gone in an instance," Katt says, snapping her fingers. "Consider yourself warned."

Narrowing my eyes, I point my sword at Katt. "Then find the cure yourself, or let me in."

Giving me an amused look, Katt reaches behind her and pulls her own sword from its scabbard. "You will have to get past me before you ever step foot inside," she says.

Chester, the warden of the garden and an incredibly annoying beast on a good day, especially for an animatronic, lifts his metal face toward the sky, filling the night air with mechanical laughter. He peers down at me from atop the gate's entrance. "Be gone, lest you desire to be beheaded," he says with a wave of his paw.

As if on cue, Koh aims his scythe in my direction.

Thinking of how many have already died, I swallow back my fear and dig my boots firmly into the damp grass. "I assure you, I am skilled with the sword. My father taught me well. With one swipe I'll take down your guard, incapacitate you, and just to be rid of that smarmy machine, I'll turn Chester into scrap metal. I'm sure the Tinkers can find something to do with his scraps."

Chester hisses.

Katt laughs wildly. "Now that is something I would pay to see."

The animatronic's eyes made of cogs spin crazily. His head twirls on his elongated neck. His attempt to appear vicious fails, drumming up laughter from all around.

"You bore me," Katt says with a wave of her hand. "You heard the cat: Off with her head."

The crowd roars as Koh strong-arms my sword from me and restrains my wrists.

"This is absurd, Katt," I shout, struggling in Koh's grip.

"Those pretty gold locks will be a nice addition to my collection," Chester says, waving a paw toward the rotting skulls.

I shudder, wondering what violation the owners of the skeletal remains made to deserve such a horrendous punishment.

Koh knocks my legs out from under me. He thrusts me to the ground and rips the hood of my cloak off my head. Grabbing a fistful of my hair, he shoves me so my cheek rests on a tree stump, its dark rings stained with what appears to be blood.

"If you want a cure, you'll let me meet with Maddox," I say desperately as I struggle beneath the soldier's grip.

Katt paces around the tree trunk, casually twirling her sword. "You can't fool me. If Maddox had access to the cure, don't you think he would've given it to us?"

"He doesn't know," I reply, still pinned.

"Shut up, girl," the guard says, shoving my head even harder onto the stump.

"What's wrong, Katt? You have to have your big, strong soldier to deal with me? Can't handle me on your own, can you?" I mock.

Katt laughs loudly. "Do you have a death wish, Duchess Alyssa?"

Panic and fury twist in my stomach. It's a very real possibility I might end up dead here. I push on, forcing bravado as I say, "And you, Chester. How easy is it for you to wave your rusty old paw and make demands? You can't fight your own battles either. That must be why everyone calls you 'Chester the fraidycat.'"

Koh twists his hand, causing me to bite back the urge to yelp in pain.

"I have information about the cure. Any chance to save yourselves will die with me," I say, refusing to give into the pain.

Katt circles the stump once more and then kneels so her dark eyes meet mine. "I'll tell you what, Duchess Alyssa. I hardly believe what you're saying is the truth, but I'll grant you the benefit of the doubt. Since you've dampened the lively mood with your intrusion, why don't we make a deal—a challenge of sorts. To get back in the spirit of things. Not a challenge of brawn, since you're such a scrawny little thing, but of wit. You against Chester, the most brilliant animatronic in all of Europe. If you win, you will be granted entrance into the garden."

"Deal," I say as Koh shoves my face harder into the tree stump.

"Let her up," Katt says.

Koh grumbles as he releases me.

Katt struts over to the collection of skulls clattering against the fence in the breeze and runs a gloved finger over the skull that hangs from the entrance. "If you lose, your head joins the rest of our unwelcome guests. Since you are royalty, I'll even give you prime real estate, the beloved entrance into the garden," she says, her ice-white teeth mocking me from her twisted smile.

Dusting the dirt from my cloak, I stand.

Katt sheathes her sword and places her hands on her hips. "Can you handle this, Chester?" she asks.

The cat yawns, a single paw covering his jowls. "A battle of wits? How childish. You forget that I am configured with the latest technology. With one sweep of my eyes I can assess the slightest variation in my opponent's core body temperature, sense changes in their trivial nuances, calculate the minor shift from one foot to the other. I can detect an enemy from a mile away. I accept the pitiful challenge."

"This will certainly be entertaining," Katt says. "Okay, then: a riddle. Chester gets first stab since I'm making up the rules."

I roll my eyes.

Katt paces for a moment, then stops as a devious grin spreads across her face. "Why is a raven like a writing desk?"

"Why is a raven like a writing desk?" Chester repeats, his wired brows creasing. His springlike neck contorts, spiraling toward me until his face meets mine, peering at me upside down. As his eyes study me, I keep my features still. I can't let him know that I know the answer. Chester's copper ears twitch before his neck retracts and he sneers at me.

Excitement blooms in my stomach. I know the answer. All those years of governesses and endless studies that might have left me lonely and friendless suddenly don't seem too terrible. They were supposed to prepare me for a good match to a proper family, but, turns out, they also prepared me for this.

"Well?" Katt says to Chester. "We're waiting."

"I haven't the slightest idea," he finally hisses. "Why *is* a raven like a writing desk?"

"Duchess," Katt says, scowling at the cat, "do you know the answer?"

"Because it can produce a few notes, though they are very flat; and it is nevar put with the wrong end in front," I crow triumphantly.

The crowd growls dangerously, and Katt looks startled that I got it right. Then she turns to Chester, shouting, "You daft pile of junk, you lost the challenge. When Maddox finds out, he's going to be a storm in a teacup. He'll likely melt you down and make a lovely copper kettle out of your noggin. Your whiskers will do just nicely as a plaited handle."

Chester's face glows red with heat that I assume is from the gears revving up within his metal skull. "Never! You're a trickster!" he jeers, retracting his head back onto his body before coming for me. "A tricky, tricky trickster!"

"A machine defeated by a girl," I sing as I march for the gates.

Koh leans against the gate, arms folded, glaring at me.

"Entrance granted!" Katt declares above the ruckus. "Let her through."

"No!" Chester howls.

The iron gates swing wide, allowing Katt to saunter in. Koh bows as she passes. "As you wish."

Protests continue to erupt as I trail behind her, stepping

through the grand entrance. My heart thumps against my ribs; my skin tingles with trepidation. Koh slams the gates hard. The fence shudders loudly behind me as I listen to tumblers of the lock click into place. Chester's head swings toward me, his face now on the wrong side of his body. He grins, exposing teeth made of bits of metal, before bursting into manic laughter. "Turn back, Duchess Alyssa," Chester calls. "Turn back before it's too late. You're mad to go in there. Absolutely bonkers!"

For a split second I reconsider, fear rising in my throat.

"Let's go," Katt says. "You belong to the garden now."

When I turn back toward her, she blows smoke in my face. It smells earthy, like sage. I cough and my vision blurs, stinging from the smoke. "Wait, what?" I ask in surprise.

"When you made your deal, you never said you wanted to be able to leave again—just get into the garden. And those that enter, well, you know . . . they don't leave," Katt says with cruel satisfaction.

Horror spreads across my face as I realize what I've done. There's no turning back now.

"Welcome to the Poison Garden, Your Grace," she purrs. "Make yourself comfortable. You'll be staying with us for quite some time."

· JACK ·

Charred and splintered boards poke from the hull of the zeppelin that sits beyond the Lohr Castle courtyard. It is what is left of the ship that I salvaged before escaping after the Lost Boys torched the entire fleet. Despite the massive damage, the zeppelin endured the long journey back to Germany. My stepbrother, Hook, and I barely got out of the fiery remains of Everland. We were on our queen's mission for world domination. However, with the city turned into an inferno and our fleet of zeppelins destroyed, it felt as if we were on the losing side of a war.

The irony is a hard slap across the cheek, since it was our bombs that began it all.

From the high tower of the castle, I watch crews repair what they can of the damaged zeppelin.

A cough pulls me from my thoughts and I turn around. My stepmother takes in a shallow, ragged breath. Her lips lack the painted garnet luster they normally have. Sitting at her vanity, she runs a brush through her long, ebony-colored hair. It used to fall like beautiful waves down her back, but now it's as sickly looking as the rest of her.

Since our return, her symptoms have grown worse. In fact, all the residents of Lohr are showing one sign of infection or another. London may have been her intended target, but devastation spread farther than anyone anticipated. While the adults of London died off quickly when the Horologia went airborne, their suffering was limited to weeks or even days. Those infected farther away from the epicenter of the outbreak have seen symptoms develop slower, their pain lingering longer. It's really only a matter of time, though. Soon we all will be in the same shape as the Bloodred Queen.

Indeed my stepbrother has been ill since our time in England. His left hand is covered in blisters and oozing sores that seem to be spreading up his arm. On our trip back, I, too, developed symptoms. I scratch at my hand through my gloves, though it provides little relief and seems to just exacerbate the pain.

Despite being sick, I'm still in better shape than Hook. His right arm is no longer flesh and bone. Instead it is constructed from metal cogs, washers, and gears, making him look more machine than human. A shiver runs up my spine as I shudder, recalling his horrified screams when Gwen Darling sliced off that arm, sending it and the antidote into a crocodile pit. Between being infected with the poison and the massive amounts of blood loss, it's a miracle he survived the long journey from Everland to Lohr Castle. Why I saved his life, I don't know. Especially after he made me a traitor to Pete and the Lost Boys and marked me with the Marauders brand. I touch the scarred flesh behind my ear, feeling the pucker of the seared mark.

Dozens of times I considered throwing him from the zeppelin into shark-infested waters. Maybe *that* would've been the merciful thing to do. It was what my father would have done, sparing him from any more suffering. Instead, I couldn't bring myself to do it, and now his death will be slow and painful. Karma's patient.

Hook joins me at the window and whispers behind his hand, "She's not well."

His breath smells of rum, a scent that has become a vile reminder of his cruelty toward me over the years.

"I can see that. What do you expect me to do?" I reply, uninterested in anything he has to say. Especially when he states the obvious. "You had the antidote in the palm of your hand and lost it."

Hook turns his single dark eye toward me, the other covered in a copper-adorned black eye patch.

"No pun intended," I add, shrugging. Unimpressed with his pathetic attempt to threaten me, I return my gaze to the broken zeppelin.

My brother's men are all dead or deserted after Everland. I am the only one left. But my loyalty is not to Hook nor my step-mother. The ones who desire my allegiance don't deserve it. The ones I'd sell my soul for, the Lost Boys, don't want it. I have no family to call my own.

The Bloodred Queen sets her brush down. Her reflection gives us a condescending frown. I once sought her approval, longing for a mother—any mother—after having lost my own at birth. When my father, the king of Germany, was assassinated by my stepmother, she was all the family I had left. In spite of my anger, I still longed for her acceptance. The alternative was to end up like my father, dead. And yet there was nothing I could do to earn her love. No deed could gain her respect. So I learned to take my beatings and survive, hoping she wouldn't find a reason to have me killed, too. Bitterness festered within me, and I could sympathize with the pain of loss the Lost Boys in Everland experienced.

There's only one thing worse than being an orphan: being an orphan with a stepmother who wants you dead.

A machinelike squawk pierces the unsettling silence. Renwyk, one of the Bloodred Queen's scouting ravens, flies through the window and lands on the vanity. Its dark metal head bows before it flaps its rusty metal wings. My stepmother snatches up the bird. She slides the metal pieces of the raven into a new interlocking pattern, and a small door suddenly pops open. Reaching in with bony fingers, she extracts a rolled-up bit of parchment. Something sinister spreads across her face as she reads it. She pulls a quill from an inkwell and scrawls a reply.

"Do you really believe that one vial was all they had? With so many depending on a cure, you know that wasn't the only antidote. In fact, according to Princess Katt, the Everland children along with many others have taken up refuge at Alnwick Castle in Northumberland," the Bloodred Queen says, tapping the animatronic raven knowingly.

"Fascinating," Hook says, rubbing the scruff on his chin. "We could infiltrate Alnwick and steal the antidote."

With the note now dry, the Bloodred Queen drops it back in the raven and clicks the pieces into place. "Idiot. You had your opportunity and you wasted it on chasing ghosts, Immunes. No, I have better plans for you. Forget the antidote."

Hook's brows crook in confusion, but he still smiles at the thought of his mother giving him some new task. Hook will never learn. He's just a pawn in some unwinnable game. The Bloodred Queen dismisses the bird. It caws and flies past me, out through the open window.

"That cure isn't the only option. If we can re-create the Horologia poison, we can also create an antidote," she says.

"Seems simple enough," Hook says. "Our laboratories did create it in the first place."

I can't help but say, "If it were that simple, we'd already have the antidote." I immediately regret drawing attention to myself.

"Clever boy," the queen says. "You've always been sharper than your brother."

Hook growls at the criticism. I sigh. "What do we need to remake it?" he asks.

I try to fade from the conversation. What I need is information. Clearly, I will never win my stepmother's favor, but perhaps with access to the ingredients for a new antidote, I can use it to my advantage.

"An apple," she says, turning her stare to Hook. He casts his gaze to the floor.

I feel a small bite of terror in the pit of my stomach. She can't mean . . .

"A poison apple," she says.

Hook reaches a hand to his eye patch, rubbing the three scars that disappear beneath it, as if by instinct. "But that tree no longer exists. You had the Forbidden Garden destroyed after I . . . after . . ."

As much as I dislike my stepbrother, I feel a pang of sympathy for him. That tree, it ruined everything good we ever had. We were once more than just family; we were the best of friends. He and I spent every waking hour together. But when my father was murdered, something broke between us. Loyalties divided us. Hook refused to believe his mother was behind my father's death, but I knew better. With my mother's passing, I was all my father had. He loved me more than anything in the world and told me so each night before bed. The Bloodred Queen wore her jealousy like a crown.

From what I remember, the tree was majestic, shimmering with an inner light of its own. Lush fruit glittered among the iridescent leaves. As boys we swung from its boughs, its branches cradling us. Encompassing a spirit of its own, it was like no other plant within the castle grounds.

How something so beautiful could cause such cruelty, I'll never understand.

Hook had just turned thirteen when he brought one of the shiny ripe fruits as a gift for his mother, and in return she left him blind in one eye. Her screams, his cry for help—they both burned a memory that caused nightmares. Not long after, the tree disappeared, its forbidden fruit lost, never to be seen again.

"Not gone. Guarded so no one can accidentally get it again," the Bloodred Queen says, glaring at Hook. "The tree thrives within a labyrinth deep within the Black Forest."

It takes a moment for her words to sink in. "Labyrinth? I thought those stories were lore," Hook says.

"Far from it," the Bloodred Queen replies. "There is truth in the whispered tales."

"I'll go." Determination is strong within his words.

Pressing her lips together, the queen turns away from her son, wincing as if the sight of him pains her. "The tree was never meant to be seen again. You will have to defeat the Labyrinth, and it is no ordinary maze." Her tone makes it evident she doesn't believe him worthy.

"I don't care. I'm not afraid," Hook says, anxiety in his voice.

"It is hardly a place for the weak," she says, stirring the cup of tea in front of her. "In the Labyrinth, bravery is fleeting and fear will kill."

The Bloodred Queen drops her gaze, seeming lost in her thoughts. After a few moments she nods and announces, "I think this job is suited for both you and Jack."

Surprised, I glance at my stepbrother. As the realization that I'm expected to join Hook on another task settles over him, a renewed flush of jealousy reddens his face. The muscles in his neck cord like thick ropes as he glowers.

I, however, am suspicious. Our journey to England and the release of the poison was no accident. We were given specific coordinates to bomb by the Bloodred Queen; she knew that the laboratory would be destroyed, but then opted not to share that information with my stepbrother or me. I don't think she has any intention of us both coming back this time. Although if she needs that apple, then she must expect at least one of us to return.

Hook never wanted me along on the Everland mission, and to have to share the journey of the Labyrinth with me must be eating him up. The Bloodred Queen is pitting us against each other; she always has. It's a game I'm loath to play, but unless I intend to be the one left for dead, I'll have to come up with some plan. I certainly can't come home to Lohr after this. My stepmother will surely kill me once she has the apple—she has been working up to that for years—and it'd be too dangerous to actually let her get her hands on it. But perhaps I can use Hook's company to my advantage.

"Go to the Labyrinth and bring back the apple," she says, peering at both of us. She picks up a white handkerchief from her table and dabs at her nose. When she's done, she holds it up. The cloth is dotted with bloodstains. "Time is running out."

·PETE·

Sitting in a window seat surrounded by plush pillows, Gwen's silhouette is lit under the bright moon's glow. With her forehead pressed against the glass of the slightly opened window, she stares into the night, the luminous Milky Way painted on the galaxy beyond her profile.

Hesitantly, I walk into the room, not wanting to upset her any further. Shoving my hands in my pockets, I quietly approach.

"Are you wishing on a star?" I ask. The comment feels insensitive, but I don't know what else to say.

Her teary gaze meets mine as she gives me a sad smile. She returns her attention to the millions of stars that sparkle in the evening sky.

"You should be resting. It's been a long day," I say.

Gwen shrugs. "I can't sleep. Too many things on my mind."

"Would you like to share?" I ask.

She whips her head toward me. "Do you know what they did with my mum? She was discarded with the others. No ceremony. No funeral. Nothing! It's as if she meant nothing to them!" Gwen says furiously.

Even with the number of people dying off, it feels wrong not to mourn the Professor. So . . . impersonal. Unceremonious for a woman who meant so much to so many of us. She deserved more. We deserved the chance to say our good-byes, but with how rapidly the disease has spread, we can't take the risk. Those in charge of disposing the dead followed protocol.

She returns her gaze to the window. "And do you want to know what I'm angriest about? The fact that Joanna, Mikey, and I had already grieved her loss and now we're doing it all over again. We would have been better off if we never found her. We had already buried her in our hearts. This just feels too cruel."

I settle next to her at the window seat, placing a hand on her leg. I wish I knew what to say. The truth is, her pain is familiar. All I can rasp out is, "Gwen." I clear my throat to try again, but she draws her legs into her chest, letting my hand slip from her. Wrapping her arms around her knees, she stares at me, as if searching for lost words of her own. We sit in silence, not touching. There are no words that can bring comfort.

"Do you believe in heaven?" she finally asks.

"Heaven? As in that?" I ask, pointing to the sparkling sky.

She tilts her head. "No, you know what I mean."

My gut twists as I consider my response. I've asked the very same question again and again, having lost my entire family. While I hope that such a place exists, the bitterness of being alone, orphaned with no one to count on but myself, burns deep in my blood. But this is not the occasion to divulge my hopes or doubts.

Scooting in close to Gwen, I lean over to take in the vast sky twinkling with iridescent stars. I pick a lone star that seems separate from the others. Unique in its own right.

"See that cluster of stars?" I say. "The ones just to the left of the Big Dipper?"

"Yes," Gwen says, squinting to take in its glow.

"That is the constellation Cassiopeia. The lower right, that is my sister. And those two over there, they are my mum and pop," I say, pointing to two adjacent stars. Leaning back on the wall, I take in a breath of the cool evening air. "They watch over me."

Gwen gives me a skeptical look.

"What? You don't believe me?" I nudge her with an elbow, hoping to lighten the mood.

She turns her eyes back to the sky.

"Gwen, what if this life we live is just a glimpse? A blink of what lies beyond?"

She rolls her eyes. "You're going spiritual on me?"

Shaking my head, heat burns my cheeks. "It's not that at all. When I lost my parents and then Gabrielle, I was more than a lost boy, I was a lost soul. Everything I loved, everything I cared for was ripped . . . stolen from my life. Grief fed into anger, anger to bitterness, bitterness to resentment, resentment to misery. The day Gabrielle died, I stood in the belfry of St. Paul's Cathedral, ready to give up on it all. Ready to give up on myself."

Gwen brings a hand to her mouth, gasping. "I'm so sorry, Pete," she says in almost a whisper.

Shaking my head, I brush off her empathy. I can't talk much more about how broken I was. I won't go back to that place. The pain is too much. Her kind words force me to push it all deep down. I can't look at her. I won't let her see the shame in my eyes as I admit my moment of weakness, when there was nothing left in this world that mattered to me.

"London was destroyed, the streets littered with corpses. I was alone. What was there to live for? As I started to step off the ledge, the sky erupted into a sea of shooting stars. So numerous there were too many to count. It was as if in that one instant every lost life, every soul, lit up the sky. I've never seen the stars shine so brightly. You know what I decided that night, Gwen?"

She watches me, pain etching the corners of her eyes. She shakes her head.

"I realized that life never truly ends. How can it? How can good, kind people just cease to exist? Our bodies may wither away, but our souls don't. Have you ever looked into the eyes of a dying person? Even though their body fails them, the sparkle in their eyes is more vibrant than the brightest star." I jut a finger toward the sky. "Your mum is *not* gone; she's taken a different place in the universe."

Gwen's eyes shimmer with unshed tears. An ache festers in my chest. I hate seeing her upset, especially when it feels like there is nothing I can do to ease her pain.

"She's there with my mum and pop. With Gabrielle," I say. "See that star there? That's the constellation Libra, and that star is Justice. And over there, that's Pyro."

I turn my gaze back to Gwen's eyes. "They're always with us."

Tears finally stream down her cheeks, and I brush them away with my thumb.

"You're never alone. Not as long as the stars still shine," I say.

Gwen closes her eyes as she leans in. Her hand cups one side of my face as she presses her lips against my cheek, as if I'm just another Lost Kid. It surprises me. Her breath is quick. Hot with tears, her cheek brushes up against mine. I reach for her hand, but when I intertwine my fingers with hers, she shakes me off. Gwen snatches a pillow and pulls it into her chest, holding it tightly.

My stomach knots; I'm unsure if I've done something to upset her. Did I share too much telling her about the belfry?

"Could you check in on the infirmary for me?" she asks, scooting farther away, although she can't move much closer to the window.

"Lily's there. She's keeping an eye on Joanna and Mikey. They were almost asleep when I was in the infirmary last," I say, eyeing her.

Another tear slips down her cheek. In the short time I've known her, she's never been one who let others see her cry. And it's clear she's trying to hold them in, but I can hear her small gasps of breath. I'm alarmed at seeing so many tears, but I understand. Her mother is dead. For real this time. Gwen's an orphan for the second time.

After Hook and his men destroyed London, everything that defined her childhood was stripped away: her parents, her school, her friends. Leaving her responsible for her siblings.

There was no time for tears. And now . . . now she's grasping at frayed strings of the life she once knew. Desperate to keep some semblance of it together.

"I should be with them," she says, furiously wiping away her tears. She buries her head in her arms, sobbing through hiccups. "I should be comforting them. I'm all they have left."

A recognizable pain tugs at my heart. *I'm all they have left.* Those words are all too familiar to me. The weight is too much for anyone to carry, much less anyone who is still a few years from being an adult herself. But it is the same responsibility I placed upon myself with the Lost Kids . . . with Gabrielle.

"Gwen, you lost your mum, too. You have every right to grieve," I say, reaching for her again. I squeeze her hand in comfort, but she winces and wrenches it away.

"What's wrong?" I say, alarmed.

Another tear runs down her cheek, but I know this time it's not brought on by heartbreak. Folding in on herself, she balls her fists as her face pinches. She shakes her head, as if that would bring some relief to the discomfort she must feel.

"Let me see your hands," I say, dread growing in me.

Reluctantly, she offers me her hand, and I peel back the gloves she started wearing since working in the infirmary. Blisters cover the tips of her fingers. My chest caves, my heart sinking into the hollow of my gut. When I look back at her face, she averts her watery eyes, unwilling to meet mine.

"How is this even possible?" she asks, the tone of her voice pleading for answers. "I was the one who received the vaccinations. I'm *supposed* to be immune."

Gently, I take her hand and kiss the top of it. As my lips brush against her skin, my breath hitches.

"You're not immune, not to this," I whisper, afraid that once I say it aloud it will be real, and I can't accept that. I can't lose Gwen. My heart clenches. Sighing, I reluctantly release her hand. "Doc said that everyone is at risk, including you. I was sure he was wrong. But whatever he did to make the cure, it's made it a bigger mess. Everyone will be sick soon." I quickly explain what he told us earlier.

She stares at me with disbelief, shaking her head as if refusing to accept my words. "That's not right. That's not how this works. I'm meant to be the one who saves everyone."

"I know," I say sadly.

Suddenly, she looks up as something occurs to her. "What about you?" she demands.

"What about me?" I reply. But I know. I know what she's asking.

"Pete," she says, a warning in her voice. "Let me see your hands."

"Gwen, I'm fine." I keep my hands in my lap.

She shakes her head and grabs at my hands. I struggle, trying to pull away, but she's worked free one of the gloves. The blisters on my fingers match hers. She shoots me a look I've never seen on her face before: sheer terror. I'm unsure what to say.

She covers her mouth as she chokes back her cry.

"Look, don't worry about it. I'm fine," I say, reaching for her.

"Please just go away," she says, turning her attention back to the stars.

"Wait, Gwen," I say, trying to bring her into my arms.

She pulls away. "Go, Pete," she whispers between sobs.

My chest feels as if dozens of daggers pierce it. I stand, shove my hands back into my coat pockets, and take my time crossing her room. I stop at the door but don't turn around.

"I love you, Gwen. We're going to be okay. Doc will find a cure," I say.

I wait, half expecting her to respond, but she doesn't. It's the first time since we arrived in Northumberland that she hasn't told me she loves me, too. Her silence is far worse than her rejection. I glance over my shoulder, wondering if I should go back to her. Her eyes are fixed on the very stars that I promised were guiding her to safety, hope, and her next adventure. Stars that have betrayed her . . . and me.

· A L Y S S A ·

Torchlight casts dancing shadows on the cobblestone walkway as we venture deeper into the garden. Unlike the stench of rot that brews within the shantytown, the air here is filled with the overwhelming fragrance of flowers and forbidden fruit. Brightly colored toadstools dot the garden grounds. Pink trumpet flowers, purple foxglove, and brilliant red poppies grow in bunches on either side of the path. Shrubs filled with dark nightshade berries spill onto the walkway, desperately needing to be pruned. Katt pays no attention to them, her boots squishing their juice and leaving purple stains on the stone.

The scent of sage trails behind her as she leads me down a network of pathways. I toss a look over my shoulder, wondering if I'd even be able to find my way back to the entrance, since tall trees provide a dense canopy.

Breathless, I take in the sights. Regret catches in my throat as I realize I haven't visited the garden in years. Too consumed with my duties as the duchess, I never had time, or at least I thought I didn't have the time, for a walk through Alnwick's historic Poison Garden.

An exquisite turquoise-and-orange frog leaps from a box-wood shrub. Worried that it'll become like one of the crushed nightshade berries, I lean over to pick it up.

Katt glances over her shoulder and calls, "Tsk, tsk. Keep

your hands to yourself. Even the critters in the Poison Garden are deadly."

I'm not sure what surprises me most: that out of kindness I nearly killed myself, or that Katt stopped me, at least this time. *Silly, silly, Alyssa,* I think, chastising myself. I'll need to keep my wits about me here. I watch the frog leap across the pathway and into a small pond.

"Stick to the path. Keep your hands, feet, nose, and whatever other body parts you have left to yourself," she says, continuing on. Trails of smoke billow behind her like gray phantoms.

As we move closer to the garden's center, the music booms louder, the beat of drums pulsating in my bones, muscles, and chest. Finally, we reach a vast clearing, and it's like I've stepped into a masquerade ball. People everywhere, dancing recklessly. A five-member band plays on a raised stage. Dressed in black coats and top hats adorned with copper buttons and buckles, they play their makeshift instruments made up of scrap metal, wire, and other gadgets. The drum set consists of overturned rubbish bins and dented pot lids. The band members' eyes are lined in coal-black makeup, as are their lips.

We work our way through the crowd. I am jostled among the guests. They stare at me with dilated eyes, pupils so small I can hardly see them. Some have teeth and lips stained black, reminding me of juice stains left from the deadly nightshade. Despite the chill in the air, they perspire heavily, tainting the heady smell of flowers with the stench of body odor. Katt passes through the throng with ease, unfazed by the smells and pawing hands.

We reach two tables filled with refreshments. Handwoven grass cloths drape both tables. One contains brightly decorated cakes and biscuits. The other table contains chrome teacups filled with a steaming dark brown liquid. With a sly smile, Katt offers me a cup.

"Tea?" she asks brightly.

Hesitantly, I take it, and breathe in the fragrant scent of floral blossoms. Chamomile, I think, but I'm not certain. Others around us down the liquid in their own cups, laughing and seeming entirely fine. Perhaps this is a test of sorts from Katt.

As I tip the cup toward my lips to try just a small sip, a hand grips my shoulder and whirls me around, nearly spilling the hot liquid on me.

"I wouldn't drink that if I were you, lovie. Opium tea doesn't seem like your poison of choice," the boy in front of me says. The cup is taken from my hand and tossed over my shoulder, where it clatters against something metal behind me. A bronze embellished teacup is thrust into my hand. This time the liquid is clear and fragrance free.

"Try this. You'll thank me later."

My gaze darts from the cup to the boy. He is breathtaking. Black makeup lines his eyes, which are so gold they are as bright as polished coins. His beard is neatly trimmed, shaved close to his warm brown face. A burgundy coat with black lapels hugs his tall, muscular body tightly. Copper buttons adorn the cuffs of his sleeves, collar, and down the front of his coat. Thick bronze aviator goggles rest on the lip of his black top hat, covering a burgundy sash. I feel myself falter.

The boy reaches for the brim of his hat and tilts his head in a bow. "Welcome to the Poison Garden. Maddox Hadder, at your service, Your Grace." He exchanges a glance with Katt. "Seems even royalty can't resist the pleasure my garden brings, but who am I to judge?"

My breath catches before I regain my composure. The music, the refreshments, the purpose of this gathering . . . It stirs a moment of doubt within me and I regret not bringing help.

I've heard rumors about the boy before me, but we have never met, at least not in person. Passing glances across the castle grounds was all that was afforded to me. Mingling with the laborers was frowned upon by my parents. Maddox was the garden's caretaker, one of many whose job it was to keep the castle and its grounds running smoothly. That is, until madness struck and I no longer had time to be concerned about trivial tales of the boy who shut the garden gates, claiming the land as his own. Now this garden *is* his home, and I am not welcome here.

"How do you do?" I say with a slight bow of my head. The ghostly voices of my parents chastise me for showing honor to a commoner such as him. However, their words no longer hold weight in my decisions. It's a new world of chaos, and old social hierarchy has no place here.

"How do I do what?" he asks, his brow creasing. He rubs the closely shaven scruff on his chin with his thumb and index finger, seeming confused.

"I . . . I mean, how are you today?" I say, stumbling through my response.

"Well, it's hardly daytime anymore, so your question is irrelevant. That is, unless you want to know how my day *was*, which I assure you is definitely not a story you'd like to hear. Perhaps asking me how I am this evening would be a better question," he says.

"How are you this evening?" I ask, before finally noticing the devilish gleam in his eye. I feel like I've walked into a cat-and-mouse conversation and I'm the mouse.

"What an absurd question to ask. We're all doomed to die, me included. How do you think I am doing this evening? Drink up!" he says with a wave of his hand toward my cup.

"What is it?" I ask, swirling the contents suspiciously, dizzy with our conversation.

He gives me a crooked smile. "Water, of course," he says, before racing up a set of steps two at a time that leads to a bizarre-looking throne. Its crooked frame leans to the right before curving back to center, giving it an odd S shape. Intricate carvings scrawl across its cherrywood armrests and seat back. Burgundy leather covers the cushion and the back of the chair. Each leg varies in length, making the chair wobble as he drops into it. He leans against one armrest and throws a leg over the other. Katt grins cheekily and leans on the chair, tracing a finger along his sinewy arm.

"So, what brings you to my garden of sin? You hardly look sick enough to procure my services," Maddox says, gently brushing the lavender petals of a low-hanging wisteria vine from the enormous plant that serves as a canopy over his seat.

I think of the sores growing along my hands and feet, slowly climbing my limbs, but say nothing. I've told no one how far it's been spreading—I'll not confess to these two.

"I'd wager that the duchess has finally come to the conclusion that we're all as good as dead and she's coming to you for assistance," Katt says smugly.

Narrowing my gaze, I lock eyes with her. She isn't the Katt I once knew, who was carefree and lovely. This Katt, this is someone entirely different, whom I hardly recognize. I set my teacup down on the table before I climb the first two steps. Katt wields her sword and steps in front of Maddox, blocking my view of him.

"No one approaches Maddox unless invited to do so," Katt says with a growl. Slowly, I retreat, my fingers grazing the hilt of my own sword. Katt returns to her spot, and she begins to file her long fingernails. They look more like claws, thick and chiseled down into sharp points. Suddenly, I miss the girl I used to have tea parties with. Giggling and eating tiny cakes together while pretending to be ladies of the high court. Or dreaming up pranks to play on her older sister. Judging by the flaky skin on Katt's hands, she is well into the middle stage of the disease. Like those who surround me, she, too, will eventually succumb to the poison.

"It's true, I've come seeking your help," I say, forcing my voice to sound humble.

Maddox leaps from his chair, removes his top hat, and bows. "How can I be of assistance, Your Grace?"

I hesitate, surprised by his eagerness to help. It's my fault his garden is full of dying people. He himself is probably dying, too.

Rolling my shoulders back, I remind myself of my title. While I am only sixteen, I still must give the air of authority even though I am no less frightened than everyone else. "The Horologia illness is not what we were seeing in the early days after the bombing of London. With the introduction of the antidote, we believe that it has become something altogether different."

"Yes, yes, get on with it," Maddox says with a wave of his hand.

Startled, I clear my throat and continue. "Although those affected are living longer, the side effects are . . . " I don't finish my sentence. Struck mute by Katt's piercing glare, I take another step back.

"Are what, Your Grace?" she sneers, holding up her flaky, scabbed hand. "Worse than death? These people," she says, gesturing to the partygoers, "my sister, your Queen, are dying. Meanwhile, you're hiding behind stuffy stone walls playing royalty, waiting for some child prodigy and a dying professor to come up with a solution. We need real answers, not empty promises." Katt hurls her dagger at my feet.

Maddox places a hand on her shoulder. "Katt, go take a smoke break."

Reluctantly, she trudges over and retrieves her knife. She

bumps my shoulder hard as she passes by, nearly knocking me down. Katt joins the crowd dancing in the center of the garden. She takes a puff from the hookah and a sensuous smile grows on her face. She sways to the music, seeming oblivious to the kids around her. My heart feels as if it's being ripped apart as I watch my childhood friend become a shadow of the girl she once was.

Maddox takes my elbow and gently leads me up the stairs. "Let her go. She'll be fine."

"Why won't she just come back and take the crown? It belongs to her anyway," I say, sitting on a stool that Maddox pulls up for me.

"And do what, Your Grace? How will being the Queen of England help any of these people?" Maddox asks, resettling into his elaborate seat.

Several responses come to mind, but he's absolutely right. There is nothing more that she could do as the Queen. Perhaps being with the people, offering them companionship, an ear, joy—even if it's only for a fleeting moment—is more merciful than vigilantly seeking a cure. I glance back at Katt, her arms lifted in the air as she dances to the beat of a rhythmic song in the middle of sick but smiling people.

"They seem content, even happy," I say, taken in by the expressions on their faces.

"Don't let them fool you. We're all losing it here. I'm mad. You're mad. They're all mad." His gold gaze scans the crowd before it meets mine.

"How do you know I'm mad?" I ask, hiding my gloved hands behind my back.

"You must be," says Maddox; his brow creases as if I've asked the silliest of questions. "Why else would you risk entering the Poison Garden? You know very well why my guests come. These people, this is their last night. The last time they'll smile, partake of good food and drink, console one another . . . breathe. By morning they'll all be dead, and tomorrow's guests' entrance fee is a simple one: to help dispose of the bodies."

Maddox nods to the large bonfire in the center of the dance floor. I hadn't noticed it before, but what I once thought were tree stumps and large sections of wood aren't anything of the sort. Instead, blackened bodies lean against one another, serving as the tinder for the huge fire roaring into the night sky. Horrified, I clasp my mouth, biting back the urge to vomit as I tear my gaze from the pile of burning corpses. Pressing too hard, a sharp pain rockets through my index finger and up my arm. When I pull my hand back, a crimson stain blossoms on my white glove.

I've never been sick enough to seek Maddox's help, but for how much longer? Eventually, we'll all just be tinder for the bonfire. With the Professor gone, there is no hope for a temporary remedy to keep us all going like she provided when she was the gatekeeper for those sick kids exiting Everland. She's the only one who kept any of us alive with her treatments. When she died, we all signed our own death certificates. What's left? We're destined to become ghosts of our former selves. Maddox is right.

Soon enough, we'll all go mad unless something is done. Unless I get the apple and Doc can create the cure.

"When did they lose hope?" I ask, a wave of despair washing over me.

"Probably when the pain started, when the transformation began," Maddox says. He tugs at the fingertips of his glove, gracefully removing it. The limb he holds in front of me is not a hand at all. It's not even human. Scales weeping with an oil-like liquid cover what should be his skin. His fingers extend out, long and adorned with razor-like claws protruding from each finger.

Gasping in horror, I bolt from my seat. Realizing I never should have come this far beyond the gates of the garden, I stumble down the stairs, tripping over the last step. I land face-first in the dirt. When I lift my head, the eyes of dozens of kids watch me, cackling at my mishap.

Scrambling to my feet, I run as fast as I can toward the entrance. His voice chases me, as if he's merely a few steps away. When I peer over my shoulder, there is no one there.

I dash down numerous paths, lost.

After several long moments, I find myself at a small clearing with a simple bench. The copper armrests are green with patina, making the bench blend in with the rest of the foliage. I sit, looking for a moment of peace, trying to catch my breath. The swift beat of my heart collides with the pulse of the garden's drums. I glance toward the empty road I've just come from. Maddox is nowhere in sight, and his voice is nothing but a whisper in the breeze.

"Where are you running off to?" Maddox asks in my ear.

Jumping to my feet, I whirl toward his voice, drawing my sword and aiming at the boy who sits calmly on the bench. While I am winded, he acts as if he's been waiting here all along for me, one arm thrown over the back of the bench and legs casually crossed.

"You didn't even thank me for my hospitality," he says, and leans toward me. "I repeat: What is it you want from me, Your Grace? Why have you come to my garden?"

As his gold eyes fix on mine, my insides tremble. Instinct implores me to run again, but I can't. I need his help. I have to get what I've come for: information on the poison apple.

"There might be a way to find a cure," I say, hope lightening my voice.

His gaze darts toward mine and he sits a little straighter. "Is that so? And what does this have to do with me?"

Taking in a breath, I sheathe my sword. "The Professor, she was the one who identified the disease and was working on a cure before she died. Her notes indicate that she was missing a single ingredient to produce the cure for the Horologia virus." I shake my head. "No, not a virus. A poison."

"It's a poison? Very interesting. And just what might that ingredient be?" Maddox asks, rubbing the scruff of his chin thoughtfully.

"An apple," I say, watching for his reaction.

The corners of Maddox's mouth tip in a knowing smile.

"You know of it?" I ask.

Maddox smirks before he stands and heads down the path, leaving me alone on the bench. Surprised by his abrupt departure, I chase after him, doubling my pace in order to keep in step with his long strides.

"Wait! What about the apple? Is it here in the garden?" I ask.

"The apple you're speaking of does not exist in this garden," he says. "In fact, no one has seen that apple tree in quite some time."

Feeling as though I've been punched in the gut, I stop, unable to move. Every ounce of optimism washes away, and I feel the heavy weight of defeat crumble over me.

"However, I do know where such an apple resides," he adds.

Hope bubbles within me, and for the first time in over a year, my despair lifts just ever so slightly. "You do? Where is it?"

"Nowhere a young duchess such as you would ever venture." He winks.

Rushing over to him, I grip the lapels of his coat with both hands. "Take me there! Take me there now!" I insist.

Maddox gently removes my hands, straightens his coat, and folds his arms. "The journey is much too dangerous for a girl like you. At best, you'll find yourself in a pool of your own tears. At worst, you'll be dead by morning. There is nothing I can do for you." Then he shoves me aside, heading toward the sound of music.

My body stiffens. "A girl like me? What's that supposed to mean?"

"You shouldn't have come, Your Grace," he says with a note of actual regret in his voice.

"I'm not afraid!" I shout.

Maddox continues walking, appearing unmoved by my persistence.

"Maddox Hadder, people are dying from this disease. They've come to me for help. If I have to drown in my own tears to help, I will cry a billion worthless tears to ensure their survival."

Maddox stops but doesn't face me. He balls his hands into tight fists.

"You will help me or you will hang for treason," I bluff.

After a few moments he turns and marches up to me, stopping within centimeters of my face. He pauses, saying nothing as he studies me. Although fear wells up in me, I stare into his gold, inhuman eyes, unblinking. "I don't take kindly to death threats, Your Grace."

Shuddering, I hold my ground.

"However, I admire your boldness," he says. He reaches into his coat pockets. Opening his hands, he reveals a small green bottle with a label that says DRINK ME in one hand, and in the other sits a bite-size cake with the words EAT ME iced elegantly across the top.

"To retrieve the apple, you will face your greatest

will meet demons you never knew existed. You cower in your pretty little boots just standing here next to me, but this is nothing compared to the horrors you will face," he says.

My cheeks flush. Is my fear that obvious?

"You have a choice. Take a sip of the bottle and this encounter, this visit to the Poison Garden, will shrink away, and you'll have no memory of being here, no memory of the possibility that the apple exists. You'll wake up back in Alnwick Castle." Maddox holds up the cake. "Eat the cake and you'll fall into a brief slumber. When you wake, your dangerous journey begins, and there's no turning back."

A brief slumber? I'm not all that sure that I want to be unconscious under his care. Uneasy, my eyes dart from the bottle to the cake. I don't want to take either one of them, even if one is a way out of this wild garden. In spite of my attempted display of courage, I'm terrified.

Lifting my gaze from Maddox's hands, I meet his intense stare. "And if I don't choose?"

"You'll never leave the Poison Garden again," he says. "When you passed through those gates, you signed away your former life. No one is exempt. Not even you, Your Grace."

I swallow the lump in my throat but don't break his stare as he places the cake and bottle in each of my hands.

"And what happens if I choose the cake? If I go on this journey and succeed? What then? Will you allow me to return to Alnwick?" I ask.

Maddox frowns. "That remains to be seen."

Each beat of my heart aches as I peer through the branches of the trees and take in the corner tower of Alnwick, knowing my only sure way home comes down to a sip from a bottle. But doing so will ensure the death of us all.

"Come now. Make your choice."

My pulse races as I consider my options. I stare down at both the bottle and the cake in my trembling hands. Maddox uncorks the small bottle and smiles. "Bottoms up."

I lift the green bottle to my lips, my eyes fixed on Maddox's. He gives me a look of satisfaction, as if he knew this would be my choice all along. I pause, the bottle barely touching my lips. Suddenly, I smash the bottle to the ground, shove the sugary pastry into my mouth, and swallow.

Maddox's eyes grow wide with surprise. My world quickly spins and fatigue settles over me. I crumple, my legs failing to support me any longer. The beat of drums and music become distant as I lie on the dirt path. As my eyes grow heavy, Maddox kneels in front of me and brushes a lock of my hair from my face. From the corner of my eye, I see a small animal dart into a den just beyond a tree blooming with exotic flowers.

"Sweet dreams, Your Grace."

Darkness settles over me and I'm lost in a nightmare filled with images of oozing sores, kids screaming in pain, and the sick smell of burning bodies.

· J A C K ·

Gears whine as the Steam Crawler scrambles over the countryside beyond Lohr. It's been hours since we left the castle, and Hook hasn't muttered a word. Instead, his gaze is fixed on the monotonous scenery: villages, trees, and sprawling farms. I attempt to engage in conversation a few times, but after I'm met with primal grunts, I opt to try to mirror Hook's silence.

But the quiet leads to festering thoughts. Thoughts about what went wrong on our last trip and what's happened between us. Finally, when the quiet and the thoughts are too much, I burst out, "I could've left you for dead in Everland. Let you bleed to death or worse, let you throw yourself in the crocodile pit. And now *you're* not speaking to *me*? It was your fault we were in that mess in the first place."

Hook glares at me with his one good eye and holds up his metal-and-gear hand. "You think I should be grateful for this?"

"It's a lot better than your flesh being ripped from your bones by those stupid reptiles of yours," I say.

Hook turns away, his eyes fixed on something far off. "You should've let me die."

"Trust me, next time you'll get your wish," I say.

Hook doesn't flinch.

"Ungrateful idiot," I mutter under my breath.

Lush green hedges rise in the distance past a break in the trees within the Black Forest. Past the living walls is a world that none dare to venture into. Years ago it was the bustling town of Schwarzwald. Its cobblestone streets were a thriving marketplace for those with wares to sell or trade. Hunters gathered to sell their game, farmers their crops, and tailors their woven goods. Those days are long gone. Legend has it that overnight the walls grew and the town was lost to nature, as if it never existed. By morning, none of the inhabitants could be found. Now all that remains is a massive maze built from vines and shrubs, a labyrinth of death.

Steam rises above the eastern entrance of the Labyrinth like an ethereal blanket. Towering several dozen meters high, the structure expands so far in either direction that it doesn't appear to have an end. Then I notice a break in the hedge slightly bigger than the width of a person. As we exit the Steam Crawler and approach the entrance, darkness is all we can see within the passageway.

Hook, armed with his Gatling gun and a broadsword strapped to his back, reaches for one of the branches on the tall bush. "We could just climb over it to get a better vantage point. Maybe even find a direct path so we can get that apple and get out of there as quickly as humanly possible."

"Be my guest," I say. Hook grips the wall with his metallic hand and prepares to climb. "But that right there is poison privet. By the time you get to the top, you'll have breathed in so much of its toxic fumes you'll be dead, which will certainly make this trip that much easier."

Hook scowls as he backs away from the plant and wipes his hand on his dark trousers. "So, what? We're going through there?" he asks with a wave of his hand toward the gloomy passageway.

"Looks like it," I say, picking up a broken branch from a nearby tree. I pull out a bandage from my rucksack and wrap it around the end of the limb.

"What are you doing?" Hook asks.

"What does it look like? That place is darker than the Bloodred Queen's dungeon," I say, lighting the cloth on fire.

"A torch?" he says.

Ignoring him, I approach the opening in the wall and hold out the torch. The flames dance, fueled by a draft. Inside, boilers of all heights and shapes line both sides of the walls. Copper and brass pipes climb toward the ceiling, venting steam overhead and blanketing the room in a thick cloud. Through the sweltering corridor, torchlight illuminates the passageway at the end.

"Seems like some kind of old boiler room," I say, scanning the narrow chamber.

"Looks pretty harmless to me," Hook says, taking a step forward. "Half of them don't even appear to be functioning anymore."

It's too simple. I put my arm out, holding him back. "Wait just a second." It won't do me any good if Hook dies before we even enter. I might need him, or at least his skills as a Marauder, later. Scooping up a fistful of gravel, I toss it into the passageway. The corridor erupts in bursts of steam. Plumes of hot gas blast from both sides of the walkway, and we are serenaded by a harsh melody of hissing. Even from here, the heat of the vapor burns my skin. I shield my face as the cloud rolls out from the fortress.

"Perhaps not as harmless as I thought," Hook says.

"Another brilliant assessment from Captain Observant. Next time, you're on your own. If you think you can just strut into unknown territory, count me out," I say.

Hook sneers. "Trust me, little stepbrother, your help is the last thing I need."

With the torch in hand, I step onto the copper-tiled floor of the hallway. "It's booby-trapped, probably tripped by motion. Let's make this easy for you. Why don't we pretend we're playing follow-the-leader. Do everything I do, step where I step," I say. "Are those instructions simple enough for you?"

Hook shoves me, catching me by surprise. I teeter, trying not to misstep.

"Don't tell me what to do. Just so we're perfectly clear, I'm here only because my mother sent me," he says.

"Great, I'll stop saving your life, then. Just do me a favor and stay out of my way," I say, shoving him back.

As I head into the structure, I wave the torch, chasing away the dark shadows. Taking in the long, narrow boiler room, I notice pinhole-size spouts protruding from the tanks. When we approach the first one, a small wisp of steam rises from the end of the spout fixed on the boiler at about knee level, as if sensing our presence. Carefully, I climb over an invisible wire. Hook does the same. We continue down the passage, climbing, ducking, avoiding being in the line of fire of the boiling-hot steam.

We are nearly halfway through when alarms blare overhead, and within seconds a loud hiss erupts from the entrance. I force myself to focus on that. An echoing bang comes from the end of the hallway as a metal door on the far side starts to slide. The boilers rumble and growl on either side of us. One by one, they burst in puffs of steam, hot gas spurting in all directions. I involuntarily gasp as I struggle to take in a breath. The air feels thick and moist, hard to breathe. Over my shoulder, I notice that the hilt of Hook's broadsword is in the path of one of the spouts. It must have set off the alarms.

"Run!" I shout.

When we're nearly three-quarters through the corridor, a loud screech from the end of the hallway startles me. Drawing my attention away, I shift, my arm accidentally slipping into the aim of one of the spouts. Scalding steam bursts from the boiler, burning through my shirtsleeve and scorching my skin. My scream reverberates off the walls and metal tanks. The torch falls to the ground, extinguishing as it lands and plunging us in darkness. Although my instinct is to pull back, jumping out of the steam's path, I force myself to shift subtly, preventing myself from being completely boiled in the hot vapor. Keeping still so as not to burn myself further is nearly impossible. My arm feels as if it's on fire, the nerve endings beneath my skin bubbling in pain.

We race through the corridor, leaping over and rolling beneath the hot gas. Knowing that there is no way to get through this unscathed, I throw my arms over my face to protect it, thankful for the goggles covering my eyes, and sprint as fast as I can to the other side of the room. Hook screams in pain but continues to follow, his ragged, heavy breaths so close behind me I can almost feel them. My heartbeat keeps the cadence of every pound of our boots on the floor.

The door ahead of us is nearly shut, not much wider than a person.

"We're not going to make it!"

"Yes, we are!" Hook says. He reaches back and pulls me ahead of him. I don't recall him passing me, but in the darkness and thick steam I wouldn't have seen him anyway.

Steam continues to billow from all sides of us and there's no room any longer to try to dodge it. Every part of me cries out in pain. All we can do is run through it and hope for the best.

When we are only a few meters away, Hook shoves me through the gap, sending me hurtling to the floor. He has to turn sideways in order to fit, and the door presses against his chest. He yelps as he works to squeeze through the gap. Just in time, he pulls his arm free and falls hard onto the floor as the door slams shut with a metallic bang.

· ALYSSA ·

As the fog fades, bright blue light stings my eyes. Blinking, I find myself lying on a nest of blankets with a soft pillow beneath my head. Gears squeal nearby. I push myself upright and take in my surroundings. I am in a large metal capsule as big as a steam-train car. Levers, wheels, and dials cover the walls on both sides of me. Pipes run along the ceiling in a macramé of copper and chrome. Massive windows cover the front and back of the capsule, and what I see before me absolutely takes my breath away.

Maddox sits at a massive console, steering the capsule through a watery wonderland. Sea life of all kinds swims past, unafraid of the massive metal beast that has entered their aquatic lair. Brightly colored fish dart by, a few stopping to peek through the windows, seeming somewhat intrigued by the newcomer to their world. Stingrays and octopuses drift through the current as we speed along. Glancing over my shoulder, the dark outline of the water's edge fades away as we are propelled into the open sea.

Maddox, noticing me, checks his bronze pocket watch and grimaces. "It's about time."

Irritated by his tone of voice, I plop down into the passenger seat of the watercraft and fold my arms. Before I can retort, I notice two large metal flippers attached to the vehicle, swimming through the water like a sea turtle's legs. In the rear windows, I can barely make out two back flippers beyond the shell of the ship.

"A turtle?" I say, awed by the magnificent machine.

Maddox rolls his eyes. "This is the *Mock Turtle*."

The ship lists to one side and my stomach lurches. A wave of wooziness comes over me.

Maddox gives me a sideways glance. "Lightweight. The side effects of that little cake should've worn off at least twenty minutes ago," he grumbles.

I stand and lean on the console, taking in the aquatic scene outside. "Where exactly are we and where are we headed?"

"We are exactly in the middle of the North Sea and we're headed to Germany," Maddox says matter-of-factly.

Chills race over my body. I'm unable to breathe, to form words in protest. He's taking me straight to the Bloodred Queen. How I could have been so stupid to trust him? And now I'm stuck in a hunk of metal underwater with no escape.

Momentarily taking his eyes off the course in front of him, he gives me a puzzled look. As if finally connecting the dots, he lets out a heavy sigh. "Oh, don't get your knickers in a pinch, Your Grace. I am not delivering you to the Bloodred Queen. You can't possibly be worth anything to her. Although one has to wonder what she'd do if she got her hands on you."

Placing a hand on my chest, I try to steady my breath. "I can't even imagine what she'd do, thank you very much."

"Well, first she'd probably—"

Holding a hand up, I cut him off. "Let's just agree it would be extremely unpleasant."

"*Unpleasant* is putting it kindly. Besides, what kind of person do you think I am? I might be a mercy executioner, but I'm certainly not a traitor," he says, seeming genuinely offended.

"Then why Germany?" I ask.

"You want the poison apple, right? There is only one known tree left in the world, and legend has it that it can be found in the Black Forest, hidden within a vast maze. A labyrinth of living hedges, protecting the tree and imprisoning those who once resided near it," he says.

"Imprisoning? You mean there are people living in there?" I ask, horrified by the thought. "Can't they just leave?"

"It's not that simple, Your Grace," Maddox says. "The town woke up to the Labyrinth. One day it wasn't there, the next it was. As they slept, the hedges grew around them, and by sunrise anyone within the walls was there for good."

"How is that even possible? Bushes don't just grow overnight," I say.

Maddox's countenance darkens. "Trust me, there are ways."

"How do you know all of this?" I ask.

He presses his lips together but doesn't respond. The only possible answer strikes me, and I search his face, wondering if my thought could be right.

"You know because you were there, weren't you?" I ask.

He grips the wheel of the machine a little tighter. "My father was the Lohr Castle groundskeeper and my mother was a medicinal herbalist. Between the two of them they knew everything about every plant that you could imagine. My father collected rare species. This tree, this poison apple tree, was one of the many specimens he possessed. He figured out how to grow a tree from the tropics in a colder climate. I never quite understood how he did it. But that tree became the pride and joy of the queen's garden. It was stunning, more beautiful than you could imagine. It was my father's favorite of all of them."

A school of scarlet-colored fish flit by the window, and Maddox adjusts to avoid them before he continues.

"Then one day, the Bloodred Queen comes storming from the castle in a fury, seeking my parents." Maddox shakes his head.

"What happened?" I ask.

"The Bloodred Queen's son wandered into the orchard and picked an apple to give to his mother, which was forbidden. It was supposed to be a gift. That was the day she left him blind in one eye. He was never the same after that," he says. "In the middle of the night, a band of the Bloodred Queen's soldiers came for my father and mother, claiming it was their fault that her son nearly poisoned her. I hid beneath the wooden floorboards, and when they shoved my father to the floor, I could see his bloodied face. Through a knothole in the wood, he whispered for me to run. That was the last time I saw either of my parents."

"How awful. I'm so sorry," I say, unsure of how else to comfort him.

He gives a slight nod. "The tree was removed from Lohr's grounds and replanted far enough away that the mistake would never happen again. Once planted, the soldiers poured growth accelerant from my mother's laboratory over the entire grounds surrounding the tree so no one could gain access to it again. Nor could anyone leave."

"What about you? How did you get away?" I ask.

"I gathered a few meager belongings and did as my father said. I ran. I made it to the machine my father used for traveling and gathering his plants, this machine."

"And you came to Northumberland?" I ask.

Again he nods.

"Why there? Why not take refuge somewhere close?"

"My parents taught me everything they could with the hopes that I wouldn't end up becoming a Tinker or Forger," he says.

I bite my lip, piecing together the information. In a world dominated by machines, most ended up working with tools to build or repair them. They were commoners among us. But to have the opportunity to practice the ancient arts of horticulture and medicinal herbalism, those labors were only granted to the prestigious.

"The Alnwick Garden was one of my father's favorite gardens in the world. So much so that he had paid a hefty price to set up an apprenticeship when I came of age. With nowhere else to go, it was the only place I could think of. I was thirteen at the time. It took some convincing, but shortly after my arrival to Northumberland, the groundskeeper brought me on as an apprentice early. And the rest is history."

"What about your parents? What happened to them?" I ask.

Maddox shakes his head. "I assume they were executed."

"You don't know that, Maddox. They could be her prisoners as we speak," I say.

"Perhaps, but how was I going to rescue them? I was just a kid. Even if that were the case, what means do I have to defeat the Bloodred Queen and her soldiers? And I don't even know that they're still alive. Between her cruelty and the disease, they're more than likely dead."

"You are the bloody caretaker with access to the Poison Garden," I say, my voice harsher than I intended. "Can't you do some hocus-pocus nonsense and put the soldiers under some sort of sleeping spell? You could just pass out those Eat Me cakes, storm the castle, and rescue your parents."

"You've been reading too many fairy tales, Your Grace," he says.

"And that's another thing," I say, my annoyance fueled by his complacency. "Quit calling me that. My name is Alyssa."

Maddox lifts an eyebrow and smiles. I find myself smiling back at him.

"As you wish, Alyssa," he says.

Heat burns my cheeks as I catch myself staring into his gold eyes.

A blow to the side of the ship breaks the moment of awkward silence. I slide, falling into Maddox's lap. He catches me, keeping me from tumbling headfirst into the ship's console. His arms wrap around me like a warm blanket. My pulse quickens as I turn my gaze to his and find his face merely centimeters from my own.

Seeming flustered, he helps me to my feet.

"Belt yourself in," he says, gesturing to the passenger seat.

A hint of disappointment comes over me as I flop into my seat. I'm not sure what I was expecting, but whatever it was, this is certainly not the time for it.

The ship shudders against another hit. I fasten the harness and grip the armrest. When I turn back toward the window, I feel the blood drain from my face. In the distance, an enormous snakelike creature slithers through the water.

"What is that thing?" I say under my breath, unable to take my eyes off the approaching beast.

Maddox pulls a lever. The ship picks up speed as the flippers propel us forward. "That is one rather large sea serpent." When the creature matches our speed, Maddox shoves the acceleration lever as far down as it will go. The ship jolts and lets out a loud clang. The engine stalls, leaving us floating for just a moment. Alarms blare from the back of the hull. Maddox tries the lever again as the ship begins to slowly sink. The sea serpent rams the front of the ship, and the vehicle lists to the side as loud scraping sounds run across the top. More alarms blare from behind us. "Take the wheel," Maddox says, unbelting himself.

Reluctantly, I do as he asks. Glancing over my shoulder, I watch as he taps on dials, turns wheels, and switches levers, mumbling to himself. When I glance back to the window, the serpent circles around and heads toward us again, growing larger the closer it gets. It opens its hinged jaw, sharp teeth dangling. I realize it must think we're a real turtle—its next meal.

"Maddox?" I say, trying to turn the wheel, but to no avail. Without any sort of thrust, we're dead in the water, literally.

The serpent speeds up, its forked tongue flicking the water as if trying to smell our whereabouts. Maddox curses beneath his breath as he tugs on a wheel that appears to be stuck. Again the beast rams the front window, this time leaving cracks throughout the glass.

Maddox is thrown off his feet by the impact. He falls back, smacking his head on one of the wheels. Crashing to the floor, he moans.

"Maddox!" I scream, my voice barely audible over the blaring alarms. He doesn't move. "Get up, Maddox!"

The ship jostles again, only this time the tail end drops, tilting so the front window faces the surface of the water. Maddox's body slides, colliding against the back windows.

We plummet toward the ocean floor. Frantically, I start switching levers and pushing buttons. The pressure causes the cracks to spider out, leaving the front window in a web of fissures. The lamps flicker and go dark, so there's just the moon's reflection on the water's surface, glittering like diamonds. Unsettling quiet slices through the thinning air, silencing the alarms. Only the sound of the window splintering, the hull succumbing to pressure, and my rising pulse are left.

Suddenly, the ship stirs and lights flicker. I let out an audible sigh as I hear the machine parts grind and the flippers slowly pull back, but not nearly fast enough.

Above, the sea serpent glides toward the ship. I scan the console and find a switch labeled AQUA ROCKET just above the myriad of dials. Without hesitation I slam it. Two barrels lift from beneath the ship. With a clang they lock in place. As the sea serpent draws closer, my hand hovers over the launch button. When it is only thirty meters away, I squeeze my eyes shut and punch the button.

A roar louder than any I've ever heard violently shakes the ship. I cover my ears, hoping the windows don't shatter. My body is thrown back against the seat as the ship jets forward. After a few moments, the *Mock Turtle* stills, and all is quiet again. When I open my eyes, a faint pink cloud is dissipating in the water before me. The blast is not nearly enough to have killed the beast, but it doesn't appear to be around. I must have frightened it off. The ship has somewhat leveled itself and is moving forward, although slowly.

"Well done," Maddox says.

I put the ship on auto and look back to find Maddox sitting up, holding a handkerchief to his head.

"Maddox! Are you okay?" I ask, unclipping the harness and bolting from my seat. Kneeling next to him, I take in his injuries. A bruise is beginning to blossom on his cheek and blood drips from a gash on his forehead. "You're hurt!"

He wipes at the blood on his forehead and puts pressure on

the wound. "It's not bad. I'll have a whopper of a headache, but I'll survive."

I bury my face in my hands and breathe a sigh of relief. "I thought you were dead."

He pats my back and chuckles. "It's going to take a lot more than a scratch and a twenty-meter sea monster to do me in, Your Grace."

I pull back. "It's Alyssa. Just call me Alyssa."

Maddox reaches for his hat and places it on his head. "Forgive me, Alyssa. Now, let's get to the Labyrinth."

He stands and offers me his hand. In spite of his injuries, he is undeniably handsome. I take hold of his hand, glad to have his company. He resumes his place at the cockpit, and I return to my seat.

"Ready to get that apple?" he asks.

I nod.

"Good, because time waits for no one," he says.

· PETE ·

Having been dismissed by Gwen, I'm antsy and need something to hit in order to quiet the unbearable frustration within me. The stone walls of the castle won't suffice. I'll only break the bones in my hands, so I opt to pay Doc a visit. As is often the case, many of my troubles lead back to him. He is the underlying source of my anger. If it wasn't for him, Gwen would be fine right now, Bella would be with me instead of lying in the infirmary, and none of this chaos would be happening. If he'd just gotten the diagnosis right the first time, I'd have been able to keep my promise to Gwen that she and her family would be safe here in Northumberland.

And so, itching for a fight, I enter the laboratory. Doc is in the same position I've seen him in nearly every time I've stopped by. He sits on a stool, hovering over a blood specimen. His medispectacles extend out as far as they can go so he can observe the sample amplified in the lenses. He rubs his neck as if trying to work out the stiff muscles.

Despite myself, I decide to let him off the hook . . . for now. I lean against the doorframe and cross my arms. Disappointed that I can't knock him into oblivion for all the ways he's let me and the rest of the Lost Boys down, I clear my throat to get his attention.

He sets the specimen on the counter and lifts the

medispectacles onto his head. He clearly isn't in the mood for a spat. Dark bags line his eyes, his face sallow and thin. It appears he hasn't slept or eaten in days, and it's not a good look on anyone, much less on our only physician. Who doctors the doctor when he is ill? It's the sickest I've seen him, and I almost feel sorry for him. But, as my mum used to say about my adventuring, you can sleep when you're dead. And we'll all be dead soon enough at this rate.

"You look like something the Plungers pulled from the latrines," I say.

"Nice to see you, too," Doc says, his tone sounding aggravated by my presence. "How's Gwen doing?"

I bristle. He doesn't need to know that she more or less threw me out of her sleeping quarters. "How do you think she's doing? She's just lost her mother."

"Sorry. I guess that was insensitive of me," he says.

Strolling over to the sample, I pick up the slide and inspect the drop of blood, as if this droplet is different from any of the others. "Any luck?"

Doc pulls the medispectacles off his head, then tosses them onto the counter and leans up against it, seeming as defeated as I feel. "Until Alyssa gets back from the Poison Garden with information, I'm afraid there isn't anything more I can do."

Caught up as I was with the death of the Professor and my encounter with Gwen, I'd forgotten about the plan to inquire with Maddox Hadder about the poison apple. "Did she take anyone with her?"

Weary, Doc rubs his eyes and yawns. "How in heaven's name should I know? I've been bent over examining slides for"—he slips his pocket watch from his waistcoat—"sixteen hours straight now, aside from the few minutes you decided to turn my best shirt into a dust rag. Last I checked, the Lost Boys were all asleep."

"When did she leave?" I ask, a small spike of worry shooting up my spine.

"I don't know, a few hours ago maybe?" Doc says.

Hours? Panicked, I step up to a metal cabinet and punch it, leaving a dent, but it's not big enough. I pound my fist into it again and again, welcoming the rush of pain.

Doc grips my shoulder and shoves me from the cabinet. "Blimey, what is wrong with you? There's valuable equipment in there."

"She shouldn't have gone alone," I say, jabbing a finger into his chest.

"Let me get this straight: You wanted someone to babysit the Duchess of Alnwick and tell her that she couldn't go where she pleased?" he asks, gaping.

"Actually, yes, Doc. I do expect you to stop the duchess from entering a poisonous garden all alone where no one ever bloody returns from," I say. "I should've gone with her."

Doc waves me away and stomps back to his workstation. "You're right, Pete. Not only should I try to find a cure for all these sick people on three hours of sleep, but I also should be taking care of the sick, and chasing after the duchess."

Furious, I storm out of the laboratory. Doc's footsteps pound the floor behind me.

"Just wait a second; where are you going?" Doc asks.

"I'm going after the duchess. Her place is here in the castle, not gallivanting out there with that crazy caretaker," I say.

Doc huffs. "Oh, how archaic of you. The little woman can't defend herself so we're going to lock her in the highest tower of a far-away castle? Shall we get a dragon to protect her, too? Duchess Alyssa is capable of handling herself, which is far more than I can say for you at the moment."

Whirling on him, I throw a punch but miss. Doc shoves me hard against the wall, grips me by my collar, and gets in my face. "Stand down, Pete, or I will give you something to be pissed about, oh valiant leader of the Lost Boys."

"Go back to your lab before I show you what kind of leader I am."

Doc releases my coat collar and points a finger in my face. "You want to know what kind of leader you are, Pete? With the Queen ill, Katt off her rocker, and Alyssa gone, you're naturally the next to rule. Until the duchess returns, Alnwick needs someone to keep things calm and, as much as I hate to say it, you're the best thing. So stop whining and step up."

Doc whirls around and heads back to his laboratory. I follow.

"You know that no one returns from the garden," I say. "That is why *you* should've been sure someone was with her to be sure she got back here safely."

"Guess you'll have to go save the day again, won't you?" Doc stops, turns back toward me, and bows. "As always, I'm here for your service, leader of the Lost Boys and now Alnwick. Try not to ruin everything. Again."

He heads in to his lab, leaving me alone with the embers of rage broiling in my belly.

He's not wrong; Alnwick needs a leader. I'm just not all that sure that I'm the best choice—but I may be the only choice.

· A L Y S S A ·

Nausea grips my stomach, threatening to make me vomit. After battling the sea serpent, we puttered along for hours in the battered and broken *Mock Turtle*, oftentimes losing power and suddenly sinking only to regain power and lurch forward. After leaving the North Sea, we traveled up rivers and canals until we finally made it to the Weise River. I've never been so happy to finally be on land. With waves lapping at my boots, I lie on the bank, staring at the night sky above, doing all I can to keep my last meal inside of me. I don't know when we'll next get to eat.

Under a brilliant full moon, Maddox rips a plant from the greenery just beyond the beach and munches on the root. He stumbles toward me and offers me a bite, but my face flushes as queasiness taunts me again.

"Eat it," he says, shoving the dirt-clad plant in my face.

I brush it away. "Just leave me alone. I need to get my land legs before I eat anything, much less a weed."

Maddox pulls a multitool from his belt and cuts the tip of the root off. He rinses it in the river and brings it back to me. "Eat it or I'm going to tie you up and force-feed you. Trust me, it won't be pleasant, but we don't have time for this weak-belly nonsense."

His black-lined eyes glitter gold in the moonlight, but somehow there is a darkness within him that I don't dare challenge. I take the brown-and-gray piece of root, tentatively placing it on my tongue. Its flavor has a bite, but it doesn't take long before I feel somewhat better. He offers me another piece, and I chew it up.

He stashes the rest of the root in his pocket and heads toward a thick forest.

"Where are we?" I ask.

"Just south of the Labyrinth," he says, inspecting the woods. With his hand he brushes away scrub from beneath the trees, as if looking for something. Finally, he finds a path. "This way."

He strides through the forest, disappearing beyond the dense trees.

Reluctantly, I stand, dust the dirt off my wet cloak, and follow him.

We travel for an hour, not saying much at all. With having to climb over fallen trees, through overgrown brush, and over newly formed streams, it proves to be a strenuous journey. Something buzzes by my ear. When I turn toward it, a mechanical bee settles on my shoulder. Carefully, I cradle it in my hands.

"A bumblefly," Maddox says, sounding irritated as he glances down at my palms. "That means we're close."

"How do you know?" I ask, watching the intricate machinery spin within its body.

"My parents weren't the only ones who worked for Lohr Castle. The Apiarists along with the Tinkers created hives of those vile beasts to keep the plants thriving in Lohr. They're three times more efficient than your average honeybee."

Its copper wings beat just once. "It's lovely," I say, tracing a finger along one wing. The wire that serves as a stinger pierces my finger. "Ouch!" I squeal, tossing the insect into the air. It flits away toward Maddox, its machine parts buzzing loudly.

"Nasty buggers," Maddox says, swatting at the bee. "Worse than the mosquitobots, which have no logical purpose for existing. I'm fairly certain the Tinkers created those bloodsuckers specifically to annoy the Bloodred Queen."

"How much farther is the Labyrinth?" I ask, noticing a gold object shimmering on the weathered path. Bending, I pick up a small cog. I slip it into my pocket, curiously noticing another slightly larger one just a few meters away.

"Why? Are you in a hurry? Forgive me for not getting you there faster, Your Grace," Maddox says.

Annoyed that he's gone back to formalities, I say nothing. Instead I focus on collecting the random cogs strewn about the walkway, wondering where they've come from and what they're doing along the road. Beneath one gear is a tiny brass key, and I put both in my cloak pocket. I finally ask the question that has been perplexing me.

"Why do you help those people? The ones who come to you in the Poison Garden?"

"The same reason you chose to eat the cake. We both want to help those who are suffering. The only difference is that I recognize our days are numbered and there's not a thing that can be done about it. I've accepted our fate. The least I can do is use my knowledge of plants to make sure their suffering is minimal. Whatever lies beyond this miserable world must be a grand party, and even if isn't, it has to be better than this." Maddox stretches out his gloved fingers, clenching and unclenching his hands.

"You think living your final days in stupor and lunacy is minimal suffering?"

Maddox swings his pocket watch by the chain. "You never know which moment will be your last before you finally break"—he whirls toward me, snapping his fingers in my face—"so you better make each and every one count. The clock is ticking, Alyssa, and the timer is almost up. These are the days of self-fulfillment, of instant gratification. Wait to chase the things you want and you may run out of precious minutes."

"But you're not helping anyone," I say, frustrated. "You're drugging them."

Maddox's face scrunches in disapproval. "*Drugging* sounds so malicious. I prefer to think of it as easing their pain, providing an environment to grieve for the life they will never get to live, giving them a source of joy and . . . companionship," he says, giving me a sideways glance and winking. "One last night of self-indulgence."

I grimace as disgust rolls through me.

He smirks, obviously amused by my reaction, and turns his eyes to the road. "Which is more than you have offered them. And essentially, your solution is no different than mine. You drug them as well."

"No, I don't!" I protest.

"When it gets really bad, do you not put them in a medically induced coma so they don't feel the pain? At least my way, they have the opportunity to say good-bye to their loved ones; meanwhile, your patients die in their sleep and alone," he says.

Biting the inside of my cheek, I struggle to come up with a rebuttal, but he's right. Only the gravely ill are given painkillers, and even then the drugs provide minimal relief. Sleep is the only relief from their suffering.

"You, on the other hand, are in denial, and still fighting a battle that can't be won," he continues.

"If it can't be won, then why did you bother joining me? If death is inevitable, you could have just not brought me here or left me to get the apple by myself and gone back to your never-ending party."

Maddox snorts. "By yourself. That is utter nonsense," he mumbles, appearing amused by such a suggestion. "You'd be dead before you even stepped foot into the Labyrinth. You'd never make it alone, but with me at least you have a fighting chance to get back alive and die with dignity. If this apple is genuinely what you believe it to be—although it's highly unlikely that it is—then maybe you will prove me wrong, that there is indeed still hope."

Hope—it's all any of us have left.

"So what about you? What's driving you to survive? There must be a duke in your future, or at least what's left of it," Maddox says, giving me a playful nudge.

The comment prickles a lingering scar upon my heart. I have always been busy with the obligations of a duchess, never having time for things that pleased me. My days were filled with lessons and attending to duties. Preparing me for a proper marriage match—one that would strengthen the royal bloodline. I had no betrothed yet, much less an actual love interest. I didn't even have friends. With the state of the world as it is now, chances are, I never will. A lump grows in my throat and it infuriates me. This is not the time or place to think about romance (or the lack thereof). My job, my only job, is to help the people of Northumberland. And why on earth is Maddox even inquiring? It's certainly none of his business.

"No, I don't have time for that," I snap. I'm unsure if he's soliciting information for his own benefit, but companionship is the least of my needs.

"Truly a shame." Maddox frowns but says nothing more.

The path leads to a meadow filled with wildflowers. Under a bright moon, a rainbow of petals blooms from tiger lilies, roses, daisies, violets, and larkspur, ending at a massive hedge standing at least twenty meters high. The fortress expands as far as I can see to my left and right, disappearing into the darkness. What lies beyond is far less peaceful than the field of flowers. Instead, the only entrance I can see is filled with enormous wheels with sharp blades. They are as tall as the wall itself and spin in opposing directions, blocking passage into the maze. There are so many that it just looks like a sea of razors.

"Well, well, it appears the Labyrinth has had some modifications over the years," Maddox says, taking in its entrance.

"Perfect," I say drily.

Maddox rocks back on the heels of his boots. "I did warn you that the Labyrinth would be dangerous, and *that*," he says, pointing to the sharp blades, "is a terrifyingly dangerous entrance."

"*That?* And just how do you suggest we get through? Becoming a diced duchess was not on my agenda for today."

Maddox grabs a large branch lying just to the side of the path and launches it into the blades. The limb splinters into thousands of wood chips. By instinct we both shield our faces.

"Well, certainly not that way," I declare.

Maddox steps back, taking in the height and expanse of the barrier, and mumbles to himself, considering whether the living wall, which he claims is poisonous, can be scaled with minimal damage to our lungs, eyes, and exposed skin.

I ignore him and study the wall. I walk along it, peering as close as I dare. I notice several steel bolts and a single lever protruding from the leafy edifice. They are all different diameters but perfectly round, as if something is meant to fit on them. I kick over the accumulation of nature's debris at the foot of the hedge: leaves, branches, twigs, and dirt. My eye catches a gear the size of a dinner plate leaning up against the wall, larger than the others I have found so far. It takes both of my hands to heft it up to a pin big enough to fit it. Struggling, I slide the gear onto the bolt. I pull out the handfuls of gears from my pocket that I collected on our journey to the Labyrinth. One by one, I arrange them along the wall, making sure the teeth of each interlock with another, occasionally switching them around until they're all connected except for one missing piece. I check my pockets, but they're empty. Wondering if I possibly missed a gear along the path, I step back, taking in the vast wall. From the corner of my eye, something glints in the moonlight behind the leaves of the hedge just to the right of the gear puzzle. I brush aside vines and find a rusted antique compass clock. The timepiece reads 11:26, and the second hand appears frozen at five seconds. Although it's night, it's not nearly that late. Beneath the glass is a single cog in the center precisely the size I need to complete the wall of gears.

Just above the timepiece is a weathered plaque covered with a film of dirt. I dust away what I can of the grime and squint to read the inscription.

Turn your sight to the stars,
And choose your time wisely.
Hours will cost minutes,
Minutes devour seconds.
Death looms at all times but one.

"What do you suppose that infernal device is?" Maddox asks, looking over my shoulder.

"It's a compass clock, an old one from what I can tell. They were once used by airmen and seamen to navigate time by means of a compass and the stars," I say, placing my hands on either side of the clockface.

"How in heaven's name do you know that?" he says, his brows raised.

I laugh. "What is it you think I did behind those castle walls all day? I wasn't allowed out to mingle with the people, so instead I read books. Lots of books."

Maddox wrinkles his nose. "Books?"

"Yes, they are pages with written words on them, bound in leather. You must have heard of them," I say teasingly.

Rolling his eyes, Maddox snorts. "That's not what I meant. Of course I've heard of books. You just don't look like a bookish type person."

"What does a bookish type person look like?" I ask, trying to decide if I should be offended or not.

Maddox furrows his face up in contemplation. "I'm not all that sure, but you definitely don't fit the description."

"Looks can be deceiving," I say.

A crooked grin grows on Maddox's face. "Smart, beautiful, and witty."

Blushing, I turn and search the vast blanket of stars above, seeking out the North Star.

Maddox moves closer to the compass clock. "So how does this gadget work?"

"Well, it's based on a relationship between due north and the North Star, which is right there," I say, pointing up into the sky.

"Let me guess, you learned about star maps in books, too?" he says.

"How else would you learn star maps?" I ask.

Maddox gesturing at the star-strewn sky. "Um, from the stars?"

I ignore his comment. Glancing at the compass, I try to determine which way is true north, only to discover that the compass is faulty.

"Are you sure we're at the south side of the Labyrinth?" I ask.

"As sure as I know the difference between tea and wine," he says. "Why?"

"The compass is inaccurate. It's impossible to set the clock to the correct time," I say, tapping the glass of the compass. "Unless . . . what if this set is based on the moon instead of the sun?"

"A moondial? Right, of course," Maddox says. "Surely the Bloodred Queen wouldn't use a sundial. Too obvious. But a moondial? Who knows how to use those? Oh, wait, let me guess: You know how because you learned from books?"

Maddox is right. Of course she wouldn't make it that easy to gain entrance. Studying the stars and compass again, I bite my bottom lip. Taking into consideration where the North Star lies, which direction the compass points, and the time of year, calculations fly through my mind, deciphering what time the clock should be set to.

"Based on its current position, the clock should say twelve twenty-five, eleven seconds and counting . . . I think."

"You think? That's awfully precise," Maddox says.

Worry flutters in my belly as I take in a breath, counting off the passing seconds in my head. *Fifteen. Sixteen.* "Precise is our only option." I point to the last line engraved into the plaque. "Death looms at all times but one."

Maddox holds a fist to his lips. "Which means if we're one second off, this rusty piece of junk is going to blow us to bits."

Twenty-one. Twenty-two. "Or something worse," I say, although I can't imagine anything much worse.

Maddox takes my hand. "Alyssa, we don't have to do this. Maybe we can find another entrance."

"Twenty-eight. Twenty-nine," I say.

Nodding, Maddox picks up where I left off, counting aloud.

Grateful for his warm touch and assurance, I squeeze his hand. "I'm not turning back now. And we don't have time to look for another entrance."

Forty-two. Forty-three.

Smiling, Maddox returns the gesture. "I admire your bravery. Let's do this."

Holding my breath, I turn the hands of the clock—first the hour hand, then the minute hand. Counting out loud, I turn the second hand, careful not to pass fifty-nine seconds on the clock. I can only hope I've counted off correctly. The gadget gives a sharp snap and the glass springs open, exposing the cog beneath.

"Brilliant!" Maddox says, grabbing me in a giant hug. "You are by far the cleverest person I've met."

I let out the breath I was holding. "Not clever, just lucky."

"Luck is finding a four-leafed clover. What you did was exceptional. If it were up to me, we'd be twiddling our thumbs," he says, releasing me.

A warmth stirs within my chest, but I ignore it. Gripping the brass cog, I place it on the wall with the others and take hold of the handle, turning the gears counterclockwise.

A loud clank crashes as I pull the lever. The bladed wheels pull back, disappearing into slits along the inside walls of the matrix. Once they are fully hidden, the handle gives an audible click, locking them in place. Beyond the wall of wheels, the passageway dead-ends into a perpendicular hallway.

"Very clever," Maddox says, his eyes wide with surprise. "Perhaps you are brighter than I initially thought."

"You didn't think I was bright?" I say. "Beats your suggestion to climb a poisonous wall."

"I can admit when I was wrong," he says, adding a bow.

I laugh and then ask, "How do you suppose those gears ended up along the path?"

Maddox shrugs. "I have no idea." Then he gazes up at the slits in the wall, his expression growing wary. "Ladies first," he says, gesturing for me to go ahead of him.

"Thanks," I say sarcastically.

A noise in the brush draws our attention. Suddenly, a man wearing a soldier's uniform bolts from the trees. A glass-and-copper tank is strapped to his back, filled with a clear liquid. Tubes lead from the tank, over his shoulders and into metal gauntlets. Crisscrossing the strange tank is a modified rifle. He stops just before the entrance, taking a passing glance at Maddox and me. We're both startled at seeing an actual adult.

"Save yourselves. The Labyrinth is no place for children," the man says, before sprinting down the long pathway and disappearing into the maze.

· PETE ·

Drums echo through the night, each percussive beat louder than the last. Leaving the crude camp and its tenants behind, I follow the rhythmic call of the music. The usual large crowd congregates at the gates of the Poison Garden. I push my way through. Hands paw at me, arms wrap around my neck, fingernails rake across my skin. Beneath the orange torchlight, the mass appears to move as one steady beat, an amoeba of sweat-drenched bodies seeking relief from their festering wounds.

I finally make my way to the garden's entrance, which is guarded by Koh and his sharp scythe. We've never seen eye to eye since my arrival to Northumberland, but thus far our interactions have been somewhat civil. As I approach he stands a little taller, clearly with the intention to intimidate. However, I don't scare easily. After a year of battling Marauders, this measly punk won't stop me.

"I'm here seeking Caretaker Maddox," I say, gripping the hilts of my daggers.

The animatronic cat cackles. "No one ever enters the garden without an invitation."

"Get lost!" the guard growls.

The crowd grumbles, seeming equally annoyed by my presence.

"I'll leave when I'm good and ready," I say, my arms folded.

Koh marches up to me with his chest pushed out. "I think you're good and ready right now, Lost Girl."

I give an exaggerated laugh. "Lost Girl? How original. If I had a gold coin for every time I heard that joke, I'd be the richest man in all of England and you'd be my minion, sweetheart."

Koh sneers.

"You are Princess Katt's guard. Perhaps I should have called you her nanny instead?" I ask.

"State your business," Koh says, unamused.

"I thought I already did," I retort.

Koh doesn't respond; he just stares.

"Duchess Alyssa came to see Maddox Hadder, and we haven't heard from her since."

"Pete, so nice to see you," says a sultry voice. Katt passes through the wrought-iron gates and saunters toward me, stopping so close I can smell a hint of sage on her breath. A white rose is tucked behind her ear, almost glowing against her dark hair. "The duchess has abandoned her post, which leaves no one else left to rule but me. Or, let me guess, I suppose she's left you and your Lost Boys in charge of Northumberland in her absence."

I don't blink, refusing to turn my gaze from hers. "I guess you could say that. At least until I return with Duchess Alyssa, which I intend to do. I'm not leaving here without her. Now where is Maddox?"

Katt pulls her hookah pipe from her boot. "He's unavailable."

"What do you mean Maddox isn't available? Is he too busy drinking tea? Heaven forbid that I interrupt his party," I say, my jaw aching through clenched teeth.

"Well, aren't you feisty? Pretty, too," she says. She looks me up and down as she inhales from the hookah. Rings of smoke lift into the cold evening air with each word. "The infamous leader of the Lost Boys. Many of our guests, your former followers, speak highly of you, especially when they are conveying their happiest thoughts right before they take their last breath."

Squeezing my eyes closed, I try to shut out the images of all the Lost Boys who have died. Pyro, Justice, Mole, and his big brother, Dozer. Some lost to the Marauders, others to the disease. Those who were sick and given the antidote, many of them could not bear the pain and stole into the night, never returning. I'm certain that most, if not all of them, came seeking help from the trustees of the garden.

Katt saunters even nearer to me. Her body is so close to mine, I'm sure she can feel my heart threatening to leap from my chest. Other than Gwen, I've never been this close to any girl. But I don't budge. She may be royalty, but she is not my queen.

I keep my eyes trained on hers as she runs a sharp fingernail down my cheek. I don't flinch. Instead I smile as wide as I can, hoping my indifference will make her realize I'm not going anywhere. She smiles flirtatiously back. "Maybe I can be of assistance," she purrs.

"I'm here for Maddox, not you. When do you expect he'll be available?" I ask, my words clipped.

She slips her hookah pipe back into her boot and laces her scaly hand into my hair. I shudder. "Now, why would you need Maddox when you could have me? Certainly there's something I can do to help you," she whispers into my ear, sending chills throughout my entire body.

Koh smirks, seeming amused by Katt's advances.

"I'm not leaving without Duchess Alyssa," I say. "She came here seeking information on a rare apple and hasn't returned to the castle."

The wind is knocked out of me as Katt drives a fist into my gut, making me double over. I'm surprised by her strength. Although not scrawny, she certainly isn't overly muscular either, at least not enough to land a blow as hard as she did. She snatches one of my daggers and holds it to me. Her smile slips, turning into a deep scowl. She grips my chin hard, her nails digging into my skin. Not fingernails—claws.

"Do I look like I care? And as for that apple she seeks, you've come to the wrong garden, sweetheart. The edibles we have to offer won't fill your stomach, but you'll certainly forget that you're hungry," she says, releasing my chin and running her fingers down my chest. I wince as her fingernails tear through my shirt, leaving deep scratches in my flesh. My shirt hangs limply on my body. I rip it the rest of the way off, exposing the intricately inked gears and wheels tattooed across my chest and abs.

Her eyes light up as she takes in the artwork. "Wow, part Lost Boy, part machine. I rather like that." Katt places her palms on my bare chest.

Stepping back, I swat her hand away. "I'm not here for your indulgences!"

Chester the copper cat shakes his head. "Tsk, tsk. Such rude manners."

Katt steps toward me and slips her hand to my waist. She slowly slides my dagger back into its sheath. I don't budge.

"Your precious duchess is no longer here," Katt says, retreating from me. "Now, go back to the castle, while you still can."

Although I don't believe her, my worry for the duchess fuels my resolve. "Katt, where is Maddox?" I shout, watching her stroll toward the gate entrance.

"Maddox is gone. He left with the duchess. The Poison Garden is under my control now. Leave, Lost Boy, if you know what's good for you."

My stomach drops. I sprint after Katt, blocking her way into the garden.

"Where did they go?" I ask, trying not to give the illusion of pleading even though that's exactly what I'm doing.

Katt smiles widely and leans in close to me, her lips brushing against my ear. "Alyssa and Maddox have both deserted their people, leaving me in charge of the Poison Garden and you in charge of Northumberland. But it doesn't have to be that way," she whispers. "Hmm, I smell an alliance. What do you think, Lost Boy? You and I could rule together. It could be a beautiful union."

Snaking an arm around her neck, I pull my dagger out and press it into her throat, nicking the soft skin. A bright droplet of blood leaks down her slender neck. "Tell me where they are! Now!"

Chester hisses and the guard starts toward me, but Katt holds a hand up.

She grins evilly, as if enjoying the thought of me slitting her throat. "I'll make you a deal, Pete. You work with me to create a proper antidote, tell me what you know, and in return I'll tell you where they went."

"Why? What's in it for you?" I say.

"Aside from saving my own life?" Katt grits her teeth, rage in her eyes. "I'm not quite ready to die from the ghastly disease. I have big plans still. Your silly little duchess thinks Doc is the only one who might be able to find us a cure. So far he's been utterly useless. I'm tired of your empty promises and fabled antidote. Give everyone access to the Professor's notes, and see if someone else can find the answer."

There's a glimmer of reason in her argument. Perhaps someone other than Doc would be able to develop an antidote quicker. The more people working on it, the better the odds. But I trust Katt even less than I trusted Hook's crocs not to eat Lost Boys for an afternoon snack. "Do you know what would happen if her research was lost, or worse, ended up with the Bloodred Queen? Without the Professor's findings, we could never hope for a cure. In the Bloodred Queen's hands, only those she deems worthy would be cured. She would let the rest of us die," I say, hearing the desperation in my own voice.

"She would *let* the rest of us die? What about you and your girlfriend, Gwen? You're the ones keeping the research to yourselves. Have you seen your precious Bella lately? She's days away from losing her life, and that's certainly not the Bloodred Queen's fault. Nor are the dozens of others on the brink of death in the infirmary. That's on *you* for keeping vital information from the rest of us," Katt hisses.

Katt's words ignite a fury that courses through my veins. Bella, Gwen's siblings, and the Professor, all of them are either dead or close to it. Katt's right in some ways, but I didn't release the bomb. I didn't poison everyone in London. That bloodshed is the responsibility of the Bloodred Queen.

"You can't help, Katt! Duchess Alyssa came here to find out about the apple because that *is* our only hope. I have nothing else to offer you but my word."

Tilting her head back, Katt bursts out in mocking laughter. "Your word? Why would I ever trust you? Do you take me for a fool? You have what I need to find the cure and I will get it, Lost Boy. When I do, I will earn the respect of my people."

Good to know that I'm not the only distrustful one here. I shake my head. We're talking in circles now, and I don't have time for this. I turn and desperately start weaving among the kids, looking for someone who isn't completely out of it. Someone must know something.

"Does anyone know where Maddox or the duchess went? Anyone?" I call out over and over again. Some boys swarm me, touching my clothes, sticking their hands in my pockets, looking for things to loot. I have nothing, but I grip my daggers, not wanting anyone to snatch them from me. Others don't make eye contact. I'm feeling hopeless when I hear the mechanical caw of a raven. I turn around to see Katt open a compartment on what looks like a metal bird. I edge closer, curious. Something gleams in her hand as she pulls it from her pocket. I realize what it is when she drops it into the opening.

A vial of the antidote Doc made in Everland.

"Where did you get that?" I shout, hearing my voice catch as I race back to her.

Katt throws a glance my way. "When you're as sick as these kids are, it doesn't take much to bribe them. Even your faithful Lost Boys. Pain relief in exchange for a vial of the antidote. It's a fair trade," she says archly. "And soon, I'll have those research papers as well. The entrance fee into the Poison Garden comes at a steep price, at least with me in charge."

"Katt, what are you doing?" I ask, bewildered and angry that she's taking advantage of the Lost Boys. "You know that antidote is responsible for your condition, along with everyone else's." I reach to snatch the bird from her hands, but she twirls away from me, clicking the pieces back into place as she goes. I dash after her, but she tosses the bird into the air, where it flaps its wings and lifts into the night.

"Oh, I'm well aware of that," she says. "But until I get your cooperation, I'll seek it elsewhere."

"What have you done?" I say, defeat overcoming me.

"Ensured our survival," she says. Katt turns to the crowd of people watching our exchange. "Do you hear that, people of Northumberland? I want the Professor's papers. Until then, no one enters the garden! And if I don't get them by morning, heads will roll."

Shouts and protests break out among the kids.

Katt spins on her heels and sidles up to me, placing a hand on my cheek. "The offer is the same for you, Pete. Papers for poison. Seems like a fair trade." She tugs my fingers knowingly.

"Where are you sending it? Who are you handing the vial to?" I ask as I stare at where the raven disappeared into the night sky.

Seeing my shock, she continues. "It's very simple, really. The Bloodred Queen is determined to achieve world domination and we require a cure. Since the United Kingdom is mine to rule, I have offered her a trade. No need for her to know that you and those brats are trying to strong-arm the crown from me. Rumor has it that the Bloodred Queen has fallen ill. So, I give her the antidote, she uses her resources to create the real cure, benefiting us both. In return, I rule here as the Bloodred Queen's closest ally, thus ending years of feuding with Germany. We rebuild England while simultaneously curing those of us left. Eventually, together she and I will save the world, and with that comes universal rule. It's a perfect solution, don't you think?"

The crowd of partygoers shout their approval.

"You can't do this," I say, panic settling over me. "You know she'll never align with you. She's just using you, Katt. Germany created the Horologia disease to take over the world. The Bloodred Queen's the one who had the bombs dropped on your people in the first place. If she does find an antidote, she'll never share it with you, nor will she align with you."

Katt smirks, slipping the rose from her hair. She takes a sniff and smiles slyly. "Think about it, Pete. This is just the start. The Bloodred Queen of Germany and Queen Katt, the ruler of all of England including Northumberland. No! Not Northumberland. These are changing times, and with change comes new beginnings. New rulers. New nations. There is no longer a north or south, east or west. All of England has fallen, and under my rule, we will reunite. Everland will be just a long-lost nightmare, and Umberland will be a new era of hope and promise. Rest assured, Lost Boy, Umberland will rise up as a fierce and dominant nation ruled by me." She glances down at the blossom between her fingers before tucking it back behind her ear. "Katt, the Queen of Umberland."

"Long live Queen Katt!" the mob cheers, pumping fists in the air. Chester howls with delight. Katt bats her long lashes, her head held high and poised while she scans the crowd. Finally, her attention falls back on me.

I feel as if I've been sucker-punched again. She turns and heads back toward the garden.

"Katt, where did Alyssa go?" I plead. Koh blocks me from entering the garden, holding me back by my arms. "Where has Maddox taken her?"

"Right now you should be more worried about getting me the Professor's papers. The clock's ticking," she says. "Now, be gone, or you'll find yourself burning with the rest of the dead by morning."

The gates slam behind Katt, and the tumblers in the lock give an audible click. I wrest free from Koh's hold and grip the cold metal of the fence. "Katt!" I shout, shaking the iron bars.

"Get out of here, traitor," one boy says, shoving me into the group of teenagers. I am jostled around, lost in a sea of bodies as I watch Katt disappear down the garden path.

· JACK ·

usting myself off, I wince, feeling the hot sting of burns left by the steam of the boilers. I search my rucksack for the meager first-aid kit I thought to bring along. Fortunately, there is a tin of salve, which I rub over my injuries.

Meanwhile, Hook kneels so his face is close to mine. "Consider us even," he growls.

"Even?" I ask, confused.

He stands and gestures with his steel hand. "If it weren't for me, you'd be nothing but one big boil. That's for not leaving me in Everland. Don't get used to it."

I'm no less confused. My stepbrother just saved my life? It's an act of goodwill, but it feels too suspect.

Hook turns and jams his forged hand into a small crevice between the metal door and frame, trying to pry the exit open. He grunts expletives and finally gives up. "Great, just great. How are we going to get out of here?"

"I don't know about you, but I wouldn't go back through there if it was the only way out," I say, grimacing as I wrap bandages around my arms.

Protected by his long leather coat, Hook seems relatively unharmed. He peers down the hallway, which extends in both directions. Other passages open up along the way.

"Which way?" Hook asks.

I am about to answer when a loud clang echoes through the hallway, reverberating off the tall metal walls. Above us, large pulleys spin, dragging on an enormous chain. The interior walls shift, rearranging the pathway around us. We find ourselves surrounded by dozens of new hallways, each ending at a chrome door with a symbol welded onto it: some of them with weapons, others with earthly elements, and still others with symbols I don't recognize.

"Moving walls? This should be fun. I wish I'd brought more rum to the party," Hook says as he leans up against a metal column. He pulls a flask from his inside coat pocket and takes a long swig of it.

Walking the circumference of the room, I look down each hallway for any sign to indicate which direction to go. Reaching for my multitool belt, I tug on the chain loosely hanging from my hip. My compass pops from its compartment. I wait for the needle to align toward true north, turn to my left, and take the western corridor.

Hook's brow lifts as I pass by. "Out of the dozens of choices you have, you're picking that one? May I ask why?"

"If we're going to the center of the labyrinth, we need to continue southwest," I say, heading down the path. Carved on the door is a pickax.

Hook rubs his chin. "Any door with weapons on it can't be a good sign."

"Pick a different door. I don't care," I say, clipping my compass back into place. "Less baggage for me to carry."

With a disgruntled moan, he joins me.

I shove the door open, and we enter into a vast forest. Rocky cliffs encircle uninhabitable homes of what looks like an old mining village. Rusty tracks lead from collapsed caves to what is left of the town. Empty mining carts are scattered about the tracks as if frozen in time.

"I have a really bad feeling about this," Hook says, stepping into the wooded area.

The sound of metal upon metal sends a shiver up my spine. I glance left and see several short, stocky men emerge from the mouth of a mine. Their boots hit the ground with loud thuds as they line up in a row. They stand before us with goggle-covered eyes and most have long beards that hang to their waists, washers affixed to keep them tamed. Each one has a gold tooth that shines under the moonlight that breaks through the canopy of trees. Upon closer inspection, I also see signs of the Horologia disease in various stages on their hands. The closest man pulls out a medieval-looking weapon that appears to be a pickax, but even from where I stand, I can tell it is much more than a simple mining tool. He rams the base of the weapon on the ground, which sends a shudder through the earth beneath us. Hook and I are jostled by the earthquake, but we regain our balance.

It takes only a moment for the memory to return to me. The Zwergs were a small community of coal miners. They were a reclusive bunch, only venturing into neighboring towns to sell their wares and buy supplies. They disappeared the day that the hedges grew, their homes swallowed up by the Labyrinth.

The man closest to me spits as he meets my gaze, spinning his ax in front of him with expertise. "State your business," he growls.

I flip the switch on my belt to engage the built-in gun. "I vote you tell him what our business is," I mutter to Hook.

Hook's single eye darts from one man to the next, his lip turned up in a sneer. Taking the safety off his Gatling gun, he says to me, "Six . . . seven. Two against seven. I've been up against worst odds." I roll my eyes. Hook calls to them, "Stand down and no one gets hurt."

The Zwerg cackles, and the others follow suit. "We won't be standing down to anyone, especially to the likes of you. I'd advise you to turn back," says the Zwerg nearest to us. The others grunt in approval. Clearly, this is their leader. The other Zwergs brandish similar weapons, spinning them in figure eights, their sharp blades whizzing through the air.

"We mean you no harm," I say. "All we ask is passage to the other side."

The Zwergs collectively laugh. "Ah, passage, you say? Well, don't let us stop you, son. You may carry on, since you asked so kindly."

I hesitate for just a moment, but when I take a step forward, the Zwerg reaches for his belt, and in a flash there is a dagger stuck in a tree, dangerously close to my head.

Again the Zwergs roar with laughter. The leader shrugs. "Whoops. Pardon my aim. I was due to give Slug a close shave." He waves to one Zwerg who's cleanly shaven and obviously not needing a trim of any type. "Must've slipped from my clumsy hand. Wouldn't it be a shame if that happened again? You could lose an ear or something worse, like your liver," he says, pushing his coat back. Knives of all shapes and sizes line his belt. I swallow hard, unsure how we're going to get out of this situation alive.

"You want to play games? I'll show you how to play," Hook says, sending a spray of bullets at the Zwergs. The men blur in my vision as they swing, climb, and jump from tree to tree.

"Run!" I say, watching the men advance toward us.

Hook dashes to the right, his Gatling gun firing the entire time.

Gathering myself, I dart to the left, heading for the village, while jumping, wobbling, and slipping over the rubble of several buildings. Finally, I race up the roof of a collapsed cottage and leap. As my feet leave the thatched incline, a Zwerg appears on the roof of the next bungalow. Below me a large, cavernous crevice, the darkest shade of black, winds across the village. I swing my arms and legs, hoping to push myself farther. Instead I descend. The other side seems so far away. Time slows as I plunge toward the crack. I reach for my weapons belt and hit a switch. A grappling hook bursts from the belt, its claws springing into place and hooking onto the crevice's opposite side. I jam the brake hard, and my body jolts as the metal clamps down on the rope. Swinging into the rocky wall of the cavern, I put my feet out, hoping to blunt the impact.

Even though my boots lessen the blow, my shoulder smacks

into the wall, sending shooting pain throughout my left side. My teeth clack as I bite back a howl. When the ache dissipates, I flip another switch. The gears within my belt grind as they coils the rope, lifting me to the edge of the crevice. Finally, with every ounce of strength in me, I pull myself up and roll onto the soft dirt, barely able to catch my breath.

Someone grunts above me, and my eyes fly open. Panic grips me as a Zwerg's ax drives toward my face. I roll to my left, renewing the agony in my shoulder. Reaching for the trigger on my belt, I twist back over. Bullets fly, hitting no particular target. Struggling to my feet, I stumble as the ax swings again, this time nicking my hand as I regain my balance. The pain sends me stumbling backward, and I find myself sprawled out on the ground again. The Zwerg roars and advances toward me. I crab-walk back until there is nowhere else to go: a tree trunk behind me and the Zwerg in front of me.

"Death to the queen," the Zwerg says, towering over me, ax raised, ready to split me in half. My pulse skips a couple of beats as I realize they recognize that Hook and I are of the royal family.

As I prepare to dodge to the right, there's an explosion of sound. Despite that, I still hear the Zwerg's gasp as warm liquid splatters over my face. I wipe it away, and my fingers come back slick with fresh blood. Peering up, I shout, overcome by the gore. Riddled with bullet holes, he is no longer recognizable. His ax drops and he falls forward. Panting, I scurry away as his body hits the ground with a thud.

"Hey, enough lying around. Get up and help me!" Hook growls. At first I can't find him, but when he shifts, he is wedged between two trees, taking shelter from throwing knives as they stick into the trunks. He switches out the ammunition belt to the Gatling gun strapped to his arm, letting the empty one drop to the ground. Soon bullets are ricocheting off the trees, sending bark splintering in every direction. One bullet makes its mark, striking a Zwerg in the gut. He collapses, his body plummeting into another well-placed inky crevice in the forest floor.

Hook sprints from the trees, ducking into a partially standing cottage.

Snatching the mini-grenades from my weapons belt, I race through an enormous hollowed-out tree trunk, feeling as though I'm traveling through a tunnel. When I reach the end, I peer out. Hook leans from an empty window of the cottage and takes aim, ready to incapacitate a Zwerg. Another Zwerg peeks around the corner of the cottage, his double-bladed ax in hand.

"Hook, your left!" I shout.

The Zwerg swings. Hook ducks as the weapon nearly decapitates him. The Zwerg loses his balance, and before he is able to steady himself, Hook puts several bullets in the man's chest.

Leaping to my feet, I rush through a series of decayed, fallen trees, taking out two more Zwergs as I toss the grenades. On impact they explode, leaving no trace of the person who once stood in the projectile's way. I have no idea where I'm going, but I hope that wherever I end up will be near the exit. I count off the dead men both Hook and I have managed to stop: five down, two to go.

Turning a corner, I careen into something solid. I stumble back and find myself sprawled out on the ground. A Zwerg stands over me, grinning wildly. Despite his small stature, he is nothing but pure muscle. He kicks me in the kidney with the metal toe of his boot. I grunt in pain, feeling as though I've been hit with a sledgehammer.

"You'll never get out of here alive," the Zwerg says, lifting his pickax over his head. "I shall enjoy dispensing of you."

I roll as the ax comes down hard. Snatching my knife, I stumble to my feet and aim it at the Zwerg. "We didn't come here to fight. Just let me pass."

"It's unfortunate that your mother is the Bloodred Queen," he says, raising his ax. "With her and her kin, it's always a fight."

"Stepmother," I protest, backing up. I pull another grenade from my weapons belt. "Look, I don't have to hurt you. You could come with us. You could leave this place."

"Leave this place? Do you honestly believe we hadn't thought of that idea?" he says with a snort. Not waiting for a response, he swings his ax and misses. Frustrated, he grips the shaft of his ax tighter, his knuckles paling. "Danger lies beyond every door. We've gone from a thriving city to just seven of us trying to escape this godforsaken prison. That evil queen, she's decimated our village, captured and imprisoned our people! And now her sons shall pay the price."

Obviously, this man has never met my stepmother. Our

deaths won't mean anything to her, other than being an annoyance for the loss of time and the apple. But before I can say anything more, he swings the ax again, nearly clipping my legs as I dodge the blade. I race into the open forest. The Zwerg is only seconds behind me. As he throws himself at me, his weight hits me like a battering ram, forcing me back to the ground. His plated armor knocks the wind out of me, and I lose my grip on the grenade. It tumbles to the ground.

His knees pin my arms to the dirt, and he holds the shaft of the ax against my throat, cutting off my air. Adrenaline courses through me, and I'm desperate for a breath. I wrestle, trying to wriggle free from beneath the Zwerg. Hook's shouts draw the Zwerg's attention, and I'm able to free my hands. Gripping the worn wood of the ax's handle, I lift it just enough to take the pressure off my neck.

Hook's shouts come again from a distance, but I can't see him.

The Zwerg above me chortles. "What now, boy?" he asks, shoving the shaft of the ax back into my throat, making me gasp for air. But I keep both hands gripped on the weapon.

Hook screams again, and I shove the ax off me, throwing the Zwerg off-balance. He stumbles, and before he's able to attack, I rip off his goggles and gouge at his eyes. He shrieks in horror, releasing his weapon with a loud clatter. I bolt to my feet, grab the ax, and smash the wooden handle into his pudgy nose. The sound of cartilage and bones cracking, as disgusting as it is, brings relief. I pull a mini-pistol from my weapons belt, aim, and fire, hitting the Zwerg in the chest. Sure that I've disabled him, I snatch my throwing star from my belt and launch it at Hook's attacker.

The star strikes the other Zwerg in the neck. His knees buckle and he falls to the ground, dead. Hook, clearly shaken, stands from his position. Not acknowledging me, he retrieves his Gatling gun, which he lost during the attack.

I turn back to my assailant, now incapacitated on the ground. He bleeds profusely from his eyes and nose, staining his snow-white beard scarlet red. The bones of his skull are distorted and sunken in, no longer holding the form of what should be his face. When he coughs, bloodstained spittle dribbles from his mouth. He suddenly looks twenty years older as his face droops, the ache of surrender etching lines into his forehead and the corners of his eyes. He reaches for something in the pocket of his vest.

"I beg you, before you end my time on this earth, grant me one wish. Find my daughter. Give this to her," he says, his words gurgling with each breath. In his hand is an old key on a long chain.

"Daughter?" I say as a lump forms in my throat.

"Ginger. The Bloodred Queen took her and many others captive the night she built the Labyrinth," he says, his voice only a whisper now. He struggles for breath.

"Where can I find her?" I ask, guilt eating at my gut.

The Zwerg tries to speak, but his words are inaudible.

Placing the key around my neck, I turn away. A tidal wave

of thoughts and emotions floods me, and I feel as if I'm treading water, lost in the middle of a deep and vast ocean. I squeeze my eyes, shutting out the image of the Zwerg's bloodied body. Covering my ears, I drown out his gurgling breaths.

Those who have died by my hand, it was purely out of self-defense. It was either me or them; only one of us would come out alive. I'm not a murderer, a cold-blooded monster like my brother. After all, this man is only injured, not dead. Perhaps I should've stopped sooner, but the animal instinct to fight to the death is a knee-jerk reaction instilled in me as a means of survival.

Shots ring out, startling me. Whirling around, I see Hook standing over the Zwerg, his Gatling gun aimed at the man's head. The Zwerg lies lifeless.

"Why did you do that?" I shout in disbelief.

Hook stares at the body. "He was suffering."

"Well, you didn't have to shoot him," I say.

Hook gives me a disgusted look. "It was the merciful thing to do. He was in pain, couldn't breathe. You were just letting him drown in his own blood. Who's the evil brother now?" he says, stepping over the dead man.

Gripping his coat, I spin him around. "Don't dare compare us! I've killed no one unless my life has depended on it," I say, waving toward the bodies of Zwergs surrounding us. "Yet wherever you go, you leave behind a sea of corpses without an ounce of remorse."

Shoving me, Hook scowls. "At least I end their misery;

meanwhile, you destroy lives and then turn a blind eye, leaving your victims to suffer in your wake."

Rage boils my blood. "I have done nothing of the sort. I've only done what I felt was right, what was the best for everyone."

"Yeah, little stepbrother, and let's count the hundreds you've betrayed: the Bloodred Queen, the Marauders, the Lost Boys, me. And if it wasn't for me, this man would have lived another ten minutes suffering from his wounds," Hook says with a disgusted expression. "You're pathetic, Jack."

"His blood is not on my hands," I snarl.

Hook gives me one of his white, toothy smiles and tugs on the key hanging around my neck. "Tell that to his little girl," he says, letting go of it and heading toward the exit.

I look down at the key and see Hook's bloody fingerprints on it. I rub at the blood and tuck the key under my shirt, wondering how I'll ever find the Zwerg's daughter. When I do, what will I tell her about her father? Turning, I follow Hook, leaving behind the corpses of seven bodies.

· A L Y S S A ·

I'm sure I've dreamed up the stranger. Other than the Professor, he is the first adult I've seen in a long time.

"Wait! Come back here!" Maddox shouts, stopping just short of the entrance.

Deciding to join Maddox, I step away from the geared wall. I turn back to the elaborate series of cogs when I hear the faintest ticking sound. The lever flinches slightly but holds.

"Did you see that?" Maddox asks, wide-eyed.

"Do you suppose he's the one who left the gears I found?" I ask.

Maddox shrugs. "He must have been watching us. As soon as you solved that puzzle, he shot out of those trees like a hound chasing a rabbit. He must have known about the puzzle."

"Well, he's long gone now. We should start moving," I say, looking back over my shoulder at the geared wall. Again, I think I see the lever shift slightly, but after watching it for several long seconds, I chalk it up to my imagination.

The towering, leafy hedges give way to metal walls, which cast gloomy shadows on the pathway beneath the moonlight. I step inside the fortress with Maddox following behind. Loud clangs of mechanical noises echo throughout the passageway, although nothing appears to move. As I pass by the blades, my heart stutters hard against my ribs. The knives are larger than I originally realized, each one at least three stories taller than me. A crash of what sounds like metal doors startles me, and I jump, but still see nothing out of place. We move slowly toward the other side of the corridor in spite of the noises that reverberate off the vine-covered metal walls. Like ethereal phantoms, the sounds of our footsteps chase us.

Chains rattle ahead of us, but there is nothing that could produce that sound.

An icy chill races up my spine. "I have a really bad feeling about this," I say.

"*Now* you have a bad feeling about this," Maddox says, sweat beading on his brow.

Halfway through the dark passage, a deafening bang behind us draws my attention. My long, blond hair blows in front of my face, obscuring my vision as a gust of wind whips through the corridor. Whirling toward the sound, my heart stops as the first bladed wheel releases from the wall, only this time it spins faster than it did when we first arrived. The second and third follow. I recall the ticking sound that came from the geared wall, and my blood turns cold as I realize what it was for: a timer . . . and time's up.

"Run!" I scream. Spinning, I dash in the opposite direction. By the sound of huffing, I know Maddox is close behind. Metal blades slash against one another, scraping like sharpening knives. The terrifying noise draws closer, each blade releasing from its cradle with a loud clank.

The dead end of the passageway draws nearer. As each wheel

releases, the screech of metal builds so the shrieking pierces my ears. I'm sure that the slightest hesitation will guarantee my last breath.

"Jump!" Maddox says, giving me one last shove.

With the blades whirring at my back, I wonder if this is indeed my last moment. We slide across the stone floor, tumbling from the passage just as the final blades clash against each other, interlocking and blocking the entrance. My head hits the far wall, sending pain shooting down my spine and limbs.

My pulse beats rapidly in my ears, and I can't catch my breath. Maddox lands next to me, his wide eyes fixed on the deadly-looking blades. He collapses back, knocking his top hat from his head as he gasps for air.

"We made it!" I say, breathless.

"Well, mostly." Maddox sits up, straightens his lapels, and stands. "I may have left my dignity and my manhood back there." He bends down and picks up his hat, settling it back on his head.

Offering me a hand, Maddox helps me to my feet. I brush the dust from my tunic and leggings. The light of the full moon glitters over the tops of the metal-and-ivy walls. I take in the corridor, looking both left and right. The road seems to go on forever.

I sigh heavily. "Which way?"

Maddox nods and gestures for me to go ahead. "Pick a way. All ways are the right ways and eventually lead to the center, or at least I hope that is the case."

Reluctantly, I choose the left path and limp ahead, wondering which of the dozens of corridors before us is the next we should take.

Maddox's gaze darts throughout the passageway as we walk. Appearing nervous, he rambles on about nonsensical things such as mousetraps and the moon and memory and muchness. His nervousness mirrors the butterflies in my own stomach. Clangs ring out in the distance, sounding like metal doors locking shut. We choose another pathway that heads east just as the gears along the top of the fortress rattle and spin. I cover my ears when the mechanisms shriek. The ground vibrates beneath our feet. Wheels spin as sections of the walls shift, turning ninety degrees and blocking the way we've just come from. Other sections open, creating new passages and shutting off others. The wall in front of us shudders and slides closed.

Maddox stares at me, his dark-lined eyes wide with fear. "Chop-chop, Alyssa!"

We race down the corridor, sprinting toward the opening to the east. The metal wall creaks as it seals off the hallway ahead. We are nearly at the passageway's exit, but clearly are not going to make it. The wall bangs shut. I try to push it open, but it doesn't budge. Furious, I slap the wall. "Now what?" I say, looking back at Maddox.

He takes in the barriers that surround us. A clank of metal to my right draws my attention as another section of wall slides open, exposing a new passage.

Maddox places a hand out. "Looks like we've just one choice."

I step through the opening, my stomach fluttering. "How are we going to find our way through the Labyrinth with all of these walls shifting?"

"I don't suppose you brought a map and compass?" Maddox asks in all seriousness. "That would've been the most sensible thing to do."

"A map? I hardly know where we are, much less own a map of this place," I say.

"Well, that was terribly irresponsible of you. Why would you go somewhere you've never been without a map?" he asks.

"Seriously?" I say, throwing my hands up.

"No? Well then, it looks like we're going this way." He points to the opening next to us. "After you, Your Grace."

With a huff I say, "You could really drive a girl mad, you know?"

I'm rewarded with the sound of a deep belly laugh as I head into the next passageway.

More walls shift around us, and we find ourselves changing course every few minutes. After a while, I get used to the unpredictable shifts in direction. "So really, what's up with the walls changing? It hardly seems fair. If we're supposed to find this apple in the center of the Labyrinth, we'll never get there if we keep getting redirected."

Maddox chuckles. "Life isn't meant to be fair, my dear. A fair is where you go to buy cotton candy, enjoy carnival rides, and pet smelly goats. Life, on the other hand, is often filled with the unexpected. Sometimes the cards we are dealt cause us to have to shift our own anticipated direction. And other times fate deals us a hand that we are pleasantly thankful for," Maddox says meaningfully as he looks at me.

Blushing, I drop my gaze, unsure how to respond. Is he talking about me? Having no words to convey the brewing affection in my chest, I just nod and keep moving.

Soon enough, we come to a dead end. "Nonsense. Complete and utter nonsense. First the garden, then blades, and now moving walls. What's next? A maze of guillotincs?" I ask, frustrated.

This wall before us is different from any of the others we have come across so far. Instead of large expanses of green hedges and metal corridors, this one is a checkerboard of iron and chrome plates, each one the length of a cannon.

With a loud crash, the expanse behind us shrinks shut, boxing us into a narrow square space. Searching for any way out of this prison, I find none. My breath quickens, and I'm on the verge of hyperventilation as I feel along the wall, hoping to find a concealed button or switch, but I have no luck. "What now?" I ask as I turn my gaze toward the top of the metal walls that tower above our heads. There is no way we can scale them.

"I think I found the entrance," Maddox says, rubbing his dark scruff.

Following his gaze, I discover a small door at the bottom of one of the four walls. Had it not been for the glittering gold doorknob with a bumblefly engraved into the metal, I would never have noticed it. I rush over and kneel, testing the handle. It doesn't budge.

"Well, it was a nice thought anyway. It doesn't look like we'll be getting out through there. Besides, it's hardly big enough to crawl through," Maddox says. He grips one of the metal plates and tries unsuccessfully to pull himself up. "There's got to be another way."

He's right. Even if I could open the door, the frame is no larger than a house cat. Trying the knob again, I discover a lock big enough for a small key. Recalling the brass key I found along the road on our journey to the Labyrinth, I reach inside my pocket and pull it out. Slipping the key into the keyhole, I turn, listening to tumblers give with a snick. As I twist the knob, the door swings open and the plates on the wall fold back on one another. The opening that was once no taller than my shin sudden grows larger with each shifting plate. I have a shrinking sensation, as if I'm getting smaller.

Beyond the opening, a green field appears, seeming to go on for a kilometer or more. In the distance, past a massive chain-linked wall, the Labyrinth appears to continue. The moon and night sky are lost in the sudden brightness of the place.

Maddox takes my elbow. "Stay close," he says, his eyes darting as if looking for signs of trouble. His heightened awareness of our surroundings unsettles me.

I follow him, stepping through the walls and onto the lush green grass. Six colored arches several meters high are scattered throughout the field.

"What is this place?" I ask.

"It is said the Bloodred Queen is fond of croquet," he says.

"I enjoy a good game of croquet, but I have never seen a course quite like this," I say, hearing the quiver in my voice.

"Trust me, knowing what I know of the Bloodred Queen, this is like no croquet game you've ever participated in," he says.

I think of picnics from when I was growing up where we'd play. I have a feeling this will be nothing like those whimsical, fun games. My stomach twists in nervous knots. So far the only thing I can count on in this bizarre Labyrinth is the unexpected. And although this field is quite lovely, instinct begs me not to trust my eyes. The plated wall behind us rebuilds itself, each metal slab locking into the next until the only way out is the small door, still left slightly ajar.

"Looks like we definitely will not be going back that way," Maddox says, glancing over his shoulder.

We travel farther onto the field and find ourselves on a patch of grass painted white. Two metal disks with footprints on each sit side by side.

"What do you suppose this is for?" I ask, almost wishing I hadn't.

"You don't want to know. Let's just get to the other side," Maddox says, stepping around the disks. Star-shaped blades rocket from the ground, nearly skewering him. Startled, he leaps back as the blades create a jagged barricade before us.

Maddox glances to the side, and I can see him trying to determine if there is another way around the barrier when a wall of fire blazes on either side of us, about a kilometer in both directions.

Maddox turns to me, his gold eyes resigned. "Looks like this is our only way out. Do you have a preference?" he asks, pointing to the blue and black disks.

With the toe of my boot, I touch the blue disk, half expecting it to explode. When nothing happens, I take my place within the circle, setting my feet on the footprints. Maddox shifts uncomfortably before stepping on the black circle. Metal clips snap from the disk and wrap around each of my ankles, binding me to the circle. Maddox grunts as his disk docs the same.

"Get your sword out, Duchess, you're going to need it," he says, pulling a twelve-cylinder pistol from a holster on his belt. While most of it appears to be made of a bronze-colored alloy, the grip is wrapped in an aged leather. A decorative scope made up of thick washers sits atop the barrel. The weapon, although crudely built, is quite magnificent.

The top of the green walls opens, and balconies filled with weary and gaunt-looking spectators jut out. Insincere cheers ring from the stands above. I can't be sure, but I assume these are the townsfolk who were caught in the Labyrinth as the exterior of the fortress grew overnight while they slept. They hardly look like people anymore but rather skeletons. How they have survived this long is a mystery.

A platform resembling a lily pad rises from a murky pond in the center of the field. Standing on it is a rugged-looking boy dressed in black. A scar the shape of a heart is branded on the left side of his face. Black-threaded stitches give the old wound the appearance of having been sewn on. A glass-and-wire prison surrounds him, preventing him from escaping.

"Welcome, ladies and gentlemen," the boy shouts, his voice raspy. "Let's hear a round of applause for our players."

The crowd claps halfheartedly.

"Playing for Team A are two really stupid people, apparently with a death wish, who should never have entered the Labyrinth," the boy grumbles.

"He's right, it was a really dumb idea to come here. I blame you," Maddox says, fidgeting with his ankle cuffs.

"Shut up, Maddox," I growl.

"Playing for Team B is—" He doesn't have a chance to finish his sentence. In the distance, two large spheres, one copper and the other gold, appear out of nowhere. From this far, I can make out the distinct form of figures in each ball. They aggressively shout expletives, waving fists in the air. I get the feeling that if given the opportunity, they would try to tear me apart with their bare hands.

The ground rumbles beneath my feet. I catch Maddox's worried gaze as he holds his arms out, stabilizing himself. Suddenly, dozens of spikes rise from the circumference of the circle, spiraling out, and their tips meet just above our heads.

"Hold on to your knickers, Your Grace. We'll be going for a

ride," Maddox shouts. I look over and he's reaching for the loops of leather hanging from the steel bars. His face goes slack, his knuckles paling as he grips the black loop with his free hand. The other clutches the pistol tightly. Pulse beating rapidly in my ears, I do the same. We are trapped within spherical cages and there is no way out.

My stomach has still yet to settle from the terror of running from the blades. Somehow I know what's about to happen will not compare. My eyes lock with Maddox's, and I see apprehension in his. Suddenly, a circular section of the wall as tall as a human bursts forth, sending Maddox on a tailspin down the field toward the first archway. It quickly occurs to me that in this game of croquet I am not a player but the ball. If I thought I was sick to my stomach before, I'm going to be in much worse shape shortly.

With a jolt, my sphere is struck, and I spin out of control. I brace myself within the cage, pressing my hands and feet as hard as I can onto the bars, afraid that even one slip will send me tumbling like a rag doll within the metal ball.

Shutting my eyes tightly, I spin in a dizzying spell and am relieved when I feel my cage hit something metal. I open one eye and see the first enormous wicket pass by.

The young announcer calls out the score, but all I can hear is my rapid breath. My cage is struck again, this time from below. The sphere sails in the air, and from behind me I feel the sudden burn of heat. I scream, shielding my face as I nearly hit the wall of fire. Before I am turned to cinder, another mallet-shaped pillar bursts from the ground, sending me spiraling onto the next wicket.

Three spheres blur past me. Maddox retches inside his prison. The copper and gold spheres of the other players whirl, nearly clipping my cage. For the first time I get a good look at the figures within the opposing orbs.

It's two girls who must be sisters with their matching tawny skin and elegant cheekbones. Both are my age and wear dark suits with a single emblem just below their left shoulder: a broken and bloodied heart. As the girl in the copper cage spins toward me, she pulls out a sword and swipes at me through the bars. I duck as she chops off a single lock of my hair. I have no idea how she was able to maneuver the sword from her spinning cage into mine, but I'm certain I don't want to be anywhere near her. I reach for my own sword, but it weighs heavy in my grip, sending my balance off. I'm not sure how I can fight and still manipulate this spherical cage.

I parry right, dodge another blow of hers, and sweep up, nicking her arm along the way.

As the girl swipes at me again, her sword hits the steel bars, sending sparks showering down on me. With her attention on skewering me, she doesn't anticipate my attack as I jab at her with my sword, injuring her thigh as her cage rolls by me. She doesn't flinch, but instead reaches down to touch the blood oozing from her wound. Her face flushes with rage.

I'm eternally grateful for the dueling lessons my father gave me. The memory of him brings an ache to my chest, but there's no time to mourn. He'd tell me to be light on my feet, but inside this orb, I can hardly discern up from down.

"Lucky move, girl," she says, scowling. "But it's been a long time since we've lost a match."

"She isn't lying either," the other girl cackles, dropping into a crouch and gripping the bars by her feet. Tucked in tightly like that, her sphere spins faster and straight toward Maddox. She holds a pistol tightly in her hand as she aims for him.

"You'll pay for that, girl," the first girl says. She swings her sword, and it catches on my cloak, ripping a hole in the fabric. Thankfully, the blade misses me.

Our cages continue to roll, bouncing off each other as we take turns trying to incapacitate the other through the grid work of steel. I swing and hit her left calf. She screams and reaches for her leg, sending her cage spiraling in a different direction.

Glancing over at my other opponent, I see blood spilling from a bullet wound to her shoulder. She balls her body up and sends her sphere in a controlled spin, aiming for Maddox. I mimic the girl's moves, thrusting my weight toward the ground. My cage rolls in a wild rotation. I grind my teeth, trying to keep from vomiting. Another mallet-shaped pillar explodes from the ground, sending me through several wickets. I catch a glimpse of Maddox, dodging bullets from his opponent. He fires two quick rounds and spins away. Too busy attempting to save my own life, I've failed to count the number of bullets he's fired. Anxiety builds within me as I wonder if he's used his twelve rounds already.

I tuck and roll as the metal bars are struck from all sides, losing myself in a blur of colorful hoops, spheres, and green grass. My arms and legs are pulled in so close that the nerves in my fingers and toes tingle with energy, my hands gripping tightly to my sword.

Not soon enough, I find myself back at the starting point. Next to me, Maddox vomits violently in his own cage again. As my blue steel cage finds its way to the metal circle, I release my grip on the bars, exhausted. In the distance, I see the gold and copper balls find their place on the other side.

The cage snaps open, and I collapse on the ground, unable to hold myself upright any longer. The bars coil down, returning to the disk from where they came. Weak, dizzy, and filled with remorse, I roll over onto the grass as far as I can manage, away from the disk. Becoming the playing piece in a game for a second round is the last thing I want to happen. Bile burns the back of my throat. Maddox groans nearby, but I no longer have the energy to sit up, much less check on his well-being. The grass feels cool against my face as I fight away the overwhelming sensation of nausea. Just a few minutes. If I can only rest for a few minutes, maybe I'll wake up to find this was all just a nightmare. A bad dream and this place will never have existed but in the darkest corners of my mind.

"And the winners are . . . Team A, Blue and Black!" the young knave announces as his voice echoes through the playing field. The crowd roars with as much energy as they can muster, seeming pleased by our victory, but equally defeated.

I know I should be pleased, especially to have survived, but after nearly having lost my lunch and my life, I find nothing the least bit amusing. As I close my eyes, I am shaking. I roll over and Maddox is hovering above me.

"We have to go," Maddox says, worry evident in his tone. His eyes dart toward something in the distance. A door has opened on the other side of the playing field. "I highly doubt it'll stay open much longer. Time to move, now!"

Maddox yanks me to my feet and we are running, still flanked by walls of fire on either side of the croquet course. As I run passed the red-stained grass where blood was shed, every cell within me wants to turn back, to return to Northumberland and find another way to help my people. Instead I keep running, hardly feeling the ground beneath me. The doorway feels impossibly far away, and the more I run, the farther it seems. When we finally reach the other side, I am so eager to leave this dangerous game. While few things frighten me, this deadly round of living croquet is hardly a game I ever want to play again.

"Well done, Alyssa," Maddox says, the color returning to his face. "You make a fine croquet partner. However, let's hope this is our last game."

"Agreed, Maddox," I say, my voice barely a whisper.

Watching him reload his pistol fills me with dread. How much worse can things get? Maddox gestures toward the open corridor. Beyond the doorway lies a thick grove of trees. "Shall we?"

I step into the dark pathway with hesitance, knowing that

until we make it to the Labyrinth's center, it will only become more challenging.

"Stay close, Duchess," Maddox says, a hint of wariness in his gruff voice.

When I glance over my shoulder and peer back at the life-size croquet course, I dread what comes next.

· P E T E ·

I storm through the makeshift village outside the castle walls. It's late, past midnight, and most of the residents have either returned to their shelters or joined the party at the Poison Garden. A few stumble throughout the shanty village, nearly tripping over one another, reeking with the scent of booze and cigarette smoke. Bottles and trash litter the grounds outside the castle. I hold my breath, blocking out the smell of sewage and filthy bodies.

By the time I reach the castle entrance, a few stragglers are being encouraged to move along by Pickpocket, Cogs, and Scout. The refugees grumble but eventually return to their grubby tents.

"You all right, boss?" Pickpocket asks.

Ignoring him, I burst through the castle doors and storm up the stairs. I'm furious and I need to vent. There is only one person who can make me feel any better right now. On my way to my room I take a detour and burst into Gwen's chambers. Startled, she stares at me. I must be a sight—standing there bare-chested with bleeding gashes left behind by Katt's fingernails. If I look half as feral as I feel, it must be terrifying. Before I can say anything—explode about my rage with Katt or ask for an explanation about what happened between us earlier—she talks first.

"Where have you been?" she demands. "I was worried about you! Doc says you went to the Poison Garden. Do you know what could've happened to you there? No one comes back from there, Pete. No one! If you think I'm going to just chase you to all corners of the world to protect you from yourself, well . . . I can't."

Annoyance prickles up my spine. "Chase me? *You* sent *me* away earlier. One minute you want me and the next minute you don't. Do you know how confusing this is?"

"My mother just *died,*" she says, her voice catching. "Sorry for needing a moment to myself. You have no idea how hard it is to have to be strong for Joanna and Mikey."

"What? Are you kidding me? Of all people, I'm the one who understands the most. How quickly you've forgotten that I've lost my parents and my sister," I say a little too loudly.

"That's not what I mean. I just . . ." She hesitates. "What if they die? What if *I* die? Who's going to take care of them, Pete?"

Her words cut me. I can't believe her. "Me!" I shout. "Of course I'd take care of them. What kind of person do you think I am, Gwen? I wouldn't just abandon them or leave them to die alone. I'd take as good care of them as I would any Lost Kid."

The look she gives me is like a stab. Like she's thinking of all the others I let down. Like I'd do the same to her siblings.

"Gwen," I say, my voice cracking.

"Don't, Pete," she says, holding a hand up and turning her gaze away. "The reality is that we're all sick. We're all going to die. I can't be worrying about you, especially when you so recklessly risk your life with no regard for those who care about you, for those who depend on you. I can't watch the people I love die. As it is, I'm terrified of losing Joanna and Mikey. My heart doesn't have room to lose one more person. And neither does yours."

My anger deflates as quickly as it exploded. I reach for her. "It wouldn't . . ."

She shakes her head at me and steps away. "Pete, no," she says softly. "Please leave."

Panic claws at my throat as I realize she's trying to end things between us. And she thinks she's doing it for my own good, too. Like it'd be better for me to lose her now instead of later on. But she'll have to say the words. She'll have to look me in the eye and tell me it's over. Not that I'll give her the chance if I can help it. I will fight for her heart no matter what it costs me.

"I went looking for Duchess Alyssa," I say, stepping around what she hasn't said. I can't accept it. Won't accept it. "She's been gone too long. Someone needed to check in on her."

"Did you find her?" Gwen asks, her blue eyes hopeful. "Doc and Lily are concerned. They say she's been gone awhile."

I realize too late that it didn't help things to bring up Alyssa. It will just leave her feeling more hopeless. "Maddox has taken her somewhere, but Katt wouldn't tell me where," I admit. "But maybe he took her to the apple?"

Gwen shifts from foot to foot. "Maybe," she says, although I can tell she doesn't really believe that. I wonder if she says that only to appease me in hopes that I'll leave quicker.

An imaginary knife in my gut twists. "I should have gone

with her. Not him. We don't know him, and the way he's killing off kids doesn't exactly make him seem trustworthy."

"Alyssa can hold her own with Maddox. She's smart and strong. Your place is here. If you'd gone with her, who would be in charge and hold us together?" But she doesn't quite look at me as she says this, which undermines any confidence I have in her words.

I suck in a deep breath. "Katt has taken control of the Poison Garden. I think she intends to declare war on Alnwick."

"What? Why?" Gwen asks.

"She wants your mother's notes," I say. "She's as desperate as any of the refugees to get her hands on a cure."

Gwen's face pales. "Desperate? How desperate?"

Sighing, I let the events of the night run through my head one more time. "I don't know, but her deadline is dawn."

"She's trying to take the throne, isn't she?" Gwen asks.

"She knows we'll never let her do that. Even with Alyssa gone. And we certainly aren't handing over the research papers. Her intentions with your mother's notes are to share them with everyone. That means not only would the chemical makeup of the Horologia poison be leaked to anyone, but any new antidote could be used as leverage. Especially by the Bloodred Queen. Can you imagine what would happen if she were the only one to possess the formula for the cure? Especially since her country created the poison in the first place. They may still have access to the apple."

Understanding washes over Gwen's face. "The entire world would be indebted to her."

I nod. "Indebted to the woman who tried to murder us all. We can only guess how bad that could be. Katt can't claim the royal crown. We can't let her, nor can she get her hands on your mother's research. She's already sent the Everland antidote to the Bloodred Queen. Who knows how long they've been in contact and what Katt's shared with her already. If Katt's support of what is going on within the Poison Garden is any indication of how she would rule, we have to do everything in our power to protect Alnwick until Duchess Alyssa returns."

"What are we going to do? You saw that crowd earlier. Had they gotten any angrier, they would have stormed the castle, even without someone leading them. We'd be outnumbered," Gwen says.

Chills race through me. "We need to prepare to defend the castle, recruit as many as we can, and hope that Duchess Alyssa returns with something that Doc can use to develop the real cure."

"And if she doesn't come back?" Gwen asks.

The thought makes a lump grow in my throat. Gwen watches me, waiting for me to give her an inkling of hope, and it wrecks me that I have nothing to offer. I promised in Everland to protect her and her family. Northumberland was supposed to be a new home for us, one of hope and a future, except it's everything but that. I should never have convinced her to join me,

Bella, and the other boys in the Lost City. She probably would've been better off without me. Gwen is tough, the toughest girl I've met. Without me, things might have been better for her, too. Maybe Gwen's right to leave me. A flurry of panic fills in my stomach. I swallow hard, trying to not to lose it at the thought of life without Gwen.

"Do you think Alyssa will be okay with Maddox?" I ask, changing the subject.

A small smile appears on Gwen's lips. It's the first glimpse of hope throughout this entire conversation. "I don't know Maddox, but if anyone can handle him, it's the duchess. I've sparred with that girl and trust me, I would never want to cross her. My daggers are nothing compared to her sword-wielding skills."

I feel a hint of relief. At least this is one bit of good news.

"Pete! Gwen!" Doc shouts from the hall. "Where are you?"

"Gwen's chambers!" I shout back, dashing to the door.

Fear blanches his face as he skids to a stop.

"What is it?" I ask.

"It's Bella. She's not well," Doc says through ragged breaths.

I freeze, unable to take in a breath. "What? What do you mean?" I ask, sprinting toward the castle doors and into the cool night air toward the infirmary. My fists are clenched so tight I can feel my fingernails digging into my palms.

"I don't know. I've never seen symptoms like this," Doc says, following close behind me.

When I reach the infirmary, Bella's bed, the one closest to the window, is empty, the blankets in a pile on the ground.

Mikey has climbed into Joanna's cot with her. He sniffles as Joanna squeezes him, both arms wrapped tightly around his quaking body. Joanna peers up at me, tears streaking her rose-colored cheeks.

"She's there!" Joanna says, pointing to a darkened corner.

A single beam of moonlight shines through a crack in the structure's boards. The pale light falls on Bella's face, her expression one of agony. I rush to her side and try to pull her to me.

She swipes at me with her hand, her long, clawed fingernails scratching me in a ribbon of bright pain. I reel back in shock and brush my fingers across my skin. Blood stains my fingertips.

"Bella?" I say, hearing the uncertainty in my voice.

She opens her eyes wide. Instead of the brilliant blue irises I expect, her eyes are a greenish gold. When she sees my face, her jaw drops.

"Pete, I . . . I'm sorry," she says.

I wrap my arms around her, unafraid. "Hush. There's no need to apologize."

She weeps bitterly in my arms while I pull her into my lap and rock her. What is happening to her eyes? Out of instinct, I look to Doc to explain. But he just stares at me, confused, as I realize he didn't see what I saw.

"Shh, you're okay. I'm here now," I say, not sure how my presence will be of any comfort.

Glancing over, I notice that Gwen followed us and is consoling her own siblings next to the empty bed that once was their mother's. The finality of the Professor's death strikes me speechless. Just a short while ago, she was someone; she had a physical presence. Now someone has taken the responsibility to dispose of her body. No good-byes. No funeral. Just . . . gone.

Resting my cheek on Bella's head, I hold on to her as tight as I can, unwilling to let go because if I do, she may be the next to die.

The infirmary is filled with quiet sounds of whimpers and whispered words of assurance that all will be well when a shadow is cast along the floor, blocking out the moonlight in the doorway. Turning, I see the strong Indian warrior I met in Everland standing in the doorframe, sobbing. I can hardly breathe as it is, but the sight of a broken fighter chokes what air is left within me.

Doc rushes to her side. "Lily?"

Lily covers her eyes and crumples to the floor, her black sari spilling into a shadowed puddle. Doc kneels next to her, offering what comfort he can.

"Lily, what's wrong?" he asks, placing an arm around her.

Lily slowly drops her hand, turning her eyes toward me. Her entire body convulses with tremors. At first I don't know what's wrong until she peers at me. "What is happening to me?" she says.

Her irises are no longer brown but instead the shade of spun gold, and her pupils are dark slits, like those of a snake.

· A L Y S S A ·

We step through the break in the wall, and I've never been so grateful in my whole life. The melodious song of birds and distant howls of animals echo through the vast forest. Thick branches tower in a blanket of intertwined red, orange, and yellow leaves, concealing the sky beyond them. But the path is not well lit and I wonder if we should light a torch. I turn to ask . . . but quickly forget who it is I'm addressing or what the question was. In fact, I realize I have no idea where I am or what I'm doing here. I feel a flutter of panic. In the distance I see a boy in a burgundy suit jacket and a top hat. I take caution and pull my sword from its sheath, unsure if this boy is friend or foe. He seems vaguely familiar, but I don't recognize him.

Hearing a stick snap beneath my feet, he spins toward me. Appearing equally confused, he catches my gaze and snatches a fancy pistol from his hip. Wood and bark shower down on me as bullets smash into the tree to my right.

Realizing that I am clearly ill-equipped for this battle, I dodge behind a tree. My heart beats so hard I feel my pulse in my hand as I grip the hilt of the sword tighter. When another bullet sounds, I duck, feeling more wood slivers rain on me.

"Who are you? Did the Bloodred Queen send you?" the boy shouts. The crunch of dry leaves draws closer. The crack of his gun echoes through the forest. "Well, you just tell that evil monster that I, Maddox Hadder, am not hers to claim. I escaped her clutches once, and I'll do it again."

Another bullet ricochets off the tree. Sheathing my sword, I bolt from my hiding place, dodging from one tree to the next. A murder of crows caw from the treetops as they take flight, frightened by the gunfire.

"I'll never return to Lohr! Never!" the boy named Maddox screams. Two more shots are fired, and even from this far I can hear the crack of twigs as he searches for me within the woods.

Low-lying branches hang from a nearby tree. I race toward them, grab the bottommost branch, and start climbing. Using every notch and limb, I scurry up as high as I can. A vision of following a laughing, dark-haired girl up a tree flashes in my mind. I don't know who she is or where that was or if the memory is even real. I shake my head and focus on climbing. The boy dashes into the clearing, panting as he spins. Something catches his attention. He holsters his gun and gives chase through the forest. "Mother! Father! Wait for me!" he shouts, brushing the branches of shrubs aside as he dashes after people I can't see.

Not soon enough, I find myself alone, still panting. When the boy's shouts fade so they are no more than a whisper, I climb down from my hiding place. Dark gray smoke rises in the distance beyond a break in the trees. Thankfully, it is in the opposite direction from the one the boy has run off to. Hoping to get directions out of here, wherever here is, I follow the thick plumes until I stumble upon a cottage. W. KANINCHEN is embossed on the metal mailbox. Following the stone pathway, I climb the steps and knock on the door. No one answers.

Against my instincts, I open the front door to the cottage. When I see the kitchen entryway, my stomach rumbles. A clock nearby reads one o'clock. It's been a while since I've last eaten or slept; at least I think it has. I can't remember what has happened in the last few hours, much less the last day. There's no time to stop for the simple indulgences of food or rest, so I ignore the pangs of hunger and exhaustion. The clock is ticking, a count-down to something. What it is I don't know, but I'm sure it's urgent.

I step into the sitting room. A dark brown leather couch and high-backed chair face an old trunk. A sheet of glass covered in a fine dust sits on top of it. Fire flickers within a potbellied stove, chasing away the chill of the outdoors. Against the far wall is a large mirror framed in cherrywood and black wrought iron.

My reflection stares back at me, pale with mussed-up hair. I comb my fingers through the tangles and weave it into a side plait, a few loose strands framing my face. Although I know the girl looking through the mirror must be me, I hardly recognize myself. As I push my hair from my eyes, I notice the white gloves on my hands, unsure where they came from. I don't recall hav-ing put them on. Wincing, I slip the gloves off, exposing blackened fingernails and boils over my palms. I feel sick staring at the wounds. I have no idea what caused them. Maybe they aren't real. Maybe I'm just imagining them. Gritting my teeth, I pull the gloves back on, protecting the open wounds.

Whispers sing from the mirror. My reflection no longer stares at me, but instead I see a castle. It looks familiar, but the name buzzes just out of my grasp. Surrounding the stone fortress, tents and lean-tos cover the grounds undisturbed beneath the cloud-covered night sky. A peacefulness resides over the dilapidated town, but it's broken when an explosion rocks the image before me. I watch as the castle goes up in flames, along with the town around it. Everything is on fire, and even from here I feel the heat against my cheeks. Screams erupt and I cover my ears, trying to shut out the pleas for help. I feel panicked and furious that this castle is under attack. But I don't know exactly why.

Suddenly, the ground beneath my own feet shakes, rattling loose dust from the rafters. I stumble backward, coughing, telling myself this is only a dream, part of whatever is happening in the mirror, but then the walls around me burst into flames. Running as fast as I can, I race across the living room. I clasp the doorknob, then pull my hands away as the heat bites into my palms through my gloves. Using the sleeves of my cloak, I grip the knob again, jiggling it within the angry red doorframe, but it doesn't budge. I try the windows, too, but they are also scorching hot. Evil laughter erupts from the looking glass. When I look back, the girl's face that appears is more than familiar. She's family.

It's the girl climbing the tree in my memory. But she is not the same—this version of her is terrifying. I feel guilty looking at her. Like somehow her destruction is my fault.

Something cracks loudly behind me. A small splinter appears

on the far wall and spiders out in every direction. Hot red embers glow within the fissures. The floor rumbles beneath my feet again, but this time the house lists.

I duck, covering myself with my arms as the ceiling drops several feet, stopping just above my head. As the walls cave in, I'm forced to the floor, curling up into a ball. There is no room to move. No escape from the crumbling cottage. With my lungs compressing beneath the pressure of the building, I search for any way out. The floor begins to break beneath my feet. Planks of wood buckle and drop into what looks like an underground cave. I struggle to find solid ground, but there is nowhere to go. The floorboards splinter as the walls and ceiling buckle. My heart races as I watch the boards split. With a loud crack the plank breaks, sending me hurtling down a dark tunnel. I hit the dirt ground hard. When I turn my eyes up, I watch the house cave in on itself and disappear.

I stand, brushing the dirt off my clothes. In the distance light shines in the cave. Following the pathway, I discover an opening several meters above the floor. Scrambling up the face of the craggy rock wall, I make my way toward the opening.

When I reach the top, I throw my arms onto the ground to crawl up from the hole. I find that I am back in the woods, only this time they are covered in a blanket of untouched snow. Flakes fall from the sky, clinging to my cheeks and eyelashes.

Standing, I brush the slush from my cloak. The cottage is nowhere to be found. All that is left is the decorative metal mailbox declaring that this was once the residence of W. Kaninchen.

"Alyssa!" My name reverberates throughout the forest. Snow shakes from the tree branches, settling on the thick powder on the ground. That voice. I recognize it immediately this time.

"Maddox. Where are you?" I shout, searching within the shadows. Tree trunks blur by me as my boots sink deep in the ankle-high snow.

"A . . . A . . . Alyssa," someone says, my name whispered from every direction in the dense forest. When I turn my head, the bark in the tree next to me forms into Maddox's face. My heart beats so fast that I'm sure he can hear it. I touch his face, feeling the slope of his chiseled cheeks and jaw beneath my fingertips. "Maddox?"

"Allllyyyyssssaa," he hisses.

A twinge climbs up my spine, and I take a step back. "Maddox?"

Maddox's face contorts, his features morphing into the Bloodred Queen's, staring from the trunk of the tree. She smiles terribly before two hands made of thick vines slither from the trunk, wrapping around my neck. A gasp catches in my throat as they squeeze like an anaconda, unrelentingly. Stars cloud my vision, and darkness threatens to take me. As I'm ready to give in to my fate, the pressure releases from my neck. I collapse, rolling back onto the blanket of snow and welcoming the brisk air into my lungs. The leafy hands quiver like a detached lizard's tail. The green hue fades to brown. Within moments they wither and are nothing more than twigs.

Sitting up, I reach for one with caution, afraid it'll return to its vine-like state. When I pick it up, it remains a stick. I glance up to where the Bloodred Queen's face was, only to find that the bark is as it should be. Confused, I drop the stick, sheathe my sword, and stand, never taking my eyes off the tree trunk.

"Alyssa," a voice says behind me.

Turning, I see Maddox standing in the distance. I chew my lip, afraid to take my gaze off him. The last thing I need is for him to turn into the Bloodred Queen again, or something worse.

"I know the way out. Follow me." He smiles and beckons me with the crook of his finger before disappearing behind a tree. I trudge through the deep snow toward where he stood, but when I arrive, he's nowhere to be found. The powder remains untouched by footprints.

"Alyssa, this way." This time his voice comes from behind me. Maddox stands several meters away, gesturing for me to join him.

"Maddox!" I yell as he slips behind another tree. "Wait!"

My name rings from every direction of the forest. Whirling, I see dozens of people, all of them with Maddox's likeness: sitting in the boughs of trees, reading beneath a large birch, lounging on fallen logs. Confused, I don't know which one to run toward. I bump into something. Spinning, I find myself face-to-face with the boy in the top hat. He grips my shoulders hard, his fingers digging into my skin.

"Wake up, Alyssa!" he shouts, giving me a slight shake. Only he isn't just a boy but something completely different. Something monstrous, horrifying.

Revolted, I struggle beneath his grip. I knee him in the gut and break free as he doubles over. I turn and race through the snow as fast as my boots will take me. Maddox's voice follows me, but I don't look back.

"Alyssa, come back!" he shouts.

Zigzagging through the trees, I barely hear the sound of rushing water over my rapid breath. Wherever water runs, civilization is surely close by. My pulse throbs in my ears, but I don't know if it's from fear or from running.

Something catches my cloak, causing me to stumble. I crash into an icy snow berm, sending a shooting pain through my rib cage. Grimacing, I sit up, babying my bruised ribs. When I lift my gaze, Maddox stands over me, the hem of my cloak in his hand. Behind him, the forest is on fire. As the corners of his mouth turn up into a wide grin, his skin melts away, leaving only chunks of muscles and bone. Blood pulses through shiny arteries and veins. I scream in horror, covering my eyes and retreating. But Maddox still grips my cloak, and as I try to pull it free, I fall back. When I open my eyes, the snow is gone and I am surrounded by briar bushes bursting with flames. I try to move through the branches, but they snatch at my clock, the thorns catching and snagging, the flames licking at the fabric. I pull my arms out of the sleeves, shedding the cloak before it catches fire.

Again, I hear my name rumble through the woods. I scramble to my feet, dry leaves crunching beneath my boots. Branches whip at my face as I run as fast as I can. Warm liquid stings my cheeks. Blood, but I don't bother to stop, only race toward the sound of water. To freedom.

Under the light of the starry sky, a break appears in the trees ahead. With every breath, every ounce of energy left in my aching muscles, I hurry toward the opening. Not slowing, I burst through the tree line, unable to stop myself. Suddenly, I find myself in flight, a raging inferno behind me. My scream is swept away by roaring water. Having launched myself off the side of a cliff, I'm now plunging down the face of a cascading waterfall. Water pounds me from all sides, and below me, a navy-blue lake reflects the moon and billions of stars.

My heart skips several beats. More horrifying than seeing Maddox decompose before my very eyes is the prospect of plunging into the middle of a lake, weighed down by my heavy sword. Worse yet, I have no idea how to swim.

I struggle to release the strap of the leather-and-copper sheath, but it's far too late. Ice-cold water takes my breath away, and I sink to the bottom of the frigid lake.

· PETE ·

It takes nearly an hour to convince Lily that she's going to be okay, although I feel as if I'm only mollifying her. I have no idea if she'll recover, and even if there's a possibility that she will, I'm uncertain we'll have an antidote in time. Even though they should be in the infirmary, Doc insisted that the two girls settle in Lily's quarters so he can keep a closer eye on them. The concern etched on his face makes it clear he cares for them both.

The onyx early morning sky beyond the castle windows taunts me. It won't be much longer before dawn reaches for the horizon. A few hours at best.

Gwen, the only one among us who seems to have a way with calming the usually fearless warrior, sits with the girls. I have always faced difficult times with sarcasm and wit, and if that doesn't work, with authority, delegating duties to others to get things done. But Gwen, as fierce a fighter as she is, she's a gentle and compassionate caretaker. My heart swells, watching her speak to Lily and Bella in reassuring whispers, promising that everything will be all right. This side of her is one I've always admired. I can't imagine my life without her. I refuse to accept that everything we have together is over.

Gwen looks over her shoulder, noticing Doc and me loitering in the doorway. She shoos us out with the wave of a hand and returns to soothing the girls' fears with kind words, all the while holding their hands. Taking her not-so-subtle hint, Doc and I exit the room, waiting for Gwen in the hallway.

"What is happening to them?" I hiss.

He stares at me with an anger that must reflect my own. His lips press together in a thin line, as if to keep from saying something he'll regret. How he manages to hold his temper in check I will never understand. He knows that anything he says will only escalate the situation; it always does. So instead of gratifying me with a response, he leans up against the wall and crosses his arms, waiting for me to pull it together. I hate when he does this. Especially when I'm itching for a fight.

I pace the hallway, stopping once as I notice my reflection in a large mirror hung on the wall. Hair disheveled, unshaved face, circles so dark beneath my eyes they look almost like fresh bruises.

How can I be a good leader when I've let so many down? Alnwick deserves better. And maybe even Gwen deserves better.

Something explodes within me, breaking the restraints I've been trying to use to hold my temper. My fist smashes the mirror, sending shards of glass cascading to the floor. My knuckles burn, chunks of glass piercing my skin, but it feels good. The sting in my hand draws away from the pain of failure within my head and soul.

"You done?" Doc says, lacking even a hint of surprise at my outburst.

I glare but say nothing, evidence of my quiet surrender.

He motions for me to sit. Moving out of the pile of glass, I lean against the wall and sink to the floor. Doc kneels by me and pulls out a mini-medikit from his waistcoat pocket. Gripping tweezers, he removes pieces of glass from my skin. Each tug stings but doesn't compare to the sharp ache within my chest. I try to stop thinking of the look of sheer disappointment in me that flashed across Gwen's face earlier, but her expression is burned into my mind.

"Are you ready to hear my theory on what is happening to those treated with the antidote?" he asks, focusing on my hand, not bothering to make eye contact.

"If it's any better than your solutions, fire away," I say, irritated.

"The patients first develop unusual blisters that thicken into permanent calcified scabs with time, becoming almost like scales," he says, plucking a sliver of glass from my fist. I jerk my hand from his grasp. He rolls his eyes and gives me a look that I clearly interpret as "you big baby."

I raise my eyebrows nonchalantly. "It doesn't hurt."

Narrowing his eyes, he yanks another glass shard from my hand. I visibly wince, and he smirks, taking pleasure in this sign of weakness.

"Next they develop a core temperature drop beyond what any human can stand, and yet they survive."

"Survive? You call lying sick in beds surviving?" I mutter.

Doc rips out more glass without the care he typically gives his patients. Grimacing, I regret my snarky remarks. When it comes to upsetting Doc, I always find myself remorseful for my actions when I need his expertise. Today is no different.

He frowns, noticeably irritated with me. "Are you going to let me finish?"

I don't offer an answer, sure he's waiting for the opportunity to make this process more painful than it already is. He takes that as a cue to continue.

Doc yanks out another sliver. I grit my teeth.

"And now Lily's and Bella's eyes? I've never seen anything like that," he says.

"So what's going on, Doc? What do you think is happening to them?"

Doc shakes his head. "It has to have something to do with the lizard protein. Instead of just healing them, repairing body parts, it's turning them into something inhuman, something almost animal."

Scales, lower than normal body temperature, slits for pupils. I let out a long-held-back sigh. "Something reptilian," I say.

Worry creases his brow as he meets my gaze. Reluctantly he nods.

"Unfortunately, that's my conclusion as well. I think the lizard protein, combined with Gwen's antibodies, may have created something different. A different poison or disease altogether."

"How do we reverse it?" I ask.

Doc shakes his head. "Same as I said before: replicate the toxin, create the proper antidote, and hope it works."

"How long will it take for you to come up with an alternate antidote once we have that apple?" I say.

Doc runs a hand through his messy blond hair. "I have no idea, but time is running out fast. And we don't even know if it will work." He looks as helpless as I feel for a moment, before he says, "I sent the younger Lost Boys out to catch lizards so I can figure out why the lizard protein is reacting like it is. Gabs has needed some coaxing to give up his lizards. Says he wants to keep them as pets and has even been naming them."

"Naming them?" I ask.

"Yeah, they all have *L* names. Linus, Luther, Larry, Loretta, Lola . . . All *L*s except one he calls Bill."

I open my mouth to respond, but Doc holds a hand up. "Don't ask me why. We are talking about Gabs."

My involuntary laugh shocks me. It's been a long time since anything has made me laugh. Although Gabs has a tendency to brighten any dark situation. The respite from the dire thoughts racing through my head is beyond welcome. "Why does that not surprise me?"

Doc puts the tweezers away and removes my gloves before dabbing my cuts with an alcohol swab.

"So . . . Bella?" I ask reluctantly, afraid to hear his assessment of her condition.

Doc shakes his head. "She's always been the unhealthiest of the sick, or at least of the ones who've survived. Unfortunately, the pain she's going through is only going to become much worse."

Although I know all of this, hearing him say it out loud makes me feel nauseous. Above everyone else, Bella was my responsibility. She's my sister. Maybe not by blood, but my sister nonetheless. And I've let her down, just like I let my real sister, Gabrielle, down. I have no words.

Breaking the awkward silence, he clears his throat. "I should get back to the lab. I want to have done as much research as possible by the time Alyssa returns."

"If she does return," I reply.

Doc stands and offers me a hand. I take it, wincing as I allow him to help me to my feet. He returns my gloves and starts to walk off, but stops, his back still to me. "Give yourself a break, Pete. I know what you're thinking. I've battled the same demons I imagine are eating you up from inside. The will to try so hard to help everyone and the sense that you've failed them all. In my case, I've done the best I could. I lost a piece of me when Gabrielle died. I loved her so much. If I lose Bella, too, I have to live with the fact that, not only as her physician but as her friend, I failed her. No matter how hard I try, all the education in the world isn't enough to make her healthy again."

His words pierce holes in my heart. He's right. Doc is so many things to her. A friend, a brother, a doctor . . . If she dies, he's failed in every way. I start to say something, but the words stick in my throat, because I, too, have failed her.

"It's never too late for you, Pete. We will always, always need a leader. Bella will always need you, until her very last breath."

His words strike a chord, but I'm not sure how to respond. Doc turns and disappears toward the laboratory. I'm about to follow him when Gwen steps into the hallway, quietly closing the door behind her.

"They're asleep now," she says through a yawn, reminding me that it's nearly morning. We're all long overdue for rest, but with all that's happened tonight, sleep evades me. I'm not the least bit tired.

"What are we going to do about them?" she asks.

I shake my head. "I haven't the slightest idea."

Silence hangs heavy in the air, its weight as distant as the space between the girl I love and myself. I search for words to assure her we'll be okay, but my lips fail me.

She stares at the floor, her hands clasped in front of her. Normally she'd reach for me and hold my hand, if only to bring us both some comfort.

"Pete," she says, then stops. And I know. I just know.

She starts again. "I can't be with you. I love you, but it's too much. It just hurts too much and I just . . ." She trails off and looks me in the eye.

My heart shatters as I see the sad determination there. I can't talk my way out of this one. But I have to try. "Please. Please don't do this. I love you," I say, my voice gravelly. "I need you, Gwen. I'd rather be with you until the end than be without you."

Sadly, she shakes her head. "It's over, Pete. There's nothing you can say to fix this. I can't do this anymore. I can't give you my heart only to know that I'll lose it if I lose you."

Before I can say anything else, shouts burst from the entrance of the castle. As if one more thing could possibly go wrong. I want to stay and figure this out with Gwen, but I can't. I sprint down the staircase two steps at a time and find Pickpocket bleeding from the forehead, collapsed on the floor. Cogs kneels by his side with a worried expression. Scout slams the castle doors shut, locks them, and pulls a handkerchief from his vest. He places it on Pickpocket's forehead. Outside, profanities and fists beat at the castle doors.

"What happened?" I ask.

"Revolt!" Pickpocket says between gasps.

The screaming is so loud there must be dozens of kids out there. Having been woken up by the ruckus, the Lost Boys stumble out, each holding their weapon of specialty. My pride for their bravery is overshadowed by the sadness of those we've lost along the way. Lily, Gwen, Doc, and I rescued so many and brought them to Northumberland. Now fewer than half are left, and of those, so many are weak.

"Enough is enough!" Gwen races down the staircase, flips the lock, and shoves the castle doors open. Bright light fills the entryway. She shields her eyes with her arm. The orange hue of firelight dances on her face, illuminating her expression of shock. Her bravado slips as she steps back. The outside commotion dies down. I join her, my Lost Boys standing with me, to take in the plight before us.

Dozens of kids, each showing symptoms of infection, stand wielding weapons of all kinds: guns, knives, swords, and various other sharp objects. Leading the pack, Katt wears a naughty smile.

"Good morning. I hope we haven't disturbed you," Katt says, chuckling.

"Actually, you have. We're a little busy here," Gwen says furiously, her fists on her hips. I've seen her frustrated, even angry. Right now she's fierce, filled with a rage I haven't seen her wield in a while.

"Isn't that a shame?" Katt hisses. "Too busy for the dying? Every minute, every second, is precious. It's nearly dawn, Lost Girl, and I'm tired of watching the incompetence in the leadership. First my sister, then Duchess Alyssa, and now Pete. We deserve better. I'm here to take what is rightfully mine. The crown, and with it, the Professor's research."

"As long as your sister still breathes the crown doesn't belong to you. As for my mother's papers, they belong to me. You'll have to get through me to get them," Gwen says confidently.

"I already told you that the Professor's research was non-negotiable," I shout, shielding Gwen. Her head jerks my way, as if she's surprised to see me standing by her side. "You might be entitled to the crown, but you'll never be my queen, and we refuse your rule. Alnwick and Northumberland are under my leadership until Duchess Alyssa returns. Go back to the Poison Garden."

Laughing, Katt throws her head back, her long, dark hair whipping in the wind. "Your leadership? You think corralling a herd of a few dozen orphans gives you the expertise to rule over thousands of people?" She smirks. "By royal decree, this place is mine. All of the United Kingdom is mine. Step down, Lost Boy, and I'll be sure you and yours will be treated with mercy."

"Not without a fight," I say. My eyes burn with anger. There's no more time to prepare. It's now or never. "Listen up, you who have come to Alnwick seeking help. I vow to you today that I will lay down my life not only for my Lost Kids, but also for those of you who stand with the true Queen of England, who still lives. To you who pledge your alliance to Duchess Alyssa, I serve you! I promise you I will defend Alnwick until the duchess returns with the ingredient to the cure, or I will die trying. Our only hope lies in the safe return of the duchess. Choose! Choose your allegiance and choose wisely, because I give you fair warning: Once you've made your choice, you will not be welcome back. Who among you will stand with me to defend Alnwick and all of Northumberland?"

The Lost Boys shout their allegiance, drawing even closer to Gwen and me.

Murmurs rumble through the crowd, and a few people argue with one another. Scuffles break out.

"Choose now or you will be considered a traitor to Alnwick, which will come at a steep cost," I demand.

A crease forms between Gwen's brows. "Pete, what are you doing?"

"This is it. This is our final stand, Gwen. War is inevitable. It's time for everyone to pick their side," I say, turning my attention back to the crowd.

Only a handful of the refugees join us. One by one, the tired, hungry, and bedraggled kids trudge past me, joining the ranks of Lost Boys. Though Katt's group still outnumbers us, I'll take the extra hands. Pride wells in me. I know I've made the right choice to stand for not just the Lost Boys, not just the kids from Everland, not even just the people of Alnwick. I stand for all of the United Kingdom and those who seek shelter within her borders.

Although initially ruffled by the retreating group, Katt paces in front of the castle, her boots clicking on the courtyard stone.

"We've heard the excuses, listened to your pathetic apologies, and vows to defend Umberland," she says righteously. "No more!"

I turn away from Katt and look each Lost Boy in the eye. It might be the last time I ever do. "Barricade all entrances and windows. Prepare for battle," I order.

· JACK ·

The trees of the Black Forest continue to loom over us as we journey beyond the Zwerg village. Vines hang from the branches, giving the appearance of snakes. My boots feel heavy, waterlogged, as we search for dry ground within the murky swamp. Rickety cottages on raised stilts appear abandoned. The water is littered with random items, as if this was once a community not unlike the Zwerg village. Toys, articles of clothing, and other items float past us. My nose tingles with the smell of rotten plant clippings and dead carcasses. The odor is suffocating. I wrap a handkerchief around my nose and mouth, trying to cut out the horrid stench.

"What's wrong? A little stinky water bringing you down?" Hook says, grinning as he slogs through the swamp.

Ignoring him, I continue southeast. With no real path to follow, I can only hope we are headed in the right direction.

"Did you lose something, Lost Girl?" my brother says, reaching for a muddy corset in the water. He slips his hand under the ribbon laced up the back of the corset, and when he tries to lift it up, he's met with resistance. He pulls harder, picking it and the dead woman wearing the bodice up out of the water. There is nothing left of her but bones and rotten flesh. What looked like floating moss and dead grass is actually her long hair.

Hook yelps, dropping the young woman into the water. His

boots splash as he scurries back, away from the corpse. Taking in the scene, I realize that many of the random items in the water aren't random at all. Boots, petticoats, and dinner jackets clothe the sea of dead bodies beneath the water's surface.

My brother seems to process the dire situation we find ourselves in at the same time I do. He turns away from the corpse of the woman and retches violently. As odd as it is, I find myself snickering. He puts on a tough front—relished in serving raw meat to his crocodiles in Everland, lived among the dead after the bombing. And this . . . this is what turns his stomach? Although I can't blame him.

"What's wrong? A little stinky water bringing you down?" I say, repeating his mockery.

My brother whirls toward me, swinging his hand in my direction. I duck just in time. Fed up, I lunge at him, looking for the first opportunity to plunge his face below the water's surface. Something nudges my legs beneath the water. I stagger away, assuming it's another dead body, but instead whatever it is leaves a large ripple in the water.

Hook, not noticing the creature, swipes at me again, this time pinning my neck against a tree with his metal hand.

"What did you say?" he says, spittle spraying from his lips.

But before I answer him, something wraps around his legs, knocking him off-balance and into the rancid water. I reach for him with the intent to rescue him—again—but realize I can't move my feet. My ankles are pinned. When I look down, the head of a large snake slithers up my legs. I grab for it, wrestling to pull it off me, but it is much too strong. It squeezes my legs tighter, looping a wide circle around me, catching my arms in its deadly grip. Slowly, it coils around my chest, and I'm unable to breathe. Stars prickle the edges of my vision. I drop to my knees, the swamp water rising to my chin. The brown-and-black spotted snake's head hovers just in front of my eyes, seeming to take pleasure as it cuts off my oxygen. With my hands pinned to my side, I can't reach my weapons belt.

Meters in front of me, Hook struggles within the grip of another abnormally large snake. His lips are blue and he gasps for air. Snakes of all colors and sizes slither from the treetops, using the vines as a means of accessing the swamp. Soon we are surrounded by terrifying hissing reptiles.

My vision darkens and my breath is so shallow I hardly know how I'm still conscious. Like a black curtain, my eyesight fails me. As I'm ready to give in to my inevitable death, my lungs expand with the rush of humid but welcome air. Blood spatters my face as my stepbrother slices the snake into two parts with a long knife.

"It's not your time yet, little brother," he says, holding his hand out to me. I slap it away and stand on my own.

"I thought we were even?" I ask, grumbling.

He pulls me by the back of my coat from the murk and leans in, his dark eyes fixed on mine. "We still are. We don't have the apple and I might need your warm body yet. When you die it'll be from my hand," he says.

He turns his back on me, and I know if I don't watch mine, I'll be dead.

· ALYSSA ·

The freezing water stings my skin like thousands of needles burrowing into every pore. Fear digs its claws into me as I struggle to swim to the water's surface. Flailing helplessly, I sink deeper into the icy depths of the lake, my sword pulling me down like an anchor and my lungs screaming for air. I kick harder, hoping to propel myself upward, but to no avail.

As I'm about to involuntarily take in a gulp that will seal my fate in this watery grave, a hand rips my sword from its sheath and releases it. My weapon sinks toward the bottom of the lake. My rescuer grips the sleeve of my tunic and yanks me upward. Clinging on to the faintest bit of hope, I keep my lips pressed together, refusing to give in to the urge for air.

The moon shines down onto the surface of the water, making it sparkle like diamonds above me. This is the second time on this journey I have found myself desperate to be above the surface. If I never see water again, it won't be long enough. I reach for the iridescent ripples beneath the moonlight, knowing beyond them is the air I so desperately need.

When my face breaks the surface, I gasp, hungry for as much oxygen as possible. An arm wraps around me as I am dragged through the lake, warm breath panting in my ear. It seems like forever before we make it to shore and crawl onto the muddy bank, coughing up water. The identity of my rescuer comes as no surprise. He's as chivalrous here as he is defiant in Alnwick.

Maddox, drenched down to his black buckled boots, huffs, trying to catch his own breath. Water drips down his face as he peers at me, and worry lines crease between his brows. He inches toward me and squeezes my hand. I'm touched by the genuine concern reflected in his brilliant gold eyes.

"Are you okay?" he asks, surveying the rest of me as if to make sure I'm still intact.

"You rescued me?" I say, and it comes out sounding like a question.

"Of course I rescued you. What choice did I have? You almost died out there," he says so loudly that I startle. He wades back into the water and snatches his hat, which floats just off the bank, and slogs back up onto the sand. "What were you thinking? Who jumps off a thirty-meter waterfall and into a lake, much less a person who can't swim? How does a duchess whose life is delivered to her on a silver platter, who has access to anything she needs or desires, not know how to swim?"

Dropping my gaze to the ground, I shrug. My chest feels heavy, and I can't quite pinpoint the feelings stirring within me: embarrassment or disappointment.

Maddox sighs and tilts my chin up. "Are you really all right?" he asks, this time a bit softer. The worry in his expression makes him appear older.

Nodding, I shiver when an autumn breeze whisks through the clearing.

He wraps his arms around me, rubbing the wet sleeves of my tunic. "You're freezing. We need to get you warm."

"I'll be fine. I just need to sit for a while," I say through chattering teeth.

"We're both going to end up sick if we don't get warm," he says. He dashes into a nearby grove of trees and gathers sticks and leaves. Soon he has the beginnings of a small campfire.

Cold bites at my toes and fingers. I curl up into a ball, setting my head on a small pile of leaves. Maddox rustles around, but with my eyes shut tight I'm unable to take in what he's doing. Soon, warmth tickles my skin.

When I open my eyes again, a roaring campfire is ablaze. Maddox is sitting on a log as he pokes at the glowing embers with a large stick. I crawl toward the fire, holding my frozen fingers as close as I physically can to the flames.

"Thank you for rescuing me," I say, glad to have his company. Had he not come along, I'm sure I'd be dead by now.

Maddox gives me a curt nod and proceeds to remove his boots and socks, placing them near the fire. He pulls his coat off and hangs it on the branch of a nearby tree. I turn away as he pulls his black shirt over his head, only catching a slight glimpse of his well-chiseled chest and abs. When I hear the rustle of laces, I know that can mean only one thing.

I cover my eyes. "What do you think you are doing?"

"What does it look like I'm doing? Getting out of my wet

clothes, and I'd highly recommend you do so as well. It's only going to get colder, at least until sunrise. You don't want to be wearing those wet garments. Trust me," he says.

"I am not getting naked in front of you," I say, flabbergasted.

"Oh, come on. I'm not being improper. You can't very well sit around in damp clothes. You're already icy to the touch. You'll never warm up," he says.

"I'm the Duchess of Alnwick, for heaven's sake," I say, my teeth chattering so hard I can hardly understand what I've said myself. "I will not be naked in public."

"Public? Who is going to see you?" Maddox says, snickering loudly.

"You, for one," I say indignantly. I scoot closer to the fire.

"Suit yourself, but you're liable to catch a case of pneumonia, and then what are you going to do? It's not like the royal physician is going to come at your beck and call this far away. You, dear duchess, are on your own out here."

Body shivering, I keep my gaze averted, afraid to look at Maddox's nearly naked body, which I know is only a few meters away.

"Would you look at yourself? You going to freeze. For the love of the Queen herself, take those wet garbs off," he says, sounding exasperated. "We can't continue on in these clothes, so we might as well warm up and catch up on sleep."

He's right. I don't know how much more shivering I can

take, and with sunrise still a few hours away, it could take for-ever to warm up. "Turn around," I say.

"Are you kidding me? We're in the middle of a deadly labyrinth and freezing to death, and you're worried about impropriety?"

"Just do it!" I say.

"Okay, fine, yes, Your Grace," he says in a mocking tone. "Shall I bring you some tea while I'm at it? Perhaps some crum-pets. Or do you desire a foot massage with your nonsense?"

"Just turn around!" I hiss.

Lifting my gaze from the forest floor, I peek at Maddox to be sure he isn't looking and burst into uncontrollable laughter. His back is turned toward me and he is completely naked aside from his white knee-length flannel drawers, which are covered in bright red hearts.

"What? Do I really look that ridiculous half-naked?" he asks.

"That is the most absurd pair of drawers I have ever seen in my entire life," I say through fits of giggles.

"Oh, really?" he says, peering over his shoulder and arching an eyebrow. "Do your royal duties often bring in you into con-tact with men in their drawers?"

I blush furiously but retort, "That is not any of your concern."

"Ah, the duchess is not as innocent as she portrays herself to be," Maddox teases.

"Hush, you!" I say, laughing.

"Would you just hurry up? My front side is starting to get cold and trust me, it is not a pleasant feeling," he says.

With trembling hands, I quickly pull off my tunic, boots, leggings, and socks. I hang them on a nearby branch and sit by the fire. Left in only my undergarments, I pull my knees up to my chest and wrap my arms around them, hiding as much of my body as possible. I hate to admit it, but I'm instantly warmer without my waterlogged clothing.

I stare at the back of Maddox. I can't see his hands, but the blisters cover his feet and ankles. It looks so painful that it only strengthens my resolve to find this apple. For everyone.

"Are you done yet? Or are you just going to leave me standing here like this all night?" Maddox complains.

"Okay, you can turn around," I say hesitantly.

When Maddox turns, I am speechless. Despite his silly drawers, he is the definition of gorgeous. Muscles bulge beneath his dark skin, making his chest, abs, and arms look like a carefully fashioned work of art. I bite my bottom lip, flushed by the desire to run my hand over his bare chest just to see if he's real.

Maddox catches me admiring his sculpted body. "Look who's laughing now. Go right ahead, Duchess. Take in the magnificence of me." He struts around the bonfire, uninhibited, flexing his biceps.

Embarrassed, I stare at the campfire, hoping he doesn't notice the blush I feel burning up my neck to my cheeks. He settles on a log across the fire and watches me through the dancing flames. I shift uncomfortably, ignoring his stupid preening.

Pulling my knees in tighter, I try not to meet his eyes. I don't know if he's like many others his age, infatuated by the female body, or just enjoys watching me squirm, or is grossed out by the scabs spreading across my hands, feet, and up my legs. Finally, I can't take it any longer.

"What? Fine, take a good look and get it over with," I say, standing and spinning. "Are we done now?"

He looks me up and down, adding to my discomfort. He shakes his head and clicks his tongue in disapproval.

Plopping down on the dirt, I draw up my knees. Maddox continues to stare at me, unblinking. I roll my eyes. "Just say it. You haven't taken your eyes off me since you turned around. You're dying to say something else, aren't you?"

Maddox chuckles and folds his arms. "Nope. You're not going to like it."

"Seriously? Now you choose to keep your mouth shut?" I say mockingly.

"Yep. You've got a pretty smile, but your scowl is almost lethal," he says.

He's onto my flirtations, so I drop the pretense, pick up a stick, and poke at the fire. "Come on, just tell me."

"I'm better off just keeping my thoughts to myself."

"Really? When have you ever kept your thoughts to yourself, because since we started this journey, you can't seem to shut up about anything," I say.

Maddox looks bemused. "I was just thinking that you really ought to get out of the castle more often. I've lived in Alnwick for five years, and not once have we crossed each other's paths. I enjoy your company."

That is not at all what I had expected him to say. "I enjoy yours as well."

"Besides, your poor skin hasn't seen the sunlight in ages. Look at you!" he adds, laughing.

I pick up a small stone and heave it at him.

"Hey!" he says, deflecting the pebble before it knocks him on the forehead.

I stick my tongue out at him and rest my chin on top of my knees, grateful for the warmth the fire brings. He chuckles, but we find ourselves quiet for a few moments before Maddox hops up and heads toward his clothes drying on the branch.

"Are you hungry? I found us some food while I was gathering wood," he says, reaching into the pocket of his coat. When he returns, he holds out his hand. In his palm are two small bird eggs and a handful of what looks like rotten mushrooms. In the other hand is an intricate pocket tool complete with an array of knives, screwdrivers, and other instruments I've never seen before.

I look up at him warily. "Eggs and moldy mushrooms. How do you know they aren't poisonous?" I immediately feel dumb as the words spill from my mouth.

Maddox gives me a cockeyed grin. "Really? You do recall where I live, don't you?" He holds the dark lumps out to me. "These are not poisonous and they're not mushrooms. They are truffles."

I take one from his palm and inspect it. It is disgusting, but my stomach growls at the sight of it anyway. "I hope that it tastes a lot better than it looks," I say, handing it back to Maddox.

Setting the food on a large piece of bark, Maddox piles large rocks near the fire. I watch as he places a flat stone over the rocks. After rinsing the meager ingredients in the lake, he returns to cut up the truffles into bite-size pieces. Finally, he tosses them onto the stone and breaks open the eggs.

My stomach growls again as I watch him mix the food together. When he is done cooking, he uses his socks as mitts and removes the stone from the heat. Normally, I'd be disgusted by his sweaty socks so close to my meal, but on any given day I wouldn't be sitting nearly naked by the fire with a strange boy either.

Maddox places the food between us. Driven by overwhelming hunger and the fragrant smell, I reach for a morsel of the meal.

"Ah, wait! It's hot. Here, let me help you," he says, putting his socks on a nearby log. He finds what looks like a fork in his multitool, uses it to retrieve a bit of the egg-and-truffle mix, and blows on it. Once it is cooled, he lifts it to my mouth. At first I hesitate, but the smell is so intoxicating that I let him slip the food between my lips. It is possibly the best meal I've ever had. Wrapped up in the satisfaction I feel, I don't notice that Maddox is staring at me until I open my eyes, eager for a second bite. He is so close to me that my breath hitches.

"How was that?" he asks, his stare fixed on me.

"Delicious," I say, feeling heat in my cheeks. "Thank you."

"My pleasure," he says, smiling. He doesn't take his gold eyes from mine as he pops a morsel into his own mouth. I can't help but return his silly grin.

We eat in silence. With warmth and a full belly, I take in the area around us. Darkness covers the forest, and thousands of sparkling stars embedded into the obsidian sky entertain us. Fireflies perform a dramatic show of light. Surprisingly, this strange place is quite beautiful.

Once we have eaten every last crumb, Maddox stands and returns to his clothes, reaching into the pocket of his trousers. He returns with a flask. Opening the bottle, he offers it to me. The pungent smell of liquor stings my nose.

"I hardly think moonshine will help us through the Labyrinth, do you?" I say.

Wrapping his lips around the opening of the bottle, he takes a long swig, smiling the whole time. When he's done, he wipes his mouth with the back of his hand. He tilts the bottle toward the dark sky. "Until the sun rises, we're not going anywhere."

As eager as I am to get to the center of the Labyrinth, I'm happy for the brief rest. Yawning, I feel satiated from our meal, and I turn my attention to the fire, watching it dreamily.

"Besides, you could use some sleep," he says.

He's right. I have no idea how long I've been awake, but after days and nights tending to the refugees, exhaustion has caught up with me.

"You sure you don't want a swig? It'll help you sleep," Maddox says, offering me the flask once again.

This time I accept, gripping the flask. "Cheers," I say, tilting it his way.

"Cheers," he says in return.

I take a small sip, and the fiery liquid immediately warms me. I cough and sputter before taking one more drink and passing it to Maddox. My muscles thaw, tension releasing from them within minutes. Something brushes up against my leg. When I peer down, Maddox's knee is so close to mine, we are nearly touching. I realize I am not hiding my half-nakedness any longer, but have relaxed, enjoying the food, the drink, the fire . . . the company.

"Maddox, back in the forest . . . I . . . I saw . . ."

"Evil things," he says before taking another drink. His eyes narrow, as if remembering something dark of his own. "No good ever comes from those evil woods."

"You knew about the woods?" I ask.

Maddox nods. "They've always been there, always part of the Black Forest. That was where the Bloodred Queen sent traitors to the crown with nothing but a gun and a single bullet. There are plants and trees in there that are so poisonous that merely breathing the air will cause their victims to lose their minds. It doesn't take long for them to take their own lives."

"I forgot my name, Maddox. I had no idea who I was, where I was, where I was going. I forgot you. I saw you, but couldn't remember who you were or why you were with me," I say. "But . . . there were other things I saw, too."

Frowning, Maddox nods, and for the briefest of moments, I think I detect grief in his downcast expression. "Not surprising. Those woods will not only steal your memories, they remind you of your greatest fears. They take away the things you should remember, the good thoughts, and feed your mind with the ones that cause heartbreak, or worse yet, terror."

"So was anything I saw in there real?" I ask, remembering Alnwick in flames.

Maddox hands me the flask, and I take a sip, readying myself for his answer. I pass it back to him, and he chugs what's left.

"Who's to say what is real and what isn't," he says. Maddox rubs a hand over his eyes, clearly aggravated.

"And the bad things we saw?" I ask hesitantly, recalling his shouts to the Bloodred Queen: *Well, you just tell that evil monster that I, Maddox Hadder, am not hers to claim. I escaped her clutches once, and I'll do it again.*

Maddox hurls the flask into the fire as his jaw tightens.

Cautiously, I scoot closer to him. "What did you see?" I ask.

He peers down at me, his gaze flitting from my eyes to my lips. I can smell the liquor on his breath, no longer pungent but sweet. I shiver, but not from the cold.

"Some nightmares should never be spoken out loud," he says. The sound of crickets chases away the awkward silence between us.

Eventually, he says, "You should get some rest. We have a long journey tomorrow. I'll keep watch."

I nod and curl up on the ground, edging as close to the fire as I dare. I leave my back to him—it seems safer somehow. But then I feel the lightest of touches on my head, his fingers combing through my hair. I close my eyes and let his touch send me drifting off into a deep sleep.

· PETE ·

Gwen barricades the castle doors as the Lost Boys talk among themselves. Scout bandages the wound on Pickpocket's head.

"What are we going to do?" Gwen says, worry evident in her expression.

"Oh boy, oh boy! They've gone bonkers out there. Totally lost their marbles. The whole lot of them. Especially the Queen's coo-coo sister. What in the Queen's name is she thinking threatening you like that, Pete? Doesn't she know you're going to kick her bum from here to Everland?" Gabs says.

Pushing past Gabs, I place both hands on Cogs's shoulders. "I'm putting you in charge of the Lost Boys. Prepare to defend Alnwick. It's about to get ugly. We don't have time to lose. Gabs, gather the rest of the Lost Boys as quickly as you can. Take them to the armory and tell them to prepare to fight," I say, my heartbeat stuttering as I wonder how much blood will spill by sundown.

Gabs's voice wavers as he says, "The rest? But, Pete, this is all we've got. The others can hardly get up from their beds. This *is* all that's left."

Counting heads, I realize there are far fewer boys than I had originally thought. Only a few dozen are left.

"Count us in!" Lily stands at the top of the stairs, sword in hand. Behind her, Bella cinches her bag full of steel bearings onto her hip, slingshot in hand. They both look weak, but I'm grateful for their support.

Cogs sidles up next to Gabs, his bright red hair poking up beneath his lifted welder's mask.

"It's your call, Pete. What will you have us do?" he says in a thick Irish accent.

I take a breath in and meet each Lost Boy's gaze. I know that many will not come out of this alive. "We will defend Alnwick, or we will die trying."

Gabs rolls his shoulders back, suddenly exhibiting a fierce bravery that I've known he's possessed since the day I found him launching rotten eggs at a group of Marauders in Everland. He might be small and talk entirely too much, but he is one of the bravest Lost Boys I know.

Gabs turns to the small gathering of boys. "Attention, Lost Boys, this is it!"

"Didn't you put me in charge?" Cogs says to me.

"Stand behind him and nod your head. They'll think he's speaking on your behalf. Step in to give your orders when he's had his say," I whisper in his ear. With a curt nod he stands behind Gabs, arms folded, indignant and prepared to challenge anyone who disagrees.

"Alnwick is about to come under siege, and we're going to battle hard. You will not complain, whine, or cry, or else I will be forced to tell you about the one time I stuck a piece of chocolate up my nose because I didn't want to be caught by my mummy sneaking it," Gabs says.

A collective groan rumbles from the room as Gabs carries on. "I wasn't thinking straight in the head that day, and before I knew it, chocolate was melting out of my nostril, pouring down my mouth and chin. That was embarrassing! And the moral is, don't hide chocolate chunks up your nose in order to keep your mum from finding out."

"Ew! Gabs!" one boy whines.

"Can we just get on with it?" Cogs says, suddenly appearing a little green in the face.

Gabs turns back to me and gives me a thumbs-up as Cogs begins delegating responsibilities to the other boys. They run off in all different directions, shouting rally cries along the way.

"Scout, you get to Doc and let him know what's going on. Help him pack up the research, equipment, and any other essentials. Have him barricade himself in the top tower. Tell him not to let anyone in, no matter what," I say. "Come back to help Pickpocket board up the windows when you're done."

Scout nods and races up the stairs. Although he's quiet and somewhat reserved, Scout has always been a Lost Boy I could depend on. With our numbers dwindling, I'm glad he's still around.

"Gwen, you, Lily, and Bella help evacuate the kids in the infirmary to the basement. Take the tunnel beneath the bailey to get everyone out. Bring a few of the Lost Boys with you; you'll need the extra hands," I say.

"What about you?" she asks, turning toward me.

"Pickpocket and I will guard the front doors," I say.

Gwen frowns. My heart aches seeing her worry. Leaning in, I try to kiss her, but she steps back. Tears brim in her eyes, and she refuses to look at me.

"I told you, Pete, what you and I had together is over," she says, stepping farther away from me.

"Gwen, you can't mean that." I hardly recognize my own voice as hurt laces my tone.

She glances at me and then back to the floor, crossing her arms in front of her. "I've lost too much already."

"But I'm right here," I say, my voice rising. "I'm not going anywhere. I promised you that I'd always be here for you."

"That's not really a promise you can keep now, is it?" she says, her voice cracking. She turns and joins Lily and Bella, leaving me alone in the cold, dark foyer.

· ALYSSA ·

A rumbling near my neck lures me awake. Warm air brushes against my cheek, followed by a startling snort. I blink, shielding my eyes from the ray of sunshine shining into my face. Shifting, I try to sit up but am pinned down to the cold ground. I'm frozen with fear; my eyes follow the bronze arm to its owner. Maddox groans, pulling me tighter into him.

I bolt up, snatching my tunic from where it hangs from a tree and pulling it over my head. Maddox grunts and flails about, clearly startled from a deep sleep.

"What? It can't be time for tea already," Maddox says groggily.

I back up. "No, it is not time for tea! What were you doing lying next to me? With your . . . your arms all over me?"

Maddox sits up and rubs his bleary eyes. "You were shivering. I was trying to keep you warm. There's no appreciation for chivalry anymore."

Under the morning light, I notice that his ridiculous drawers are ragged and holey. "I hardly think snuggling up next to me practically naked is chivalry."

"I'm not naked," he protests.

I point at the tear in the leg of his drawers. "You might as well be."

Maddox pokes a finger in the hole and rolls his eyes. "I beg your pardon, Your Grace, but some of us can't afford fancy silks and satins and seamstresses," he says indignantly. He snatches his trousers from where they hang. "Must be nice to have clean knickers that don't need mending."

Maddox continues to retrieve his clothes, grumbling while he yanks them on. "Miss Fancy Panties is too good to be near the likes of a filthy commoner. Next time I ought to let her freeze her royal assets off." He pulls his shirt over his head, tugging at the bottom hem, but is unable to get his head through the proper hole. He continues to complain under his breath, his arms waving about through the air.

Unable to help myself, I burst out in laughter. Maddox peers from an armhole. "What exactly is so funny?" he growls, which sends me to the ground laughing even harder. My sides ache and tears roll down my cheeks.

Maddox manages to get his shirt on, along with the rest of his clothes, and sits next to me, his lips jutted out in an exaggerated pout. I take a breath, trying to hold back a giggle.

"I'm sorry," I say, nudging him with an elbow.

A wide grin grows on his face, and I realize that his dramatic display was all a show. I give him a gentle push. "You did that on purpose, didn't you?"

He gives me a shocked expression and presses his fingertips into his chest. "Are you saying that my interpretive dance with my clothes and the temper tantrum that would put a toddler to shame was all an act? Well, now I'm really offended."

Shaking my head, I chuckle.

Maddox leans his head on my shoulder. "You still mad at me?" He turns his gaze up to me and flutters his eyelashes. My smile slips when I look into his golden eyes. His pupils are no longer circular, but rather slits, appearing almost reptilian.

"What's wrong with your eyes?" I ask, half wondering if he's been nibbling on the strange flora surrounding us.

Confused, although speaking as if clearly sober, he says, "My eyes?"

I pick up his multitool and release the knife, then hold it up so he can see his reflection in the blade. He rubs one eye, as if he could wipe the distorted pupil away. When his reflection peers back unchanged, he rips his glove off with his teeth and holds his hands up. The skin on his hands has become rougher . . . scalier than it was before.

Maddox rushes to get the rest of my clothes. "We'd better get going. The sooner we get that apple, the sooner we can get back to Alnwick and find a cure."

He holds the rest of my clothes out to me, but instead of taking them, I place my hand gently on his face. Confusion? Uncertainty? I'm not sure what it is I see in his stare, but he meets my gaze with an expression I can't interpret. His warm palm covers my hand, and in spite of his scales, his fingers are soft against mine as he intertwines them. I lean in, lightly pressing my lips against his cheek.

"You're going to be okay. I promise," I say. "I'll make sure of it."

He gives me a sad smile. I wish there was more I could say to assure him.

"Thank you for coming with me. I couldn't have done this without you," I say, my attention fixed on his handsome face. His gold eyes dart from my mine to my lips. I drop my arms and take a step back, but don't shift my gaze. Maddox licks his lips, and I think I detect disappointment. Or perhaps I'm imagining it because that's what I feel in this moment.

Maddox shakes my clothes at me. "We should get going."

As I slip on the rest of my clothes, I get the unnerving feeling that we're being watched. Searching the forest, I don't see anything out of the ordinary, but something doesn't feel right. Even the occasional bird or squirrel seems to have taken cover. A deep, menacing growl rumbles from behind me. Spinning, I lock eyes with a beast possessing the head of an eagle that appears to be bolted onto the body, legs, and tail of a lion. Sharp talons that look like knives protrude from its enormous paws. Metal wings fan out in at least a four-meter wingspan. A twig falls from a nearby tree, and when I look up, a dozen of the winged creatures stare down at us from thick branches.

"Gryphons," Maddox says, pulling his handcrafted pistol from its holster. "This is going to get ugly."

Instinctively, I reach for my sword, but remember that it lies on the bottom of the lake. Maddox draws a blade from his belt and hands it to me.

"What do we do?" I ask, aiming the knife at the gryphon slowly approaching us.

Maddox checks the ammunition in his gun. "Fight or die trying."

The large gryphon picks up speed, its murderous black eyes fixed on Maddox. He fires, and the bullet strikes the gryphon in the neck. The beast yelps and collapses, whimpering, but doesn't move. As if on cue, the group of gryphons take flight, dive-bombing us from every direction.

One leaps toward me, its hooked beak aiming for my neck. Using its weight for momentum, I tackle it, driving my knife into its side as we both fall to the ground. Its beak snaps at me, nicking my cheek. I stab my blade into its thick fur repeatedly until it no longer moves. Just as I sigh with relief, talons sink into my arm, forcing me to drop my weapon. I scream in pain. I try to pull my arm from its grip, but it digs its claws deeper into my flesh. With a clenched hand, I punch the beast's face as hard as I can with my left fist, but that doesn't even faze it.

A bullet whirs passed my cheek and plunges into the gryphon's skull. Immediately, it drops dead next to me, releasing my arm as it falls. I glance up as Maddox reaches down and pulls me to my feet. He aims just over my shoulder, taking out another gryphon. Behind him, a wounded gryphon gets to its feet, shakes the dust from its fur, and pounces on Maddox.

"Maddox!" I snatch my knife from the ground and throw it. It sticks in the gryphon's side, but it doesn't slow the beast down. It growls and snaps as Maddox fights to keep the gryphon's bloodied beak from hooking into his flesh. Leaping over the smoldering fire, I tackle the beast, knocking it off Maddox. My shoulder feels as if I've tackled a brick wall. With two sharp talons, the gryphon grabs me and throws me to the ground. The massive creature growls. I pull my knife from its side and plunge it into the gryphon's heart. It goes limp on me, pinning me beneath it. Nearby, I hear Maddox fire another round. From the corner of my eye, I see him pull the trigger, but the gun only clicks, empty of bullets. Before he has a chance to reload, he is cornered by three gryphons.

"Alyssa," he says, panic evident in his voice, and a gryphon grabs him by his long coat. Maddox is dragged to the ground, where he hits the animal with the butt of his gun.

"Just keep fighting," I wheeze as the weight of the gryphon prevents me from taking in a deep breath. I struggle to get out from under its dead body, but the monster is too massive.

Bursting from the trees, a man lifts his rifle, the sharp bayonet pointed right at the beast. A bullet whizzes by me, striking the gryphon above Maddox in the neck, killing it instantly.

"So, you're hungry? Come and get me, you vile beasts!" he shouts, taunting the gryphons. It's then that I realize that this isn't the first time I've seen him. His dark, wavy hair and beard are familiar, and it takes me seconds to place him. He was the man who darted into the Labyrinth ahead of us. Only this time, his shirt is shredded and shallow cuts mark his skin beneath the fabric, evidence that he's faced his own dangers within these deadly walls.

Suddenly, the gryphons converge on him in one large pack. With the skill of an elite warrior, he takes them out one by one, using both ammo and blade to neutralize them. Gryphons fly through the air, bleeding and yelping in pain. Finally, the few survivors retreat, howling as they flee into the forest.

The man helps Maddox to his feet.

"Has anyone ever told you that your timing is impeccable?" Maddox says.

"Yes, once or twice," the man says in a clipped British accent. Together, they push the dead gryphon off me. Maddox and I give each other an incredulous stare. Standing, I brush the dust from my clothes. The ground is littered with dead gryphons, their blood staining the earth.

"Who are you?" I ask.

The man pulls a wilderness knife from his rucksack and saws off the hind leg of one of the gryphons. "You can call me Colonel," he says.

"I'm Duchess Alyssa of Northumberland, England," I say.

His head whips toward me, shock evident in his gaping mouth. Soon enough he lets his expression slip, suddenly seeming uninterested as he wraps the leg in burlap. "You're the duchess? You're awfully far from home."

"Indeed. We've come a long way," I say. "But so are you."

He glances at me warily. "I'm indebted to you for opening the Labyrinth's entrance."

"Were you the one who left the gear pieces to the Labyrinth's puzzle?" I say.

He ties the wrapped meat to the top of his rucksack and slips his arms through the strap. "Yes. I couldn't solve the puzzle. I've spent weeks trying to unravel that thing. When I saw you two land on the shore, I hoped one of you could figure it out. Thanks again for the help." He starts to trudge off, but stops and turns toward us. "Look, the Labyrinth is no place for a bunch of kids. The sooner you get out, Duchess, the better it'll be," he says, plodding off into the woods.

"Well, that was certainly awkward," Maddox says.

"Let's go before more gryphons arrive," I say.

We travel for nearly ten minutes. Ahead of us, the forest appears to continue on; however, I run into a solid structure. When I put my hand out, it is met by a wall with trees painted on it. I follow its length with my hands. Maddox does the same in the opposite direction.

"Alyssa! Over here!" Maddox calls.

I make my way over to Maddox, climbing over dry logs and through thick brush. Ropes hang from a pulley several meters above and attach to a large basket. "Looks like we're going up," I say, climbing inside the basket.

Maddox hesitates.

"What's wrong? Aren't you coming?" I ask.

Nodding uneasily, he starts to climb in but retreats again.

Confused, I watch him as he takes in the expanse of the wall.

"Is the brave and mighty Maddox Hadder terrified of heights?" I tease.

"Yes, and spiders, which are everywhere in the Poison Garden, but mostly heights," Maddox says, peering at the top of the wall.

"You're kidding me. Would you just get in here? I promise it won't be that bad," I say, holding a hand out to help him in.

"Wishful thinking," he grumbles under his breath. Reluctantly, he throws a leg over the edge and settles into the basket.

"You take that side, and I'll take the other." We spin the handles of the large wheels on either side, letting the mechanism guide the ropes through its braking system. The basket lifts only a little at first, but then we rise several meters off the ground.

We continue to spin the handles. Although Maddox is clearly nervous, his hands shaking with every turn, his sights are set on the top of the wall. Something snaps loudly and the basket drops a few meters, listing to the left. Maddox nearly falls over the side, but I reach for the back of his jacket with one hand, my other holding desperately on to the lip of the basket. The lift swings lopsided over the forest floor. Maddox squeezes his eyes shut and clings to the side.

"This is a prime example of why one should keep his or her feet firmly placed on the ground at all times," Maddox says.

Above, the rusted brackets holding the pulley in place have bent, skewed at an awkward angle.

"Trade sides with me," I say.

"Gladly," Maddox says, taking over my position in the basket. It shudders as we switch, but fortunately, we fall no farther.

The wheel on this side is nothing more than springs, washers, and other metal parts. The rope hangs loosely within the wheel of the pulley. I grip the rope and wrench it, lifting my side of the basket.

"If we get out of this alive, remind me to refrain from going on any further adventures with you," Maddox says.

Between the two of us we manage to lift the basket up the wall. We finally reach the top of the hedge wall and tie the ropes onto two hooks. Maddox climbs out first and helps me from the basket. When we are safely out, Maddox lies down and throws an arm over his eyes.

Standing, I take in the view of catwalks before us. It is absolutely stunning from this high up. The early morning sun shines down on the brightly colored treetops. Their leaves are a blur of reds, oranges, and golds, and beyond them are the brilliant azure waters of the lake we encountered. A large tree marks the center of the maze, shimmering in the daylight. I'm certain it is the pwazon pòm tree that we seek. From where I stand, the catwalk on this section of the Labyrinth looks like an elaborate maze: starting and ending in various places.

"The bad news is that we are not there yet," I say.

"And the good news?" Maddox mumbles, his arm still thrown over his face.

"If we can figure out which of these catwalks will get us closer to that tree, we might have the apple by sundown. Assuming we don't meet any other creatures or deadly obstacles up here," I say.

"That is the best news I've heard in a long while," Maddox says, finally standing.

The catwalk rumbles beneath our feet, and I hold on to the copper railings. The walls of the Labyrinth move, creating new walkways and paths to follow. The eastern path shifts, and within seconds, new pathways merge together.

"This isn't so bad. At least this way we can see which way we need to go," Maddox says.

"Yeah, but nothing here is as simple as it seems," I retort.

Loud clanks echo throughout the Labyrinth as we make our way along the shifting catwalks. Suddenly, a horn blares so loud that I have to cover my ears. Nearby, something rises from beneath the floor. At first all I see are spikes, but as it surfaces, I realize it is a human-size ball with sharp barbs affixed to its surface, poking in every direction. It reminds me of the vicious ball at the end of a mace. More metallic clangs reverberate around us. Dozens of similar spiked balls rise throughout the catwalk.

The walkway shakes beneath our feet, making it nearly impossible to stand. The nearest weaponized sphere wobbles and rolls off its stand, straight toward us.

"Time to go," Maddox says, pushing me to a perpendicular walkway. We don't get far before another sphere rolls in our direction, the tips of each spike glinting in the sunlight.

We dash down walkways, running into dead ends, backtracking to others, and struggling to stand straight as the walls shift beneath our feet. I step out onto an adjoining catwalk but am yanked back by Maddox as a spiked sphere nearly skewers me. Some of the orbs pick up their speed as they spin through the loops, giving them momentum as they swing out the other side.

It seems no matter what direction we turn, we find ourselves either farther away from the Labyrinth's center, or in the path of the maze's weapons. I take Maddox by the hand, noticing a walkway that appears to be empty and leads straight to the west of where the apple tree stands. We sprint, our boots pounding on the metal grates beneath our feet.

"We're almost there!" I say, breathless. "Just one more corridor."

As if on cue, a hatch opens beneath our feet, and we fall down a shaft that appears to hold the inner mechanisms of the rotating walls. We are surrounded by machinery that blurs in the gas lamplight as we descend quickly. I can hardly catch my breath, much less scream. Panic settles over me as I wonder what lies at the bottom: something to catch us or kill us. I shiver, thinking what that might feel like.

Finally, something shimmers beneath us. Maddox and I hit a silky parachute-like material at the same time. It pulls from the wall, but we hit another and another. With each one, our descent slows. Maddox turns his head toward me, fear washing away, replaced by awe. He smiles brilliantly as the fabric billows above us. I smile back, grateful not only for not being splattered like a broken egg on concrete, but also for Maddox's company. Exhilaration replaces the terror I felt only seconds ago. I throw my hands out in front of me, enjoying the fall.

"Wahoo!" I yell, my cheeks hurting because of how hard I'm smiling.

Maddox shakes his head and laughs.

Our speed slows down to a crawl. When we finally hit the bottom of the shaft, the jolt tosses me and I find myself on top of Maddox, my arms pinning either side of him.

"You may very well be the craziest person I have ever laid my eyes on," Maddox says, resting his hand on my cheek.

"It takes one to know one," I say.

Our lips are so close, too close. It's the first time I've noticed that he smells of cream and sugar. Of course the host of the grand Poison Garden Tea Party would smell of ingredients to add to tea. Leaning in, I close my eyes. Just as my lips graze his, voices interrupt our fleeting intimate moment.

"Well, who do you think it is?" a female voice says.

"I don't care. Probably that darn dodo bird playing pranks on us again. Do you know how long it's going to take me to re-attach those chutes?" another voice says, only this time its male.

Something paws at our shelter of nylon. Maddox pulls me close, his arms wrapping around me protectively.

"Chip, you're always complaining. What if it's something good this time?" the first voice asks. "We haven't had a decent catch in weeks!"

Maddox and I shield our faces as the material covering us opens up. The bright sunlight shines down in our faces, obscuring the face hovering above us.

"What do we have here?" the female voice says. Blinking, I see two metal hands spread open the rest of the material. A kind face made completely of brass clock parts peers down at me. Rust colors her lips red, and long black wires serve as her eyebrows and lashes.

"Oh my!" she says, cocking her head to the side. "It's okay, dears. Don't be frightened. We won't hurt you."

Her head spins wildly and when it stops, another face scowls at me. The same black wires are affixed to this face as well, only it appears to be a beard and mustache. The machine holds up his metal arm and a barrel lifts from a hidden compartment.

"Chirp, step away!" shouts Chip, aiming a red light in between my eyes. "We don't know who they are or where they've been."

Again, the machine's head spins, this time stopping on the female face. The barrel disappears back into her arm.

"Nonsense, Chip, they're just wee children," she says, offering her hand. "Come, come, you two. You must be terrified."

Chip moans from the back side of her head. "Heaven help us," he grumbles under his breath.

I don't have a chance to respond before the machine is shaking my hand vigorously.

"I'm Chirp, and that grumpy old thing on the back of my head is Chip," Chirp says.

"I'm Alyssa," I say. "This is Maddox."

Maddox bows his head.

"Such a pleasure to meet you," Chirp says.

"At least for one of us," Chip groans.

"Oh, shush!" Chirp says. "What brings you here?"

Maddox straightens his coat, brushing out the wrinkles. "We're looking for the pwazon pòm tree."

Chirp's eyes grow. "Oh, no, no, no, my dearies. No one should enter the orchard. It is much too dangerous. Why, you'll end up like the rest of the challengers that have come here.

Nothing left but your inner parts exposed and your outer parts melted away like thin pieces of aluminum."

Reaching for his top hat in the pile of fabric, Maddox guffaws. "Giant blades, shifting walls, human croquet, memory wiping forest, and spiked spheres . . . I'm sure there is nothing in or near that tree that can be any worse than what we've experienced."

Chip's face spins toward us, smiling widely. "You hear that, my love? Who are we to deny them entrance? Let the strangers continue on their journey."

As if not of his own will, Chip's hand smacks himself hard in the forehead with a loud clang.

"Blast! What'd you do that for?" Chip whines.

Chirp's face spins back. "Chip, I'll have none of that barbecuing the Labyrinth guests. It leaves such a wretched smell." This time she turns a key in her neck, locking her head in place. "That's much better now. I think our visitors have had enough of the likes of you."

"I hate when she does that," Chip murmurs. "Do you know what sharing a body with a feisty woman is like?"

"Ignore him. Come with me, my dears. Perhaps we ought to talk about this over a warm cup of oil," Chirp says, leading the way out of the shaft.

Maddox's brows draw together. "I don't suppose you have tea, do you?"

I elbow him in the ribs. "Don't be rude," I whisper.

He sticks out his tongue and gives me a disgusted look.

"Maybe just some hot water with lemon and honey?" he asks hopefully.

As Chirp leads the way, Chip glowers at us from the back of her head. Leaving the shaft, we end up in a flourishing plot of land. In the middle is a building that looks like a large steel-and-brass furnace. Steam lifts into the sky from a copper pipe on the roof. Grated windows glow red. A fire dances just below the doors of an open basement that looks like a kiln. An overflowing pile of coal sits nearby.

"What a lovely home you have," I say, a weak attempt to be polite.

Chirp's bronze cheeks redden. "Why, thank you!"

"Yes, Chirp's very particular about our home. Sometimes even to a point that it's a pain in my—" Chip starts, but Chirp smacks the back of her head.

"Knock it off, you!" Chirp says.

"—brass," Chip moans.

"Follow me," Chirp says, seeming flustered, her hands flitting about.

"Do you think she intends to cook us?" Maddox teases, gesturing toward the glowing red embers flickering within the basement.

The rusty hinges wail as Chirp opens the caged front door of her house. "Please, come on in. Make yourself at home."

· P E T E ·

As the sun rises on the horizon, the Lost Boys take up posts in the towers that surround the inner and outer baileys, each armed with slingshots, pistols, and bows. Peering out the window from the duchess's sleeping quarters, I watch the refugees below prepare a battering ram in front of the castle doors.

"What do you think they'll do if they get through?" Gwen asks, joining me.

Although I'd asked her to protect those that arrived from the infirmary, she refused, claiming that Lily and Bella were enough protection for them. I try not to read too much into it. By instinct, I reach for her hand, but stop, reminding myself that she ended things with us. Swallowing the lump in my throat, I settle my hands onto the hilts of my knives.

"It's going to be a bloodbath if they do," I say.

"I wish Alyssa were here," Gwen says. "I hope she's okay."

"I don't know that there would be much that she could do either," I say.

Gwen faces me. "Pete, let's just give Katt access to the castle. No one has to die. We can hide my mother's research."

Standing this close to Gwen and knowing I can't touch her strangles the breath from me. "And then what? When she doesn't find what she's looking for, do you think she'll just walk away?

She'll take us out one by one, use us against one another in order to get information. We'll die anyway. We have to stand our ground."

Pressing her lips together, she shifts her weight to one side. "Then let's get out of here. Evacuate the castle. We'll take the *Jolly Roger* and just go somewhere else."

"Where, Gwen? Where in the bloody world are we going to hide?" I say, frustrated. Hook's zeppelin might still fly, but there's no way she's big enough for all of us. "There's too many of us. Between the sick, the Lost Boys, the Queen, and the duchess's staff, do you really believe we'll all be able to make it to the ship before Katt catches on to what we're doing?"

Gwen casts her gaze over the growing number of refugees gathering around the castle. While I want so badly to hold her, I also feel anger flickering at the edges of my heart. I can't understand how she can so easily give up on what we had together.

"We're out of options. We have to fight or die trying," I say, shoving all the emotions deep down.

"To die will be an awfully big adventure?" she asks sadly. It's the very thing I said to her the last time I was sure I'd never see her again. Now she stands with me and we're facing death a second time in just a few short months, only so much has changed between us. If I'm going to survive this, I have to protect myself. Brick by brick, I try to build a wall around my heart. Ironically, I know Gwen is doing the same.

As if reading my mind, Gwen takes my hand in hers and

squeezes. Confused, I stare at our hands. "Pete, I can't take much more loss." And again, my hope sinks. She gazes down at the crowd before turning her eyes back to me. "But if this is our last day, I want to spend every moment by your side."

I pull my hand from hers and step back. "Gwen, you either want us, or you don't. I want you by my side always. But if you don't . . ." It kills me to say the next words, but I make myself anyway, no matter how bitter they are. "Then you're right: It's over. Either way, get off the fence and decide, because my heart can't take losing you."

Before Gwen can respond, Katt yells from below.

"Aw, well, isn't that just sweet. I've caused a lovers' quarrel," Katt hollers. She is dressed all in white with a laced-up corset, a holster riding low on her hips with a matching pair of pretty pistols, and a flowing skirt trailing behind her. Her long hair is pulled up in a twist and held in place with what looks like a knife. If I didn't know any better, I'd think she was the bride at a deranged wedding. "Last chance, Lost Boy! Step down as leader and hand over Professor Darling's research."

"Katt, you look lovely. What's the occasion?" I say flirtatiously.

"Your funeral if you don't give me what I want," she says, bitterness cutting through her words.

"Seems awfully early to be planning funerals, especially mine, since I have no intention of dying today," I say.

Katt narrows her eyes, clearly not amused. "Hand over the research or face the consequences."

"Northumberland is under my rule, and I won't bend to your threats," I say with conviction.

Katt flashes me a sultry smile. "As you wish. The blood that spills is on your hands, Lost Boy." She whirls around, her snowy-white skirt flowing behind her. "People of Umberland, you have suffered enough under the reign of my sister and Duchess Alyssa. They have both failed you. The Queen is ill, unable to protect you. Duchess Alyssa has abandoned you, leaving outsiders in charge. Will you stand for that any longer? Will you continue to lie down and die while they withhold the information vital to the cure?"

The crowd roars in support. A scrawny boy approaches Katt, kneels, and lifts an elaborate crown to her. Katt places it on top of her head. Spikes rise from the black wire base, adorned with jewels. A diamond is embedded in the center of the band.

"Long live the White Queen!" a voice cries. The crowd thunders its approval.

"Rise up, Umberland. Follow me into battle!" Katt yells.

Again the crowd cheers her on, waving their weapons in the air. Their shouts take my breath away. We are outnumbered threefold.

"Tear it down, stone by stone, and don't stop until you find those papers," she says with a wave of her hand.

The refugees swarm the castle. A first shot rings out, whizzing past my head.

"Take cover!" I say to Gwen.

Sprinting out of the duchess's sleeping quarters, I throw

myself down the staircase, skipping multiple steps at a time. The Lost Boys have barricaded the doors and windows. Their bodies shake each time the battering ram hits. Fear etches lines in their young faces. Through a broken and boarded window, kids scream, trying to pry the wood slats from the opening. This close, the magnitude of their illness settles over me. Those that have joined Katt's army, they are the worst of the sick.

Their eyes glow gold, their pupils hardly visible. Instead of fingernails, sharp claws grow from their hands. Every inch of their bodies is covered in thick green scales. Most are them are bald, or have only a few tufts of hair left on their heads. They hiss at me, and that's when I see their forked tongues.

Their transformation must nearly be complete.

But their alarming appearance isn't my biggest concern. With the swiftness and agility of snakes, they seem to slither from one window to the next. Others crawl like lizards, some of them attacking on both hands and feet. They rip at the boards with the force of angry crocodiles barreling down on their prey. My remaining Lost Boys attack from the surrounding towers, shooting arrows, stones, and bullets at the rampaging swarm. Their ammunition bounces off the tough scales covering the reptilian creatures without leaving a scratch.

A handful of the kids or reptiles or whatever they've become turn their attention to the boys in the towers. They claw at the doors, trying to gain access to the stairs that lead up to the keeps.

"Lost Boys, fall back!" I shout, just as one of the creatures snaps a board in half and leaps through the window.

Not expecting the attack, I am knocked to the ground. A growl rumbles in the lizard boy's throat. He opens his mouth wide, exposing razor-sharp teeth. With a snap, he bites down on my shoulder. His fangs tear at my flesh. I scream in agony as I plunge my dagger into his soft underbelly. Appearing unfazed, he snaps at me again, and misses. He hisses violently in my face, and I gag at his breath, which smells of decayed bodies. His pulse throbs beneath the dry, sickly skin at his throat. With a knife in each hand, I aim for his artery. The tips of both blades puncture through his thick outer layer. The reptile screams and attempts to clamp his teeth on me one last time. Before he can make contact, I twist both blades in the creature's neck and scream with remorse. This creature was just a kid. A child I swore to protect. But from two gaping holes, hot, sticky blood spills, covering my weapons and hands. Gasping, I shove him off and stand.

The Lost Boys battle bravely against the army of lizard people, but it's clear that we stand no chance against the creatures. Just as I'm about to repeat the call for the Lost Boys to retreat, Katt appears under the archway where the castle doors are broken, a cloud of smoke billowing behind her. Next to her are the remains of what once was a person, only now, crawling on all fours, it resembles a crocodile. She pets the leashed beast as if it were a dog.

Cries of pain erupt from the kids surrounding me and are washed out by the hissing of the beasts.

"Katt, you have to stop this!" I shout.

She cackles, throwing her head back and holding her stomach as if what I've said is nothing but a joke. Finally, she tilts her head to the side, her lips pouting, as she resumes petting the crocodile beast. "What's wrong, Pete? You don't like my timsah?"

"Timsah?" I ask.

Katt sneers and points a claw at me. "Because of you, they're no longer human. You gave them the antidote. You turned them into these things! Into slithering, reptilian creatures."

Gwen breathes heavily as she sneaks up behind me. "We can't win this, Pete. Over a dozen Lost Boys are dead. We have no other choice but to evacuate," she says, panic lacing her voice.

My chest feels hollow. Over a dozen Lost Boys? I look around and sure enough, bodies of both the younger and the older kids lie still in pools of blood. My heart sinks when I see Scout in a bloody heap. The bite marks on his neck leave no question in my mind that he's no longer with us. This was a mistake, a huge mistake. We should've run. We should've left Alnwick. Found safety somewhere else. Now it's too late. And it's all my fault. Again. Guilt wells up in me. I have to save whoever's left.

"Gather everyone from the castle. Get them to the ship immediately. And get your mother's papers," I say.

Gwen breathes faster, her eyes darting from me to Katt. "And you?" she asks.

"I'll be there soon. Just get everyone to safety, now!"

She gives me a small nod and a fast hug, but quickly pulls away. "Hurry," she says softly.

I try to respond, but she's already gone, calling for the Lost Boys to follow her. Those who have survived the assault battle their way through the back of the foyer, seeking the closest exit to where the *Jolly Roger* waits. Gwen waves the kids ahead of her, and when the last Lost Boy runs in, she glances at me once more with a worried expression. As the timsah close in on her, she darts through a door on the far side of the room.

Katt juts her chin. "Aw, poor Lost Boy, your girlfriend left you. That's quite all right. I'll take good care of you." Katt unhooks the leash on her crocodile friend. He growls approvingly. Katt pets him between the eyes. "Patience, my pet. You'll get your snack. A tasty morsel, even if he is a pathetic excuse for a leader." She looks at me with a wild glimmer in her eyes.

I swallow hard, glancing down at the ferocious animal that is barely under Katt's control.

The timsah gnashes its teeth and claws, growling at me. I grip my daggers tightly in my fists. Time is what Gwen and the rest of them need to get to safety. It's the least I can give them, since I've failed them in so many other ways.

"While the dinner invitation for your beast is tempting, I think I'll have to pass. I'm afraid my daggers are a bit sharp for its digestive system," I say, narrowing my eyes at Katt. I flip my dagger in my left hand, looking for the first opportunity to plunge it into her skull. "The castle is all yours. Let us leave in peace."

Katt paces, her boots clicking on the stone walkway. "Oh, not quite yet, Lost Boy. I still haven't received what I'm here for. I want the Professor's papers," she screams. "Her research is going to prevent me"—she holds up her scaly hand—"from turning into that!" She points at the timsah. The reptile hisses in disapproval.

"My plan is this: I take you and as many others as I can as my prisoners. One by one, I'll feed you to my timsah until one of you spills the location of her journals. I will find them, trust me, Lost Boy. One way or another. I'll use her research to create the cure, and then I will reign as the Queen of Umberland with my loyal subjects by my side."

When she glances down at the timsah, I take my opportunity. With a flick of my wrist, I throw my dagger. Katt doesn't flinch. Unsurprised by the weapon hurtling toward her forehead, she flips a hand up. The dagger hits the scales on the back of her hand and flops to the ground. Casually, she lifts her head, smirking. "Stupid, Lost Boy. You still don't get it. Your time is up."

The whir of an engine purrs outside of the castle. The *Jolly Roger* buzzes just beyond the castle doors. Her gold skull-and-crossbones figurehead glimmers in the sunlight. Above, a cigar-shaped air balloon keeps the hull of the ship afloat.

"Pete! Pete, come on!" Gwen says, throwing down a rope ladder.

"No!" I shout, feeling as if the air in my lungs has been sucked out. "Gwen, get out of here!"

"Tsk, tsk. Our dinner party isn't over yet. Alas," Katt says, pulling one of the handcrafted gun from the holster. She aims it straight at me. "Good-bye, Lost Boy!"

I squeeze my eyes shut as she cocks the hammer. Before I hear the release of the trigger, Katt shrieks in agony. When I open my eyes, blood pours from her nose, spilling onto her white gown. Katt holds her face and screams.

"Run, Pete!" Gabs hollers from behind me. "I'm fed up with this crazy princess. No one threatens to kill the leader of the Lost Boys and lives to tell about it."

I look back and see him holding a slingshot in his quivering hands.

"Gabs, get out of here! That is an order!" I say, gripping him by the arm, tightly.

"I'm not leaving you," Gabs says fiercely, ripping himself from my clutch.

"This is your last warning. Get on that ship now or—"

I'm cut off by a loud bang, and I never get to finish my sentence. Gabs's dark eyes grow wide, and his mouth drops open. He falls to his knees, and I catch him before he hits the floor. As I do, blood blossoms on his shirt. I can't breathe as I look up to see Katt's gun still pointed at the young boy.

"No!" The grief-stricken holler sounds distant and not of my own doing.

Gabs gasps. "It's okay. It hardly even hurts," he says, wincing. I know he's trying to be brave.

Hyperventilating, I rip my shirt off and try to stanch the blood gushing from his wound. "Stay with me, Gabs. You're going to be just fine. We're going to get you out of here, and Doc is going to fix you up just like new," I say, my voice wavering.

"It's all right, Pete. Don't be sad," he says. "I'm going to see my mum."

Hot tears burn my cheeks. "No, Gabs! Don't you dare leave me. You're going to be all right. You'll be just fine." I peer up and see the *Jolly Roger* hovering just outside the castle doors. "Doc! Doc, get down here now!" I shout.

"Tell Gwen thank you for being my mum, even if was just for a short while," he says. His final words are barely a whisper as he goes limp in my arms.

"Gabs! No!" I say, shaking him. He doesn't flinch, doesn't blink.

"Sweet dreams, Lost Boy," Katt says, with a sly smile.

"Bloody witch!" I scream, snatching up my dagger from the floor, where I must have dropped it when I caught Gabs.

Four timsah surround her, daring me to challenge her. She rips at the hem at the bottom of her dress. Using the torn fabric, she wipes the blood from her face.

Katt takes in the chaotic scene within the castle as her troops tear it apart. Seeming satisfied, she turns and exits, her timsah following close behind.

"Like I said, their blood is on your hands," she says, not turning back.

Fury floods through me, and I chase her from the castle into the inner bailey. Eyeing the back of her head, I lift my dagger. I pull my arm up, ready to throw the knife just below the base of her skull, when someone grabs my arm and yanks me back.

"Pete, hurry!" shouts Pickpocket. "We have to get out of here!"

"She killed Gabs!" I shout. "She killed him! We have to stop her." I struggle against Pickpocket, but he holds tight.

"She's gone, Pete. And we have to go," Pickpocket says. When I look back, Katt has disappeared. The timsah rush into the castle, sprinting faster than is humanly possible. Then again, they are no longer human. Pickpocket and I dash to the rope ladder. He scurries up, and I follow behind. One of the beasts bites the bottom rung and shakes it violently. I stomp on its snout, avoiding its deadly teeth, but trying to force it to let go. A well-placed boot heel to the soft spot between its eyes and it drops. My heart clenches. That was a person. A *person*.

I hold on with all my might as the ship lifts into the air, leaving behind the timsah . . . and Gabs. With the back of my arm I wipe away the last of my tears and turn my eyes to the sky, wondering which star will shine for Gabs tonight.

· JACK ·

My brother rips through the hanging vines, grumbling the whole way. We've been trudging through the muck for hours without a hint of whether we are even headed in the right direction.

"We're lost," he says. "We're going to be stuck in this blasted labyrinth for the rest of our blasted lives."

Although I'm tired, I can't help the smile that I feel twitching at the corners of my mouth. He's so easily aggravated, which made our childhood incredibly amusing. It took very little instigation to set him off in a flurry of rage.

The swamp seems never-ending. The scenery is all the same, except that the trees have become more densely packed. Their thin gray, brown, and white trunks stand like soldiers, leaving narrow paths curtained with vines.

Hook continues to grumble, then suddenly stops. Just ahead is a sheer, rocky cliff. A circular metal door is built into the rock. BEWARE OF THE BANDERSNATCH is scratched crudely into the metal, as if another traveler has left a warning for us.

"What's a Bandersnatch?" I ask.

"I don't care, and I have no intention of finding out," Hook says. He reaches for the curved handle and pulls, but it doesn't budge. An unusual keyhole sits beneath the handle. Pulling out the necklace with the key from the Zwerg, I look from the key to the keyhole, but it doesn't appear to be the right shape. I tuck it back beneath my shirt.

Muttering under his breath, Hook flicks his metal index finger and the tip opens up, revealing a pick. Grumbling, he works on the lock.

"There must be a key nearby," I say, searching the crevices in the cliff. It seems we've finally found the entrance we sought, and we won't be stopped by a blasted missing key.

Something rumbles, low and menacing. Hook and I turn toward the trees, but nothing appears unusual. It occurs to me the Bandersnatch might be on *this* side of the door we're trying to open, not the other side.

"We'd better figure out where that key is, or else I have a feeling we'll be meeting that Bandersnatch soon," I say.

Hook continues to fiddle with the lock while I search the wall, wondering if perhaps I should be diving into the mud instead. We are busily trying to find our way through the door when the sound of gears breaks the quiet. Hook and I both look over our shoulders, only to find the head of a mechanical creature between us. Curved spikes serve as teeth. It snaps at me and roars when I duck.

Hook whirls around and aims his Gatling gun at the creature, but it's too late. Sensing danger, it zips away, across a small section of the swamp and up to a branch in a nearby tree.

Its coloring is that of the tree, which camouflages it within the branches. It's no wonder we didn't see it. The Bandersnatch flaps its metal wings, sending us stumbling into the door with a gust of wind. I try to regain my balance, taking my attention off the beast.

"Look out!" Hook shouts.

The Bandersnatch rears its head back before springing it forward, diving toward us. It's extraordinarily fast, its bladelike teeth slashing at the air before Hook just as he pulls the trigger on his Gatling gun. Bullets ricochet off the armored animal. I shield my face as a bullet whizzes by my head. It is then I see a strange key that hangs from the metal neck of the Bandersnatch. I reach for my weapons belt and spin it to the left, searching for the only weapon I know that will stop the beast, at least temporarily.

Hook is out of bullets. He duels with the Bandersnatch, attempting to use the weight of the Gatling gun to cripple the monster, but his weapon only bounces off the armor. Teeth gnash at him, nicking his arm. He drops his gun and reflexively pulls his arm in, crumpling to the ground. The Bandersnatch growls over my stepbrother as he holds his metal arm up, ready to fight to the death.

Finally, I find the button I've been searching for. Pressing it, the lightweight, chain-link net springs from the belt, blanketing the Bandersnatch. It screams, not expecting the attack. Before it has time to regain the upper hand, I launch myself onto the creature's back, doing my best to pin its head down on the ground.

"Get the key!" I scream.

My brother reaches into the net with his hand, snagging the

chain around the Bandersnatch's neck. He pulls and the chain breaks, leaving him with the broken necklace and key. Quickly, he unlocks the door, grabs me by the back of my coat, and drags me into the cave. He slams the door just as the Bandersnatch frees itself from the net.

"You saved me again?" I ask.

"One, I already told you that when you die, it'll be by my hand, and two, if we run into any more creatures like that, I want to be sure your handy-dandy magic belt of tricks is around. It has saved my skin more than once," he says, offering me a hand.

Cautiously, I take it. As much as I'd like to trust him, something's off about him. He's being too nice. Saving my life once—okay, I'll buy the now-we're-square logic. But this is now three times. I'm not sure what he has planned, but I don't like it one bit. At some point, I may need to look out for myself and ditch him. Can I get back out of this maze without him, though?

Sunlight floods in at the other end of the tunnel.

"Let's hope whatever is on the other side isn't as nasty as that Bandersnatch," he says, traveling up the tunnel.

It occurs to me that possibly the most dangerous beast on this journey is not a prisoner of the Labyrinth at all, but instead is my own brother. I follow behind but keep my distance.

· A L Y S S A ·

Maddox looks at me, his expression uncertain. Although my stomach flutters with nervousness, I step through the doorway.

Inside, the home is stunning. Every wall is made of polished copper so flawless that it reflects the single gas lantern hanging from the center of the room, brightening the sitting area. Two chaise longues and a sofa constructed of rosewood and covered in plum velvet sit in the middle of the room. A steamer trunk serves as a coffee table that sits between the two couches. Pictures of zeppelins, trains, and pedal-powered flying machines hang in brass frames on the walls. A large clock ticks over a fireplace, but it is no ordinary clock. It appears the mechanisms that make it run are on display around it. Surrounded by spinning gears, the second hand in the face of the clock inches forward, counting away the time.

"Would you like something to drink?" Chirp asks, standing at the kitchen entrance.

Maddox holds up a gloved hand. "No oil for me. I'm trying to quit, but thanks. How about you, Alyssa?"

He smiles as if daring me to accept.

"That's awfully kind of you. Perhaps next time?" I say.

Sitting on the opposite chaise longue, Chirp settles herself in. It is then I notice the purposefully set mirror behind her.

Chip's reflection peers at us with a scowl. Behind me is another mirror, in which Chirp smiles brightly. How clever of them.

"Please excuse the mess. We don't have company often," Chirp says, brushing the nonexistent dust off the trunk in front of her.

"We *never* have company and all she does is clean. I'd be shocked to find a spot of rust in this entire place," Chip growls.

"I beg your pardon, but I hardly see you lifting a finger to help out. Besides, there isn't much to do here in the Labyrinth. It's too dangerous to venture beyond our little home." Chirp frowns. "What I wouldn't give for just one day outside these wretched walls."

"No use dreaming for things you . . . we can never have, Chirp, dear," Chip says, sounding equally as disappointed. His reflection frowns.

I search for some response, something to give them hope for life outside of the Labyrinth, but nothing comes to mind. The world beyond these walls is in shambles. I'm not sure they'd be better off than they are in their current circumstance. It occurs to me that as awful as the Labyrinth is, perhaps it's better than what waits for them outside the walls.

"Now, where were we?" Chirp says, interrupting the awkward silence. She sips from a copper cup of oil. "Ah, yes, the pwazon pòm. Why on earth would you ever seek that out? It will kill you. And not to mention that it's all overgrown with nasty vines, poisonous plants, and such."

"Poison ivy, poison oak, and poison sumac," Maddox says, his chin resting in his hand.

"Plants that will make your skin itch so much, you'll scratch until you draw blood," Chip says.

"Stinging nettle," Maddox says.

"Why, yes! How do you know?" Chirp says.

Maddox lifts his eyes and smiles weakly. "My father was the king's groundskeeper," he says quietly.

Chirp gasps, holding a hand up to her lips. "Mayr, is that you? It can't possibly be. You've grown like a weed!" she exclaims, rising from her place.

"Mayr? No, this is Maddox," I say to Chirp.

"Maddox Hadder was the name I gave myself when I arrived at Alnwick. Remember, I was hiding from the Bloodred Queen," Maddox says.

Maddox gives me a small sheepish smile and stands. Chirp wraps her metal arms around him and kisses him on the cheek. "You've been away so long that we thought one of the Bloodred Queen's henchman took you along with your parents. How are they? Your folks, I mean?"

Maddox's expression darkens. "I don't know. I haven't seen them in nearly five years."

"Oh my. Poor dear," Chirp says, resting her hand on her cheek. "You must miss them terribly."

"I've managed okay," Maddox says, grinning, and I can't help but grin as well. Having lost his parents, escaped with his life, and been on his own at such a young age, I imagine seeing a familiar childhood face must bring some comfort.

"You know each other?" I ask, raising a brow.

"Know each other? Why, I wiped that boy's bottom when he was just a wee little boy," Chirp says, waddling back to her seat and plopping on the chaise longue.

Chip lets out a hearty laugh. "He was such an ornery lad. Chirp and I were in charge of looking after him while his parents worked on the castle grounds. That boy gave us such grief!"

"I see nothing has changed," I say lightly.

"I wasn't all that bad," Maddox protests.

"Oh, really?" Chip says. "What about that time you sprinkled morning glory seeds in the streusel your mother made for the garden helpers? Your poor mama and papa were chasing near-naked people for hours."

"I have no idea what you're talking about and I'm sticking with that," Maddox says airily.

"Likely story," Chip says.

"So you've both been here the whole time?" Maddox asks.

"Oh, yes! Twasn't anywhere to go. When the Bloodred Queen shut everyone out, she made sure those of us stuck in the Labyrinth couldn't leave either," Chirp says. "We were gearing down for the night when the soldiers arrived. When everything was said and done, your folks were gone, Chip and I woke up here, and the apple tree was shielded by an array of poisonous plants."

Maddox, suddenly seeming interested, leans both elbows on his knees. "Overgrown with poisonous plants, you say?"

Chirp's wire eyebrows lift. "Why, yes. All specimens from your parents' greenhouse."

"You know what that means, Your Grace?" Maddox asks.

Chirp leaps up and claps, her palms sounding like cymbals. "Oh! Did you hear that, Chip? There is royalty among us." She bends into a deep curtsy and bows her head. "Welcome to my home, Your Grace. Whatever is mine, is yours."

"Goodness gracious, woman. Get ahold of yourself," Chip says, his face staring straight up at the ceiling.

I cover my mouth, holding back a giggle.

"Where are my manners?" Maddox says, standing up and tugging me up with him. "*This* is the Duchess of Northumberland." He bows and waves a hand at me. "Go on now. Curtsy or whatever it is you royals do."

"Oh, for heaven's sake, Maddox," I say. I can't tell if he's being sincere or if this might be a joke to him. I sit back down on the sofa and yank him with me.

Chirp fans her face with her hand, her fingers literally spinning in circles. "I beg your pardon, Your Grace. I've never been around royalty. Well, other than that awful Bloodred Queen, but I'd hardly call that devil royalty of any sort. She's more of a taskmaster."

"Taskmaster?" I ask.

"Indeed; our job is to keep the machinery functioning,"

Chip says. "There are numerous other shafts like the one you fell through. It's our job to be sure they're all running smoothly. Oiling the joints and gears, fixing and repairing broken parts, that sort of thing."

"And if you refuse?" I ask.

Their shared body rattles, the metal joints clanging. "Terrible things will happen," Chirp says in a hushed voice. "If the walls stop moving, if the doors are left ajar . . . if the Labyrinth stops working, all that is evil will be let loose within and beyond the fortress."

"Have you ever attempted to just leave?" Maddox asks.

Chirp weeps bitterly.

"Not this again, my love; please don't cry," Chip says.

"Oh dear!" I say, searching my pockets for a tissue.

Maddox pulls a black silk handkerchief from his coat pocket and offers it to Chirp.

"Thank you," Chirp says, taking the cloth and dabbing her eyes. "You're a lucky girl to have snagged this boy for a husband, Your Grace."

Maddox, looking surprised, quickly corrects her. "Um, I'm not . . . eh . . . we aren't married."

"And why not?" Chirp says condescendingly through a sniffle.

"Let the kids be. It's none of our business," Chip says.

"Uh, well, let's just say her kind rarely mingles with my kind," Maddox says.

Although what he says is the truth, his honesty stings. My

cheeks flush. Maddox has grown on me, even stirred feelings within me that I've never felt for another. A friendship between royalty and peasants would be frowned upon, and a union would certainly be out of the question. However, with the world in the state it is in, the lines between royalty and commoner have become blurred. But perhaps Maddox has realized that already and this is his polite way of stating he's not interested in me in such a way. Then again, we may never make it out of here alive.

"What a shame," Chirp says, dabbing her eyes one last time, before returning the handkerchief to Maddox. "Thank you, dearie."

Chip clears his throat, changing the subject. "You asked why we haven't left the Labyrinth. There is only one way out from this point on and it's at the tree."

"We can't go back the way we came?" I ask.

"No," Chip replies. "Do you remember how the maze reconfigured as you went along? It's impossible to trace your steps back to the place you started. Besides, the entrances into the Labyrinth can only be opened from the outside. You'd be stuck at the door even if you did find your way."

"But what about you—can't you leave through the exit at the center?" I crane my neck, trying to see his face. "The one that lies in the garden?"

Their hand reaches for their neck and turns the key the opposite direction, allowing Chip to face us. He frowns. "For Chirp and me, I'm afraid this is forever our home. We'd never survive what's out there. Come, follow me."

Chip rises and leads us up the staircase. His feet clang on the metal stairs with every step. The stairwell spirals up several stories high, copper as far as I can see, which leads to a tiled domed roof. When we reach the top floor, it is fairly empty other than a leather chair and an elaborate telescope set upon a tripod. The sun casts a bright light into the room through a circular window.

With a wave of his hand, Chip gestures toward the telescope. "Take a look."

I step up to the telescope and peer through the eyepiece. A black metal dragon tugs at its chains on the far side of the maze. The massive machine with spiked horns and claws roars, fire and smoke erupting from its nostrils, mouth filled with jagged teeth and deadly fangs. Surrounding the platform where it sits is a pit filled with pipes with flames bursting through the opening in the floor.

"What is that?" I ask, stepping back.

Maddox peers through the lens and his face blanches. "That is a terrifying beast."

Chip's expression darkens as he speaks. "That is the Jabberwock, the guard of the western entrance to the tree you seek. There are four entrances to get to the tree. Each guarded by a beast that tests a warrior's strengths or weaknesses: the Bandersnatch at the north tests kindness, the Jubjub Bird at the south tests patience, and the Murderous Crow at the east tests love."

"And the western entrance?" I ask.

"Bravery," Chip says.

Maddox groans. "You mean we need to be brave enough to get through that hunk of metal to get to the tree with the apple?"

"Worse yet, you need to get through that hunk of metal if you ever hope to get out of the Labyrinth," Chip says, his frowning face turning toward us. "The monsters are the reason why we've never left the Labyrinth. We'd be nothing but a hunk of metal if we stepped foot in those lairs."

"Tell us about the Jabberwock," Maddox says.

Their metal body shudders, and Chirp's face spins toward us. "Frightening creature. Many have tried to enter, but none has succeeded. That machine, that dragon, brings out the greatest fears in the bravest of women and men."

"Which is what?" I ask.

"Why, death, of course," Chip says sorrowfully as his face returns to the front. "What greater fear is there than no longer existing? Chirp and I are just a machine made up of gears, springs, and other random machinery, parts that can be repaired or replaced. But you mortals, your last breath comes with the last tick of your heartbeat. There's no coming back. And that creature's only goal is to make sure that ticker inside of you," Chip says, tapping his finger over Maddox's chest, "comes to an early end."

As I consider what Chip said, I realize it is the ultimate test. Death is precisely why Maddox and I are here. We're trying to prevent it. We're risking our own lives to save more lives. At that realization, I feel determination deep down in my gut. We have to do this. No more trying. We're nearly there; just one more creature.

Chirp's face spins forward, and she hurries back down the stairs. "We have guests now. Actually, I suppose they're not guests since they will be staying with us indefinitely. Oh my! So much to do. I'll have to prepare the spare bedrooms. Plant a vegetable garden since it's apparent you are not fond of organic oil at all. Chip, dear, you'll need to take up hunting. How are you with a rifle?"

"Wait!" I say, chasing her down the stairs. Maddox follows closely behind. "But we won't be staying. We have to get that apple and return to Alnwick."

"Of course you're staying, my dear. That's a fool's errand right there," she says, still bounding down the stairs.

"I must return to Alnwick with that apple," I repeat.

"Nonsense. We just told you no one has ever beaten the Jabberwock," Chip says. "I've seen grown men take that beast on and still the result is always the same. Barbecued knight in shining armor. It takes days for that rancid smell to dissipate."

"And you don't even have any armor," Chirp adds.

I stop suddenly, and Maddox nearly runs into me. "I *will* defeat the Jabberwock," I continue, the resolution in my voice unwavering. "However, you're right that I'm in need of armor and weapons. Can you help me?"

"*We* will defeat the Jabberwock," Maddox interjects. He looks me dead in the eye, daring me to argue. I won't. If Maddox is prepared to offer his services, I'll take all the help I can get.

Chirp halts midstride and Chip stares at me, his mouth

gaping. Then their head whirls a full three-hundred-and-sixty degrees, their geared eyes spinning wildly.

"Wahoo! Can I? I've got the finest weapons in all of Germany," Chip says. "Follow me!"

His head twirls forward, and he bounds down the stairs two at time. Chirp smiles at us. "Well, if you're going to do this, you've come to the right place. He just adores tinkering with bits of metal and tools. He's created a fine collection of weapons. A very fine collection indeed."

We descend the rest of the staircase. "Chirp, Chip, when we destroy the Jabberwock, you will come with us, right?"

Chirp pats my cheek. "Aren't you kind, Duchess? Why, that is the most thoughtful thing anyone has ever done for us. But where would we go? There is nowhere out there for us. The Labyrinth is our home." She looks at me, and I realize she's right. Where would they go? To Alnwick? To do what? Become a servant of the castle? That's what would be expected of them, as all the animatronics are expected to work. I nod my head sadly. "But don't you worry about us," she adds. "For now, your mind must be on getting past that Jabberwock."

Chip leads us out the door and toward a large building that looks like a warehouse. Smiling, he opens the double doors.

The sight before me is breathtaking. Racks and racks of armor and weapons fill the space except for a small worktable cluttered with tools.

"Do you think you can find what you're looking for in here?" Chip asks, pride beaming in his smile.

"I think we can work with this," Maddox says, leading me inside by my hand.

"It's either this or we're the main course on tonight's dinner menu," I say.

Maddox whirls his head toward me. "Let's hope the beast isn't hungry."

· PETE ·

The hiss of the reptilian swarm fades beneath the whir of the *Jolly Roger*. I throw my arms over the railing of the ship, my feet dangling. Gwen grips my arms and pulls me over to the starboard side. As I take one final glance at what has been our home, a deep ache, a darkness I have never experienced overwhelms me. Again the kids that I'm responsible for are homeless, including me. Loss is a familiar and bitter friend, and it haunts me once again.

Bodies of a dozen Lost Boys lie lifeless, like fallen tin soldiers. Tears well up in my eyes as I bid those brave kids farewell on their final adventure: a journey I, too, will see one day.

I watch as the army of timsah overruns the castle. My knuckles pale as I grip the railing, digging my fingernails into the wood. It stings, but I welcome the distraction of pain. Unable to contain my rage, I scream until my throat tastes as if it bleeds from the inside. Finally, when I no longer have the energy, my knees give out. I bury my face in my hands, pressing my palms into my eyes as hard as I can.

It should be my blood spilled on the cobblestone courtyard.

The air is thin, and I can hardly catch my breath. Reality feels as distant as a lost dream. No. As if I'm in a horrible nightmare that I'll never wake from.

Gwen gently places an arm around me. Normally, I would

welcome her warmth, but every cell in my body is numb. She is silent, and I revel in the quiet she brings. There's isn't anything she can say or do that will bring me consolation, nor do I deserve it. I've failed the Lost Boys, only this time it cost me Gabs, Scout, and so many others.

When I finally come up for air, dropping my hands into my lap, the world I once knew is long gone. I bite back the bile and, clenching my fists, I stand to take in the survivors. They are bloodied and battered. Dozens of sick lie swaddled in stained and shredded blankets. Hatred beyond anything I know brews in me. My stomach roils, making me want to double over in disgust, when my gaze catches Doc lying up against the ship, dazed. Bella presses a cloth to a gushing gash across his cheek. Although his blue eyes glisten with tears, I feel nothing for him.

"How many did we save?" I ask.

Gwen balks and gives me a worried glance, not answering. She doesn't have to. Our crew is few, and many of those who made it can hardly stand.

"Joanna? Mikey?" I press. "Bella?"

"They're safe," she says.

"The Queen?" I ask.

Gwen nods. "One of the few we rescued."

"And Lily?"

"Yes, Lily made it out, too," she says, pointing to the bow of the ship. Lily stands at the helm, guiding the zeppelin away from Alnwick.

Although the sun warms my face, I feel nothing but cold and darkness brewing within me. "And the Everland cure? Your mother's notes?"

Gwen's voice cracks. "They're gone, Pete. All of them."

My legs feel weak and I support myself with the ship's railing, barely able to steady myself.

My eyes scan the faces of the passengers. There are so many missing from the group.

Gwen drops her head on my shoulder, sobbing, and I stiffen. She wants my comfort, but I no longer know where we stand.

"Pete, we couldn't save them all. We had to leave them behind," she says.

As the dead and missing toll rises, my last hope for our world ever having a happy ending diminishes. There is nothing left for us here now, and I have no idea where to take the survivors, much less where they will be safe. Even if we find ourselves another home, how much longer do we really have? Weeks? Days? Without an antidote, it'll be sooner rather than later. And I still have no idea where Maddox and Alyssa are. I had hoped they were retrieving the apple, but now how will we ever find them?

Pulse sprinting, breaths shallow, I race to the helm, asking Lily to step aside, and turn it hard to the right. The zeppelin lists and heads east.

"Where are we going?" Lily asks.

Staring over the land spread before us, I say:

"Lohr. To stop this battle where it started."

· JACK ·

Hook and I emerge to find ourselves in a virulent garden. Although it's somewhat overgrown, it thrives in a rainbow of colorful flowers. Within the center stands the tree. It has doubled in size since I was a boy. Chains hang from one of the thicker branches, supporting a metal bench swing. Memories flood back to me, of the days when Hook and I were actually friends rather than foes. Hours of swinging on the bench as high as it would go just to see if we could make it circle over the top of the branch.

However, the bench has been modified. No longer is it a swing, but an enclosed vehicle of some sort. An elaborate panel with dials and levers is attached. A propeller is affixed to the top of the capsule. I can only assume that this is how we escape the Labyrinth.

If we could reach it.

Hook's dark stare falls on the tree. His expression is pinched and distant, as if he's reliving the nightmare of his thirteen-year-old self. He picks up a large stone and hurls it at the tree, but it only lands within the ring of briars and brush. Again and again, he launches his assault with an arsenal of rocks—most of which never even come close to hitting the tree. I lean back on the wall and cross my arms, captivated by his tantrum. His last toss makes him lose his balance, and he falls to the ground on his hands and knees, panting.

"Are you done?" I ask.

He glares at me, stands, and brushes the dirt from his black trousers. "If I never see that tree again, it won't be long enough. Let's get that apple and get out of here," he sneers.

I nod to the briar patch before us, its sharp thorns in the midst of the flowers and vines. "Any ideas on how to get through that mess?"

Hook pulls his long sword from the sheath, struts up to the foliage, and slams his weapon down. Sap sprays across his dark coat, sizzling as it corrodes the thick fabric. He howls, drops his sword, and rips his jacket off, throwing it the ground.

"It appears the tree isn't eager to see you again either." I laugh, relishing in the situation.

Pressing his lips together, he marches over to me and holds his geared fist up to my eyes. "What exactly do you think is so funny?" he growls.

I resent the threat and push back the fabric of my coat, exposing my weapons belt. With the press of a button, the mini-blowtorch releases from its holster. I pass by Hook and head toward the apple tree. "We've come this far, and instead of finding a solution to our prickly and apparently corrosive problem, you'd rather duel to the death?" I take a step back and bow. "By all means, brother, let's do it!"

Hook grits his teeth as he backs down with some reluctance. "So what do you suggest?"

Pulling my goggles over my eyes, I turn toward the briar patch. I take the handkerchief from the front pocket of my waistcoat and wrap it around my nose and mouth tightly. The lack of air is uncomfortable, but it's better than breathing in the fumes the plants are sure to give.

"What are you doing?" Hook says, following suit with his own handkerchief.

"Just stay behind me," I say. Flicking a lever on the mini-blowtorch, the end of the barrel ignites in a burst of fire. Immediately, the plants heat up with a fiery red glow, melting before our eyes. The smoke that rises smells acrid, and I attempt to hold my breath.

I burn my way through the foliage, until we reach the base of the tree. The bright green apples litter the ground. Holstering the mini-blowtorch, I drop my rucksack and kneel, gathering up as many apples as I can. I have no intention of returning to the Labyrinth again. If the Bloodred Queen wants a poison apple, she can get it herself. If I take it west to Alnwick, Doc and the Professor might be able to do something with this apple. It's the only way I see to get back in their good graces. The Lost Boys were the closest thing to family I've ever known. I never should have revealed the Lost City's location to Hook. I thought I was saving them, but I only made things worse.

Tying off the rucksack, I don't notice Hook approach me until it's too late. His thick leather boot kicks me in the jaw, sending me sprawling on my back. Searing pain throbs in my cheekbone. I'm certain it's broken. Before I regain my senses, Hook is straddling me, his entire weight on my chest, pinning my arms to the grass beneath me, ripping the handkerchief from my face. As I blink back tears, my vision comes into focus, and I feel as if my heart stops beating altogether. His metal fingers puncture an apple. Then he grabs my jaw, forcing it open. Bones crack in my face, and it hurts so much I think I might throw up. I try to press my lips together, but it's no use. The juice of the apple drips into my mouth as he shoves the fruit in. Holding it in place, I feel like a stuffed pig about to be cooked over a fire. I thrash, trying to break his grip, but his legs lock my body in place and his other hand reaches to pinch my nose tightly. My eyes widen in horror. He's blocked my airway, and I panic at not being able to breathe. I keep thrashing, but it's no use.

"Thanks for all of your help, little stepbrother. I probably wouldn't have made it this far without you. At least you can die knowing you have my gratitude. Our mother . . . well, *my* mother will be so proud. She might even weep when she hears how you died, by my hand, with the very fruit that is going to save her life. Well, maybe she won't weep for you, unless it's tears of joy. She'll be so pleased with your death—now you'll never take the crown," Hook says.

At first I can feel nothing but the ache in my jaw. As the apple juice slides across my tongue and down the back of my mouth, the muscles in my throat contract. Hook continues to prattle on, boasting about what a great son he is and what a horrible brother I've been. Only a few of his words make sense. The rest blur into the ringing in my ears. I helplessly gasp for air, but soon enough I'm overwhelmed with exhaustion and sleep threatens to take over my thoughts. My vision fogs, and I can only make out the fuzzy outline of Hook hovering over me.

"Rest in peace, Jack," Hook says as the world fades away.

· ALYSSA ·

Armed with a brand-new sword finer than the one I lost in the lake in the woods, I swing wide, testing its weight and balance. The armor that Chip has given me is surprisingly lightweight and slips easily over my clothes.

"Are you sure this is strong enough to protect us?" I ask.

"Of course it is!" Chip says. "That's a vorpal blade. It's the strongest blade I've ever forged."

"And the armor?" Maddox asks doubtfully as he straps the chest plate to himself.

"Absolutely!" Chirp declares. "If my Chip made it, you can be assured it's made from quality material."

Maddox flicks at his flimsy-looking armor and whispers to me, "Do you expect me to believe that this aluminum foil is going to protect us from that hunk of a beast?"

"That there is the strongest and most lightweight material you will find anywhere in this entire structure. Possibly all of the world," Chip says.

He picks up a sledgehammer and whacks Maddox's chest armor. Not expecting the blow, Maddox stumbles back. The crack of metal on metal startles me and a flock of birds roosting nearby.

"What was that for?" Maddox snarls.

Chip points to the metal. "See! Didn't even leave a scratch on ya."

"Next time give me some warning, will you?" Maddox says, inspecting his armor. "What do you call this stuff?"

"Chirpdanium," Chirp says proudly. "Chip named it after me."

Maddox rolls his eyes. "Obviously."

"It's an alloy only found here within the Labyrinth. Unlike my sweet Chirp, it is waterproof, rustproof, lightweight, durable, and can withstand heat up to six hundred degrees Celsius, which is what you're going to need if you plan to take on that dragon."

"I'll show you who's a lightweight," Chirp says, flicking Chip's nose.

Chip howls.

"And what about this?" Maddox asks, holding up an elaborate gun.

Chip's eyes spin wildly as he rubs his nose. "That is my best invention yet! It's a Chipblaster."

He takes the gun from Maddox's hand and aims toward a rocky embankment. With barely a flick of his finger, it discharges. A flash bursts from the barrel and the pile of stones blows up, leaving nothing but a crater and pebbles.

Chirp squeals with delight. "I love it when he does that."

Wide-eyed, Maddox snatches the gun back and shoves it into the holster at his hip. "This'll do."

Once we're geared up, Chip leads us to a lift.

"All aboard," he says, guiding us to a wooden platform that sits in front of the prickly hedges. Maddox and I step on the rickety lift. "Hold on to your britches."

Maddox eyes it warily, and frankly I can't blame him. The lifts in the Labyrinth haven't been so kind to us thus far.

Chip feverishly spins the handle of a wheel. The valley of their home comes into view. It is breathtaking, with gurgling springs, patches of forests, and fields of flowers. Their home takes center stage of the colorful work of art. It occurs to me that all the foliage before me was planted and cared for by Maddox's parents.

"It's beautiful," I say, resting my hand on Maddox's as he grips the railing of the lift.

"It looks a lot like Lohr before the Bloodred Queen's rule," Maddox says, his eyes lost on the garden his father toiled over. "That city was nothing but forest until my father cleared and landscaped it as the town grew."

His adoration for his parents' work warms me. As ominous as the Labyrinth is, it truly is a masterpiece. If it were not such a deadly prison, this land could very well be paradise.

I feel a nudge and find Maddox grinning at me. Smiling back, I interlace my fingers with his. My breath hitches, and I realize that I don't want these to be our final minutes together. In fact, we haven't had nearly enough time together. This boy who I'd dismissed as crazy and uncaring, he's shown mercy to the sick, and risked his life not only for my people, but for me.

The lift shudders as it comes to a stop. Suddenly, I feel as if I can't breathe. Maddox squeezes my hand.

"You ready, Your Grace?"

"It's just Alyssa," I remind him.

Maddox drops his gaze and smiles shyly. He's incredibly charming and handsome. I wish I could stay in this moment forever.

"Okay, Just Alyssa."

Chip flips levers and switches, mumbling to himself down below.

Realizing that this is possibly the last time I'll ever have a chance to convey my appreciation, my gratitude for all Maddox has done, I squeeze his hand. I'm certain I would never have survived without him. And then what? If I died, so would hundreds, thousands, millions of people, because we all depend on that apple. Maddox isn't here just for himself, or me; he's here for all of us. The entire world.

The hinges of the pulleys squeal as I take Maddox's face into my hands. "Thank you. I am forever indebted to you."

Maddox nods. "You have changed me, Alyssa." He removes his hat and bows. "*I* am forever in your debt." He places his hat back on his head and brushes a thumb across my cheek.

As the lift comes to a halt, we are met by a ledge. Beyond it is a hole in the wall fitted with a circular opening just barely big enough to sit in. The tube curves down, disappearing into darkness.

Maddox's hands grip my wrist, his gold eyes fixed on mine. I nearly take off his head with the vorpal blade, a subtle warning to mind his manners, and give him a brazen smile. Ignoring it, he wraps his arms around my waist and pulls me closer. As he draws me to him, I drop the sword and crash against his chest. Eagerly, I rush to meet his lips. Locked together, I can't breathe. His fingers feather through my hair. His mouth presses urgently against mine, and I am lost in his arms, weak beneath his touch. An ache grows in my chest. I kiss him as if tomorrow will never come.

Disappointment swells as Maddox pulls away.

"I believe we have a Jabberwock to slay, Alyssa," Maddox says, handing me my fire-resistant shield.

I take it from him, ignoring the hornet's nest of nervousness in my stomach. "Indeed," I say, and my voice sounds unsure even to me.

"Farewell and good luck," Chirp shouts, waving. "Your papa would be proud of you."

A tinge of pink tints his bronze cheeks. Together, Maddox and I step into the tube. He sits behind me, holding my waist before pushing us off from the ledge. We slide, spiraling down the pipe. It is so black I can't see anything in front of me. Light finally appears in the distance. The tube spits us out and we find ourselves within a fiery cavern, which makes sweat instantly bead on my forehead and back. A black iron spiral staircase splits in two directions, leading down to the ground. The ground is made up of gears of all varieties, shapes, and sizes. They spin, the teeth of each interlinking into the others. Some are as small as tea saucers, while others are bigger than the face of Big Ben. Gaps in the floor expose a pit lined with a pattern of pipes. Gas ignites the rows and rows of flames beneath the mechanical floor. On the far side, the Jabberwock is curled into a ball. Its automated wings twitch, and it stretches out its bladed claws.

A dormouse appears from the hedge, hesitates, and dashes across the spinning floor. Less than a few meters from the edge, the cog drops, plunging into the fiery inferno. The dormouse lets out one squeak before disappearing into the flames.

Maddox sighs. "We should've stayed back at the Poison Garden. Tea sounds a lot better than this."

"We?" I ask.

Maddox gives me a wide-eyed stare. "Um . . . me . . . ah . . . I . . . I should've stayed back in the, back in the garden . . . unless, well, unless you'd want to join me."

I smirk. "I can't say I blame you. Teatime does sound awfully good."

His head spins toward me. "Stay away from the poppy tea. It's terrible stuff. Tried it once and found myself swimming naked in the garden fountain. No poppy tea for you, missy," he says, waving a gloved finger at me.

Shocked by his admission, whichever one that is—the fact he's only tried it once or that he was skinny-dipping—I gape at him. "I was kidding!"

As if backpedaling, he sucks in his bottom lip. "Um, so was I?"

Before he can say more, the Jabberwock stirs, yawns, and unfurls its dark metal wings and limbs. It sniffs the air as if searching for the scent of intruders in its lair. Its ruby-red eyes fixate on me. My hair blows back as it rears and roars so loudly my ears ring. The smell of sulfur stings my nose. The beast flaps its metal wings, sending gusts of heat our way as it takes flight. The flames in the pit respond in a turbulent dance. Steam rises from the Jabberwock's nostrils.

"Time to go!" Maddox says, rushing down the stairs toward the spinning gears.

I follow suit, dashing down the opposite staircase, barely dodging a streak of flames spit by the mechanical beast flying above our heads. Reaching the bottom of the stairs, I leap from one moving wheel to the next, nearly losing my balance, but regaining it before toppling into the fire pit. The gear drops beneath my feet as I hurdle to the next one.

"Just keep moving, Alyssa," I say, my heart ready to burst from my chest. I duck, holding up my shield as another explosion of flames from the mechanical beast turns the wheel beneath me fiery red.

I am nearly halfway to the other side of the room where the door into the garden stands. I take a step onto a gear that my foot barely fits when it gives and drops beneath me. With my arms waving, I fall forward. My shield plummets into the fiery pit below and my sword skids across the gear ahead of me. I reach out, hoping to catch the edge of the next wheel. My left hand slips through one of the teeth of the cogs, but my right hand finds its mark. I dangle from a single prong of a gear as the wheel turns and the Jabberwock roars from above.

"Maddox!" I scream. The large gear spins slowly, each tick one notch closer to the next wheel. Maddox throws himself across a wide gap, aiming for the gear I hold on to. He doesn't make it. Instead, he plunges into the blazing pit below, but I reach for him, catching his hand with mine just before he's incinerated. His top hat tumbles off his head and bursts into flames as it plummets into the inferno.

"Maddox," I cry in panic.

He glances up at me. "That was my favorite hat."

My fingers slip slightly, and I tighten my grip on his wrist. His added weight is too much. I can't hold him—*us*—much longer. Struggling to hang on to both the gear and Maddox, I growl to muster the strength to hold on.

"You're too heavy," I shout. "I can't pull you up."

Maddox peers down, taking in the fire and brimstone that burns below. When he looks back at me, flames cast a golden glow on his face. "Let me go, Alyssa."

"No!" The brutal scream that comes from me echoes throughout the chamber, and I don't recognize my own voice.

His gold eyes meet mine. "Let me go, Alyssa. It's my time."

Pressing my lips together, feeling him slip even more in my hand, I shake my head. "I won't. I won't let you go."

With his gaze fixed on mine, he wriggles his wrist, loosening my grip on him.

"No, Maddox! Stop," I plead, my voice cracking. "Please don't do this."

"It's been an honor accompanying you," he says. He tugs his wrist once more, and my grip on him is gone.

"No!" I scream.

· P E T E ·

As the ship flies deep within Germany's borders, a vast woodland area comes into view, and within it is an enormous network of pathways and walls expanding as far as the eye can see. A magnificent tree inside some kind of mazelike structure stands in the middle, glittering in the early evening sun. With a monocular, I peer into the distance. I can't see it, but I know Lohr Castle stands dark and foreboding.

"What is that?" Gwen says, joining me at the helm and motioning to the forest.

"I have no idea," I say. "Whatever it is, we're sailing over it."

The zeppelin flies over the wall, and when I glance down I see that we're passing over a vast maze filled with corridors and pathways leading in every direction. Forests, rivers, and lakes are partitioned off by tall metal and what seem to be living green walls. I steer the ship toward the massive tree that stands in the center of the labyrinth. It sparkles in the sunshine, the light refracting on the shimmering leaves into brilliant colors.

As we come closer to the tree, I look through the monocular again to get a better lay of the land. My blood runs cold when I see cannons shift on the top of the walls that surround the magnificent tree. They aim right for the *Jolly Roger*. Before I have a chance to react, an explosion bursts from the nearest cannon. Shoving the monocular into Gwen's hand, I grip the helm, turning it so the ship tilts violently as I change our course, heading south in hopes of flying the ship out of the maze. A cannonball whizzes by, nearly hitting us.

The crew scatters, each taking a post. There are so many missing that not all the stations are filled. I feel sick knowing that their bodies lie in Umberland, left for dead.

Another cannon fires, sending a cannonball straight for the zeppelin. There's no time to divert the ship; she's a little too big and a touch too slow to maneuver that fast. The hot metal sphere pierces the balloon, igniting the hydrogen in a ball of flames.

"Abandon ship!" I yell.

Still seeming somewhat dazed by his head injury, Doc rises and stumbles to the emergency chute box. Handing out the parachutes, he shouts instructions, assisting the littlest of what's left of the survivors as best he can, including Gwen's siblings, Joanna and Mikey.

The helm shudders beneath my grip, and I struggle to keep control.

Gwen comes to my side, holding out a parachute. "Pete, we have to go."

"Go with the others," I say.

"What about you?" she asks, thrusting the parachute toward me.

I bite my lip, knowing she isn't going to like what I'm about to say. "I have to get the Queen off this ship. She's too weak to do it on her own, and as captain, it's my job to make sure we all get out alive."

Wide-eyed, Gwen shakes her head. "I'm not leaving without you."

I don't bother pointing out that she's already left me. Instead, I say, "And I'm not leaving without the Queen. If she dies, Katt really is in charge. That can't happen. You told me of your father's devotion to the Queen. How the day the bombs fell, he left you, telling you he had to protect her. There is honor in that. Your father was a brave man. He stayed with her until he no longer could. I will do the same."

Tears brim in Gwen's eyes. I've struck a nerve.

"Please, Gwen, go now."

Suddenly, she kisses me, hungrily. As confused and angry and hurt as I am, I pull her into me. Knowing this might be our very last kiss, I don't want to let her go. When she finally breaks away, there is a determination in her stare. "You better not die, Pete."

I have no words, nothing that I can say to convince her. She's made that clear. All I know is that this is my ship and if it's going down, I'm getting everyone off alive.

Gwen gives me one last hard stare before turning. Only she and Doc are left on the deck of the ship. Doc struggles to buckle his parachute. Gwen helps him and gives him a hand as he climbs over the railing.

"Don't forget to pull the cord," she says, tapping it lightly to show him where it is.

He nods before throwing his weight off the ship. Gwen sits on the ship's railing, staring at me. Clipping her chute, she watches me, her eyes searching mine, as if this is the last time she'll see me.

I give her a weak smile before she leans back and falls over the side.

The ship shudders again, and smoke billows from the zeppelin above. The fire spreads wildly. Panic grips me as the nose tilts. If we hit the ground, I'm not all that sure that either the Queen or I will survive. To the east, a murky river flows. I whirl the wheel of the helm, guiding the ship to the water. It's my only hope to extinguish the blaze. What's more, it's the only way either of us will survive.

· ALYSSA ·

I squeeze my eyes shut, not wanting to watch Maddox be incinerated. The Jabberwock roars nearby, and I'm sure I'm next to be burned alive. Instead, Maddox lets out a grunt. I open my eyes. Maddox lies on a rotating gear above me in the fetal position, his arms wrapped around his gut.

"Son of a bloody devil, I don't know whether I want to kiss that hunk of metal or kill it," he says through a groan. "Stay away from the tail. It's got a mean sucker punch."

Elated to see him alive, I struggle to pull myself up as the cog continues to turn. As I round the corner, I realize the adjoining disk is not like the others. Instead of regular teeth like the other gears, it is a blade like that on a circular saw, spinning faster than the other geared platforms. I can hardly breathe.

Shifting my hands to the left, I hope to buy myself time. Maddox crawls toward me and grips my wrists, ready to pull me up, but behind him the Jabberwock flaps its mechanical wings. It pulls back as if taking in a breath.

"Gun! Give me your gun!" I say.

Maddox snatches it from its holster and hands it to me, holding on to one of my wrists. I aim. Maddox ducks just as the bullet whizzes passed his head, striking the Jabberwock in the face. Metal shards scatter, raining down on us. Half of the Jabberwock's face is gone. It howls, the exposed portion appearing like a titanium skeleton beneath its armor. Taking flight again, the Jabberwock circles above us. Just as the blade draws nearer, Maddox pulls me up, but not in time. The blade slices my thigh as I throw myself over the edge.

Blood trickles down my leg, pooling into my boot. Although it stings, adrenaline presses me on. Handing Maddox his pistol, I grab my sword from where it lays on the gear. Having lost my shield to the pit, I keep an eye on the Jabberwock, not wanting to get into the direct path of its angry flames. Maddox takes my hand, and together we hurdle over the remaining gears until we reach the far side of the room.

"The door!" Maddox says, aiming his pistol at the Jabberwock.

Reaching for the wheel on the door, I spin it as fast as I can until I hear the tumblers click. I wrench the door open.

"Thank heaven's stars. Let's get the bloody . . . "

Maddox doesn't finish his sentence. When I turn back around, his eyes grow wide. A metal barb protrudes from his right leg.

"Maddox!" I scream, wielding my sword.

The Jabberwock lifts him up, its horn skewered through his leg, and throws him against the wall. Maddox hits it hard and crumples to the floor. I leap onto the beast's head and drive my sword into what's left of its face and neck. It screams, but I don't stop. I pull the sword out, then plunge it in again and again. Sparks burst from its gears like fireworks, and I keep stabbing until the head is held on by nothing else but a few slender rods.

I slam my sword down on them, severing them. The head tumbles into the fire pit and the Jabberwock's body goes limp, crashing to the ground. Steam rises from its broken pieces as it lies in a puddle of oil.

"Maddox!" I shout, leaping from the machine. He screams in agony. Blood rushes from his wounds, pooling beneath his body. I rip the sleeve from my tunic and make a tourniquet around his leg wound. When I tie the knot on the crudely made bandage, he winces, although I can tell he's trying to not to let his pain show.

"Go get the apple. I'll be all right," he says, trying to quell my worry. "It's just a scratch. Go."

His wound is hardly superficial, and I know he needs medical care immediately. But ultimately that apple is the only thing that will rescue him . . . will rescue any of us.

Placing a hand on his cheek, I lean in and press my lips against his. Afraid that once I take my eyes off him, he'll be gone forever, I memorize every detail of his handsome face, from his gold eyes to his full pink lips, the warm tones of his skin, and the dark scruff of his closely shaved beard and mustache. It's hard to breathe and I'm dizzy with fear.

"I'll come back for you. I promise. Hold on, Maddox."

He gives me a weak smile and nods. I race to the door and swing it open wide.

Beyond the Jabberwock's lair, I stagger into an exquisite garden filled with brightly blooming flowers. Flowers that are all too familiar. Blossoms I last saw within the Poison Garden. In the center, the largest tree I've ever seen reaches toward the sky; its leaves glitter with an iridescent sheen. The base of its trunk is easily as wide as an elephant. Ripe apples cover the tree, but they are no ordinary fruit. They sparkle with a brilliant glow, as if containing a life force of their own. Searching for a path to get to the forbidden fruit, I circle the foliage. Overgrown and uncared for, the bushes, trees, and vines spread wildly, intertwining with one another so it's indiscernible where each plant ends and where the other ones start. There is only one way to the tree—through.

Wielding my sword, I hack away at the vines closest to me, careful not to touch any part of the plant. I slip through the small opening I've carved out. Afraid to breathe, to risk the rise and fall of my chest in the narrow path I've created, I hold my breath. It's just as well. Pungent smells rise from the broken stems, and I have no idea if the fumes are poisonous or not. I pray they aren't.

It is difficult to keep slicing my way through, but I manage as best I can. When I'm nearly through, I bring my sword down on a writhing vine. Sap splatters over me, burning holes in my clothes and searing my exposed flesh. I scream, trying to wipe the liquid off my body, but to no avail. It eats through the fabric of my gloves, seeping into the sores on my hands and fingers. I grit my teeth, fighting back the urge to scream again. My knees feel weak, but I know I can't sit down. Beneath my boots are the clippings of the plants I've hacked through.

Gripping my sword tightly, I continue to chop through the vines, using the excruciating pain to press me onward. Not soon enough, I stumble out of the dense foliage and onto a thick grassy patch that sits below the tree. The grass looks like ordinary grass, and I collapse on the ground, rolling around, hoping to brush some of the searing sap off me. Finally, I lie back and stare up at the tree, admiring the rainbow sheen on the leaves. Exhaustion threatens to steal me away from my mission. I've come so far from home, battled this insane deathtrap created by the Bloodred Queen, only to have the apple within reach, but I can hardly muster the strength to sit up. From the corner of my eye, I notice a fallen apple glowing nearby. I reach for the fruit and cradle it to my chest, a prize I've fought so hard for. It's real; it's actually real. Hope bursts in my chest. No one else has to die. I have to keep moving. Sitting up, I gather as many apples as I can carry, ripping off the bottom of my tunic to carry them in. An explosion rings through the air. Atop the massive wall that surrounds the garden, cannons fire at something in the distance. Sprinting, I follow its aim.

Horror digs its sharp claws into me as I watch a ship I'd recognize anywhere, the *Jolly Roger*, nose-diving into the Labyrinth. Flames consume the zeppelin as dozens of people parachute out. I can't see where they land, so it's hard to say if they're okay or not. I have no idea why the ship is here, but whatever the reason, it can't be good. As tempted as I am to race to the survivors, I won't leave Maddox alone.

I rush back toward the Jabberwock's lair, and suddenly smell what I think is a campfire: burnt wood and leaves. Smoke hangs thick in the air. Waving it from my face, I cough. As I run back around the bend, I discover the source of the smoke. The Colonel stands at the base of the pwazon pòm tree. That strange glass-and-copper tank is strapped to his back, the liquid inside bubbling furiously. He aims metal gauntlets toward the giant tree, and then I realize that fire is spewing out of the palms of his hands.

"Stop!" I shout. "What are you doing?"

The Colonel peers over his shoulder, wearing a welder's mask. "Destroying the last pwazon pòm tree on earth!" he shouts, his words muffled.

"But why?" I say, still shocked and unsure what to do.

"This tree has brought nothing but death and destruction. It's taken everything. Everything from me! My Queen, my country . . . " He shuts the flames off with a click of his thumb and raises the mask. Anger burns hot in his eyes. "My wife and children."

He turns back to the tree, which is now a wild blaze. Embers and ash rain down on us. "It's time to rid this world of its evil forever!"

Afraid of what he'll do with the apples I retrieved, I clutch my makeshift satchel behind me.

"Alyssa?" Maddox says.

Turning, I find him standing at the entrance of the Jabberwock's lair, holding himself up. I dart over to him and hand him my sword to use as a crutch. Slipping his arm over my shoulders, I pass him the apples and hold him by the waist.

The Colonel, meanwhile, has fallen to his knees, his eyes turned up to the blaze that was once a beautiful tree. All that remains of its radiance is blackened boughs and trunk.

"We have to go. That tree is liable to fall any moment," I say to the Colonel. By now both Maddox and I are coughing. Fumbling together, Maddox and I start moving away from the fire, trying to find the exit Chip and Chirp mentioned.

The Colonel pays no attention to me.

"You knew long ago about the dangers of this tree. That in the wrong hands the world could be destroyed, and no one listened. No one believed you, but I did. I've always believed in you," he says tearfully. "This is for you and the children, my darling Marie. Gwen, Joanna, Mikey, I love you. May the four of you rest in peace."

I still. The names are all too familiar. I can hardly believe it myself, but, trembling, I ask him the question that I can't hold back.

"Was your wife Professor Marie Darling?" I hold my breath.

Finally, he turns to me, his eyes wide. "You know her?"

"Yes! She's been in Alnwick since Everland was destroyed," I say.

The Colonel throws his hands up and exclaims, "My Marie! She's alive!" He beams, his smile so wide that I realize my next sentence is going to steal this moment of joy from him.

Shaking my head, I bite down hard, not willing to tell him the truth. His smile slips when he sees my expression.

"I'm sorry. I . . . " Words catch in my throat, and none of them seem to be the right ones.

He nods, and at first I'm surprised by how calmly he's taking the news until he screams, his face contorting into unbridled rage. The Colonel rips his heavy gloves from his hand, tears the tank off his back, and launches it at the tree. It explodes, fueling the flames even more.

A roll of heat washes over us. It's time to go. "Your children are alive."

The Colonel gasps and wipes away fresh tears. "Where, where are they? Also in Alnwick?"

Nodding, I say nothing more. He doesn't need to know how sick Joanna and Mikey are. Gwen, too. Not right now. We just need to leave.

Another explosion draws our attention. We both turn our eyes to the sky, watching an odd machine equipped with propellers lift into the sky. A single occupant sits at the controls, and my blood turns to ice. The dark-haired boy with the eye patch is all too familiar. Although I've never met him in person, he meets the exact description of the treacherous Captain Hook of the Bloodred Queen's army of Marauders.

"Hook's got an apple," I say, breathless. And another thought crosses my mind: The Bloodred Queen most likely needed the apple just as badly as we did. This is not good.

"We have to stop him! That's our only way out of here!" the Colonel yells, racing after the machine and disappearing beyond wild brush.

"We'd better follow him," Maddox says, wincing.

"I don't know if he realizes it's the enemy in that ship," I say, wrapping an arm around him as he limps forward. "You're in no shape to fight Hook. Let the Colonel take care of it. Besides, the *Jolly Roger* just went down not far from here, which means a crew from Alnwick is here. We should see if they need help."

"Good idea," Maddox says. "Maybe if the damage isn't that bad, we can get that ship back into the air, and back to Alnwick."

I don't have the heart to tell him that from what I could tell, the ship is beyond repair. Instead we travel east, listening for any signs of life.

· PETE ·

Aiming east, I head for the rushing river that runs near the massive tree. Flames engulf the zeppelin, causing the ship to descend faster than I'd hoped. Knowing that the landing is going to be rocky and I'll have only moments to save the Queen, I sprint toward the captain's quarters.

She sleeps peacefully. I wonder if she's aware of the tragedy that has struck her kingdom. If she dreams of the horrible events of the last year. From outside the window, the river draws closer. It'll be a matter of seconds before the ship will be submerged. Racing to the Queen's side, I wrap my arms around her, bracing myself for the crash.

When the ship hits, it sounds like an explosion. The Queen and I are tossed from the bed, thrown apart as we crash to the floor. As I regain my footing, water roars in from every crack and crevice of the broken ship. Before I can reach the Queen again, the water is up to my neck. I search the cabin, but she is nowhere to be seen.

With only a few inches between the surface and the ceiling, I take in a large breath and dive down into the murky water, grasping with my hands. After several long moments, I swim back to the air pocket to take in another breath. Again I search beneath the water, unable to see anything beyond my reach. I poke my face into the small space of air that is left. Suppressing the panic that threatens to consume me, I slow my breathing, taking in as much air as I can before there is no longer air to take. When the water seeps into my mouth, I plunge beneath the surface, swimming frantically around the room. Still, I can't find the Queen. With my lungs aching, my heart imploding, I swim toward the door of the captain's quarters. As I reach it, an angel floats before me, her long locks haloing her pale face. She is still unconscious, and I know she doesn't have much time. Pulling hard with my hands, I swim toward her, grabbing her from underneath her arms. Thankfully, the door is ajar and I maneuver her through the opening.

We burst through the water's surface where only the remains of the zeppelin reside. Outside the captain's quarters is a war zone. Flames scorch the air around us, giving me the sensation of being in a furnace.

With the Queen in my arms, I abandon my ship, kicking with all of my strength. The Queen's chin rests in the crook of my arm as I pull her onshore and lay her in a grassy field. She is cold to the touch. I watch for the rise and fall of her chest, but it never comes. Choking on water myself, I clear my own airway and press my lips against the Queen's, pinching her nose closed. After a few breaths she doesn't respond. I try again, but she does not stir. Resting my hands on her chest, I give her quick compressions, feeling the bones beneath my palms crackle.

I give her two more breaths, and she lets out an involuntary cough. Relief washes over me as I roll her to the side to let the water spill from her mouth. Although she remains unconscious, I'm grateful to see her attempting to fill her lungs with air. She stills, but the rise and fall of her chest assures me that she is very much alive.

Sighing, I roll onto my back on the soft, grassy riverbank. Ash falls over me, reminding me of my last day in Everland. I sit up. The magnificent tree is a fiery beacon, flames dancing in the darkening sky.

Suddenly, a man emerges from the forest with an arrow trained on me. I reach for my daggers, but they're missing. I must have lost them in the river. Instead, I hold my hands up and study him cautiously. It's been a long time since I've seen an adult.

"Why, you're just a boy," he says as he draws closer, dropping his weapon. He approaches, taking in me, the Queen, and the sunk zeppelin. He cracks a smile. Wisps of silver sprinkle through the dark hair at his temples. Wrinkles line his warm eyes. "Mighty fine landing there, lad," he says. "How'd you learn to maneuver a ship like that?"

"It's like riding a bicycle. Once you take the handlebars, it's all downhill. And in this case, quite literally," I say, watching the *Jolly Roger* burn.

He chuckles. "I'll say. My name is Hunter," he says with an outstretched hand.

"Pete," I reply.

"And who is this young lass that you so admirably rescued?" he says, peering down at the Queen.

I press my lips together. Surely here in Germany, the English Queen would not be welcome. Before I can answer, shouts erupt from the forest. My crew from the *Jolly Roger* emerge from the trees, calling my name. Upon seeing me, Gwen breaks into a sprint and throws her arms around me, panting as if she's run a race. "Are you all right?" she whispers urgently into my ear.

Hunter clears his throat. When I turn my attention to him, he's got the Queen in his arms.

"I don't suppose you both could hold off your reunion until we get back to the village," Hunter says. "This one is in need of warm blankets and medical attention right away."

Gwen pulls herself away from me and stares in surprise at Hunter. "Village?" Gwen asks.

Nodding toward the setting sun on the western horizon, he grunts. "Won't be much longer before the sun is gone. The Labyrinth is nowhere to be wandering around at night. You and your crew will be returning with me. Come along now."

Gwen gives me a wary look and mouths, "Who is he?"

I shrug. "It's better than freezing out here. I'm sure we'll be fine," I say. I hope, anyway.

"Pete!" someone shouts. Duchess Alyssa emerges from the trees. Maddox limps toward us, his arms slung over Alyssa's shoulder.

"Duchess!" I say, relieved to see her relatively unharmed.

Pickpocket races over to help her hold up Maddox.

"And what are we going to do with this bloke?" a strange man asks, emerging from the trees carrying an unconscious Jack.

"Will you look at that, the traitor lives . . . for now," I say, shocked to see the former Lost Boy so far from Everland, along with another adult. Finding two different adults alive seems suspicious, especially when one of them is carrying the enemy.

"I found him lying on the ground like this. Nearly tripped over him while chasing down the boy in the pod ship," the man explains.

Gwen brushes past me, her eyes wide with shock.

"Dad?" Gwen gasps, staring like she doesn't quite trust her eyes.

"Daddy!" Mikey and Joanna say at the same time.

The three of them rush to the older gentleman. Upon seeing them, he falls to his knees, setting Jack gently to the ground, and opens his arms, delight evident in his brightened smile. Gwen, Joanna, and Mikey throw their arms around him. Tears flow freely as they shower one another with questions and affection. Warmth fills my chest as I take in Gwen's pure joy.

Doc limps over to Jack to assess his condition, I assume.

"It appears this party just gets bigger. The more the merrier," Hunter says.

Gwen's father rises to his feet and hurries over to Hunter, taking in the sight of the unconscious Queen.

"The Queen?" he says, dropping to one knee.

Hunter's brows rise. "Queen, you say? Well, that's even more reason to get her back to the village quickly."

Rising, the Colonel peers at Hunter, seeming to gauge

whether he is friend or foe. "I'm Colonel George Darling of the Royal Guard. I insist on accompanying the Queen to your village."

"Colonel, you say? Welcome to the Labyrinth. I have no idea what brings the lot of you here, but I'm sure it's a fascinating tale that would do well with a full meal and some brew," Hunter says. "Follow me."

Hunter trudges off into the forest, and we trail closely behind. Who knows what awaits us, but we're free of Katt. Which is something. At least for now. Glancing one last time over my shoulder, I bid farewell to the *Jolly Roger*, thanking her for saving my Lost Kids not once, but twice. As she smolders in the muddy water, grief burns within my gut. Loss has been so prevalent in my life that it ought not to faze me, but even the burning ship feels like the death of a close companion. Finally, I turn my eyes forward, never looking back.

· ALYSSA ·

As the sun glazes the dusk sky in brilliant pink, orange, and yellow hues, I breath easier now that this day in the Labyrinth has finally come to an end. After a short hike through the forest, Hunter brought us to an elaborate treetop village bustling with survivors of the Bloodred Queen's cage. Equipped with coal-fueled lifts, chain-and-wooden bridges, and lights energized by steam turbines, this town is thriving in spite of its imprisonment.

My heart hurts for my home. Tears sting my eyes as I imagine Alnwick and my people overrun by Katt's army. I'm grateful to see those who made it out alive—as few as there are.

A sweet melody from a flute lifts into the evening sky. I'm seated on a wooden deck surrounded by the branches of fir and pine trees. Lamplight twinkles from the boughs, illuminating dozens of treehouse cabins made of timber with thatched roofs. Walkways circle through the limbs of the trees, leading in almost every direction. Smoke rises from a bonfire in the hub of the forest town. Pete sits, staring at the dancing flames, a bamboo flute with multiple pipes held up to his mouth as he plays a sad tune. Joanna, Mikey, Lily, Maddox, and several of the Lost Boys sit sleepy-eyed, listening to the sad song.

"Are you okay, Your Grace?" someone asks. Resting a hand

on my shoulder, the Colonel stands next to me, genuine concern in his expression. My last memories drive my response.

"Just call me Alyssa. I am the duchess of nothing now. With Alnwick overtaken, I no longer rule. Here in Germany, we're all equal," I say.

The scowl on the Colonel's face fades. He lowers his eyes and nods respectfully. "Okay, Alyssa. Are you all right?"

"Well, my home, my country, has been destroyed, what's left of my people are stuck in the Labyrinth, and we've lost the Professor's notes. I'm far from fine," I say.

He waves a hand toward Doc and Gwen. Doc grips a poison apple while he talks endlessly. Gwen scribbles notes in a leather-bound notebook.

"He's sharing what he knows before he loses it. Gwen is recording what she can," the Colonel says, smiling with admiration.

Gwen turns toward us and smiles as her gaze falls upon her father.

"I'm glad you rescued those apples before I torched the tree," he says. "I didn't realize their potential importance in everything."

Grateful the apples are in safe hands, I lean against the wooden railing. "How's the Queen?" I ask.

A crease forms in his brow and he points to the highest cottage in the treetop city, far away from the hustle and bustle of the population. "She's resting."

The Colonel shifts awkwardly. "There is one tiny . . . well, maybe no-so-tiny complication," he says warily. "You'd better follow me."

Reluctantly, I follow him. I'm not sure how much more bad news I can take.

He leads me through a series of walkways, makeshift lifts, and swinging bridges. Finally, we reach a torch-lit landing. Vines of flowers wrap around a bier where a raven-haired boy lies as still as death. His clothes are torn, his hair disheveled, and a key with a faint smudge of dried blood hangs around his neck. I'm not sure what the key is for, but I decide I'd better hold onto it for safe keeping.

"Who is this?" I say, unclipping the chain from the boy's neck and tucking the key in my pocket.

"It's the good king of Germany's son, Prince Jack," the Colonel says bitterly.

Although the Everland kids shared stories of Jack's betrayal both of them and the Marauders, I still can't believe it's possible.

"Jack's dad was a kind and gentle ruler. Peace resided between our kingdoms during his reign."

"Is Jack . . . dead?" I ask.

The Colonel nods. "It's complicated, but for the sake of the argument, let's say yes. At least for now."

"For now?" I ask, confused.

"Again, it's complicated, but he's obviously in no condition to rule over Germany, and from the stories I've heard from your Alnwick crew, that may be a good thing," he says.

"They don't lie," I say, feeling defeated. "He'd be a terrible king."

"Not necessarily," he says. "According to Hunter, Your Grace, Jack was kind back when Germany and England were allies. Rumor is that the disappearance of his father broke him. He was never the same again."

"Disappearance? You mean the assassination of the king?" I ask.

"No, I meant disappearance."

"The German king is alive?" I ask, flabbergasted.

"If there is truth to the stories, he is indeed alive," the Colonel says, folding his arms.

Excitement rushes through me, filling my heart with hope like a breath of fresh air. "Where is he? Why hasn't he taken his throne back?"

"I think we ought to join the others for a drink. Hunter can explain it to you better than I can," the Colonel says.

Soon enough, the villagers and what is left of the kids from England venture off to bed. The Colonel, Pete, Gwen, Doc, Bella, and Lily sit by the bonfire. Maddox, although very groggy, also joins us, insisting on wanting answers himself since Lohr was once his home. Hunter pours beer into tin cans for each of us. When we are all served, he clears his throat.

"What can you tell us about the king?" I ask eagerly.

"Exactly where he is, I don't know. However, I do know where the ship was headed when they carried him off," Hunter says.

"How do you know?" Gwen says.

"Because he was the king's huntsman," Maddox says sluggishly. Although he's heavily medicated, he winces as he sits up a bit straighter, his leg bandaged and propped up. "Hunter was close to the king and my father's best friend."

Hunter smiles warmly. "Ah, so you remember me, Mayr? I was afraid you'd forgotten me."

Maddox smiles. "It's Maddox now. And how could I forget you? You taught me how to hunt squirrels with my bare hands when I was barely out of nappies. My parents were always sending me to you when I'd get bored."

"They were a fine couple. I miss them terribly," Hunter says.

"Me too," Maddox says with downcast eyes.

There is a solemn moment of silence for all of those who've gone missing since the Bloodred Queen's reign. Finally, Hunter breaks the quiet.

"Of the story you know about the king, what is true is that he was poisoned with the very same type of apple that was used to create the Horologia disease. And it appears young Jack also ingested the apple. It suppresses respiratory function, giving the illusion of death and inducing the victim into a deep sleep. However, the Bloodred Queen then figured out a way to use it and make it lethal. Now that Doc managed to share what he remembers of the Professor's research, my physician and Doc should be able to come up with an antidote in a timely fashion."

Doc nods. "We'll work as fast as we can. Hopefully, I can develop something to help our young prince, too," he says begrudgingly.

"We should just let him sleep forever. He'd be less trouble that way," Pete says bitterly.

"Pete," Doc says wearily. "You know I have to help if I can. I took an oath."

"Your oath is about as good as a shilling these days," Pete shoots back. Doc glares at him but doesn't have time to respond before Pete carries on. "That said, I'm sure he's got quite a bit of dirt on the Bloodred Queen that can be useful. And if he made it back, who's to say that Hook didn't make it back as well?"

"You don't think Hook is still alive, do you?" Gwen says, horror spreading across her face.

"Hook's alive," I say. "I saw him escaping the Labyrinth."

Shock darkens everyone's faces, but no one says a word.

"He's the least of our worries," Hunter says. "As long as the Bloodred Queen reigns, peace will never abound. Not here, not England, not anywhere in the entire world."

Pete leans on his knees, suddenly attentive. "So what is your solution?"

"There's only one solution," I say softly. "Kill the Bloodred Queen."

Hunter nods, the bonfire flickering in his green eyes. "That'll be tricky," he says. "The castle is impenetrable. The Bloodred Queen has a vast army guarding her at all times."

"London was once my home, until the Marauders took over. Pirates, disease, crocodiles. A few soldiers and some weapons won't stop us. It will be an honor and a pleasure to rid the world of that evil queen," Pete says.

"But with Jack and his dad under the apple's spell, who will take the crown?" Gwen asks.

"Oh, trust me, the king will rule again. It's only a matter of rescuing him," Hunter says confidently.

But I don't feel so confident. I know we have to stop the Bloodred Queen, and the only way to do that is to kill her. A few whispered stories that the German king might be alive—it's a lot to stake a future on. If there is even a future to be had. Doc still has to see if the apple can actually create a true cure to the disease. But we have no other options.

A gust of wind carries the hush through the branches of the trees, rustling the needles in the pine trees. I shiver in the breeze and at the tasks that still lie before us.

Pete cracks his neck. "Count us in. Just show me and the Lost Boys where to go."

Gwen hugs her knees and leans on their father. "I'm in," she says.

Doc scratches his unruly blond hair. "Me too."

Lily nods from next to him. "Count me in." Bella cheers in agreement.

Hunter smiles. "Brilliant! What about you, Alyssa? Maddox?"

Maddox reaches for my hand, and I marvel at its warmth and reassurance. Most of all, words cannot express my relief as I look into his golden eyes, which, although tired, are very much alive. Maddox squeezes my hand and pulls me to him. A burst of strength spreads through me as I look around the camp. And I see hope. There's still something worth hoping for.

"Down with the Bloodred Queen!" I say.

THE ADVENTURE COMES TO A
THRILLING CONCLUSION . . .

THE ONLY WAY HOME IS TO KILL THE WICKED.

OZLAND

WENDY SPINALE
AUTHOR OF *EVERLAND*

TURN THE PAGE FOR A SNEAK PEEK.

· GAIL ·

My breath rises in ghostly wisps into the cold evening air as I hold my position. Motionless. Silent. My arrow securely nocked and trained on the shoreline of the icy lake. It's after dusk, and winter has settled in early this year. The woolen cloak and gloves offer some warmth, but the chill bites the tips of my ears and nose. Still, my eyes remain fixed. The nightly cries of the youngest children, the ones that are nothing but flesh over bones, just skeletons really, shriek in my thoughts. They cry for their lost families, for the blistering pain riddled throughout their bodies as the new cure slowly heals them, for insatiable hunger; I can only help with the latter.

I'm the best of the hunters in my village, bringing in the most food out of all of us who take our weapons to the wilderness. But even so, my father, Hunter, our leader, has insisted I travel no farther than the forest's edge.

Beyond the body of water, red lights glow in pairs. They are the eyes of those that are neither human nor beast in these parts. No one has ventured past the lake and returned alive. Terrible creatures lie in wait within the dense forest. Describing them as terrible is generous. They hide in the shadows of the trees, their bodies camouflaged like chameleons—only, they've been known to snap a person in half with one bite from their powerful jaws.

The crackle of dry leaves draws my attention, but I remain still. Heart racing, sweat beading my forehead, I can't allow my fear to shake my resolve. Survival lies in what game I can bring home.

Under the glow of the moon, a shadow emerges from the tree line as the dead foliage rustles beneath the newcomer's feet. The wild sow lifts her snout into the cool evening air, in search of the slightest hint of danger. Although I've been careful, rubbing my clothes and body with oak leaves to cover my scent, my stomach twists, worried that it isn't enough. That my anxious heartbeat will divulge my location.

The sow snorts, as if declaring the area safe, before making her way to the water, only five meters from where I've taken cover.

My fingers twitch, but I don't shoot. Instead, I take in a breath. If I fire now and miss, that will be my only shot before the pig bolts back into the forest. I wait until the animal is lapping at the shoreline. Steadying the bowstring close to my cheek, I take aim.

As I'm about to take the shot, high-pitched squeals break the silence. Four piglets burst through the shrubbery and race to their mother's side on the lake's edge.

My breath catches, hesitancy paralyzing me. I lower my weapon and watch the offspring romp by the lake's edge. They are too young to be alone. With what else lives in these woods, they won't make it through the night. Not without their mother looking after them. Growling, my stomach reminds me that there are those depending on me. Yet, if I don't get back to the village soon, I also might not see the sun rise. It's either them or me.

Again, I take aim, my arrow fixed on the thick neck of the large sow, my hands steady as I pull the string taut.

It takes only a moment to recognize the familiar rumble of a menacing growl before one of the piglets is snatched up by a hideous claw. The poor animal hardly has time to squeal before it disappears into the shadows. My face grows cold as the crack of bones startles the rest of the pigs. Instinct takes over, and I keep my weapon aimed at the adult pig. But I don't have time to shoot. A Bandersnatch explodes from the trees, seizes the sow with its teeth and two of the remaining piglets with its claws. Only one escapes into the wild brush. The horrifying creature abandons the offspring and bulldozes into the trees, leaving behind splintered branches and uprooted shrubs. It takes seconds before the terrifying shrieks of the wild pigs cease, leaving the lakeside as quiet and desolate as it was when I arrived.

Cursing, I throw my bow over my head and quiver my arrow. Knowing the frightened squawks of the pigs have probably warned off any other nearby game, I pack up and take one last look at the shoreline. Everything is still. As I turn away, I hear a quiet whine.

Snatching my bow and an arrow, I target the bushes and find the young pig trembling beneath the lower branches. I drop my aim. Even if I kill it, there's not enough meat on the piglet to make a decent meal for one, much less an entire village. There's no point shooting it, at least not for now. Perhaps I could bring it home and fatten it up. It's better than going home empty-handed or leaving it alone to be eaten by predators. I sit cross-legged on the damp soil and reach inside my rucksack. Taking out some wild berries and nuts, I shake them in my hand.

"You hungry?" I ask.

The piglet cautiously steps forward before it hesitates. I toss a handful of food its way. Squealing, it dodges back into the brush.

"Chicken," I mutter.

The young pig watches as I pull out another fistful and snack on the meager morsels. It edges up to the closest berry with caution. With a guarded gaze set on me, the piglet devours the fruit and nuts. I coax the young pig toward me, holding out another palmful of food. When the warm snout nudges my hand, I pour the snack onto the forest floor. Hungrily, the piglet plunges its face into the pile. It flinches only once when I scratch behind its ear.

"What am I going to do with you?" I ask.

It peers up at me with chestnut eyes before returning to its meal. The piglet finishes off the food and begins chewing at the toe of my silver boot.

"Hey!" I say, pulling my foot away.

A roar rips through the trees. It's the same beastly howl that makes the ground tremor in the dead of night. The piglet sprints for my rucksack and cowers inside, rattling the unclipped metal buckle. My eyes dart upward, hoping the beast is too focused on its dinner to notice me, but I know it's only a matter of time before it picks up my scent.

As the growl dies out, echoing far into the forest, my surroundings become eerily quiet except for the howl of a lonely wolf. I let out a silent sigh, grateful that the Bandersnatch has gone on its way. Standing, I cradle my rucksack in my arms, ready to turn back to the village when the ground shakes again, but this time it is much more violent. Earth-shattering screams erupt from behind me—the Bandersnatch is back, and it's brought company.

I don't have enough time to draw my weapon. Instead, I just run.

The canopy of branches blocks out what little moonlight there is in the sky. I can't see where I'm going as I race between the large trunks of pine trees, dodging low-hanging branches. Twice I nearly fall, tripping over debris scattered throughout the forest floor. The piglet trembles within the leather bag clutched in my arms. The crack of tree limbs chases me like a violent thunderstorm, but I don't dare turn back to see how close the beasts are. Panting, I push my burning muscles as fast as they can go, knowing if I slow down even a little, the piglet won't be the Bandersnatches' only snack.

The Bandersnatches draw closer, and my legs grow tired. Panic riddles my body. I know I can't keep running much longer. Hiding is my only option.

Ahead, a large tree, its trunk almost a meter wide, comes into view. I slip around and press my back against the bark.

Gulping, I hold my breath, afraid that my panting will give away my location.

Three Bandersnatches roar as they sprint past me, and the gust of wind following them ruffles the stray pieces of hair that have fallen from my braids. The younger trees snap like twigs as the beasts burst through the forest. When their long, spiked tails are no longer in my line of sight, I let out the breath I was holding in a cloud of mist. It won't be long before they return. I need somewhere to hunker down until they've given up their search for me.

The pale hue of a rocky hill catches my attention. If it wasn't for the small amount of moonlight casting through a break in the trees, I never would have seen it. Taking one last glance at the destruction the Bandersnatches have left behind, I head toward the stone wall. It doesn't take long for me to find a series of caves. With the chill in the air, more than likely this network of alcoves is a home to a bear or wildcat. But I'd rather deal with a dozen bears than even one Bandersnatch.

Scrambling over the uneven stones, I choose a smaller hollow, hoping that the carnivorous wildlife would opt for someplace a bit roomier.

On one hand and both knees, I clutch my rucksack and crawl through the entrance. The damp soil soaks through my pants as I creep to the back of the cave. Finally, I sit and lean up against the stone wall, thankful for the chill it brings. I inhale deeply, trying to slow my breath. It is the squirm within my satchel that pulls my attention from the anxiety boiling in me.

Reaching inside the bag, the piglet rubs its warm snout against my hand as I search for a candle and matches. Lighting the beeswax candlestick and tucking it into a crevice in the wall, the cavern brightens. Small bones, tufts of fur, and feathers litter the rock-and-dirt floor. Based on the size of the scat, whatever lives in here can't be any bigger than a fox. Relieved, I sigh and watch the shadows dance across the gray rock.

"It's your lucky day, Gail," I mutter aloud.

The piglet peeks out of the bag and tilts its head, as if listening intently.

"Seems today is lucky for both of us," I say, scratching its soft pink ear.

With a single snort, the piglet circles my lap and flops down, lying on its side.

"How can you possibly nap after all that?"

The animal doesn't seem to hear me, but instead breathes deep and slow, lost somewhere in its dreams.

Another roar echoes in the distance. The Bandersnatch may not be outside the cave entrance, but I'm not taking any risks. Not tonight, at least. Besides, I'm suddenly drowsy, my eyelids weighted down by the aftereffects of an adrenaline rush. As the candle flickers, fighting to stay lit, I close my eyes and surrender to the lull of sleep.

Prepare for an awfully big adventure...

ACKNOWLEDGMENTS

Umberland would have never come to fruition without the love, support, and encouragement of so many.

My three sons continue to be a source of inspiration and joy. Thank you, Gavin, Keaton, and Riley for being the perfect cup of tea in my life. You all make me proud.

Stu, thank you for believing in me.

Again, I wouldn't be here today without the love and constant support of my family, especially the king and queen of my heart, my mom and dad. I appreciate all the ways you've encouraged me these last few years. Also, much love to my in-laws, Bob and Harriet.

To my awesome BBB's critique group, Jennifer Fosberry, Erika Gardner, Amy Moellering, Cameron Sullivan, Georgia Choate, and Jerie Jacobs. Without the ongoing support of my Bacon Babes, Alyssa and her peeps would be only a mad thought in my head.

I can't leave out my sweet online critique partners, Ashley Hearn and Monica Hoffman. I cannot wait to celebrate your very own book launches.

To my closest and biggest fans, Department 384. Our days working for the Mouse continue to be a source of inspiration. I miss the tea parties.

Jones, I'm simply mad about you. Thank you for being my beta reader.

To Ed Westmoreland and the staff at Eddie Papa's, thank you for the office space (the high-top table near the few outlets). And for letting me come back after I accidently dined and ditched that one time. By the way, I tipped 25 percent when I came back to pay the bill.

I had no idea how many cogs in the big publishing machine it took to bring a book together. Again, my rock stars at Sandra Dijkstra Literary Agency and Scholastic have done an amazing job in contributing to the creation of another beautiful book.

My incredible agent, Thao Le, and the Sandra Dijkstra Literary Agency team members, Andrea Cavallaro and Jennifer Kim—where would I be without my Dream Team? Words will never express how much I appreciate all that you do for me.

Jody Corbett, my beautimous (Yes, this is a word! Just go with it!) editor at Scholastic, can I just keep you forever and ever? I'm eternally grateful for the ways you push me to create a better story, even when my stubborn Irish Italian side wants to dig my steampunk boot heels in. The Everland series wouldn't be as special as it is without you.

Where do I start with the rest of my fantastic team at Scholastic? Thank you doesn't seem to say enough. My appreciation goes out to the sales team, including Elizabeth Whiting,

Alexis Lunsford, Annette Hughes, Chris Satterlund, Betsy Politi, Jackie Ruben, Jody Stigliano, Meaghan Hilton, Sue Flynn, Nikki Mutch, and Charlie Young. Special thanks to Roz Hilden, my Bay Area rep, the sweetest lady in the whole world who puts up with my shenanigans during events.

And where would I be without the creative Scholastic marketing and publicity super duo, Rachel Feld and Brooke Shearouse? You two are amazing, and I'm grateful for all you do for me.

The talented designer and art director extraordinaire, Christopher Stengel is the brilliant brain behind the gorgeous covers on *Everland*, *Umberland*, and *Lost Boy*. I curtsy to your skill.

And of course, many thanks to those at Scholastic who continue to provide ongoing support, including David Levithan, Tracy van Straaten, and Lizette Serrano. Also, I must send love out to Lori Benton, John Pels, and Paul Gagnes, who handle all things audio books.

Last, but hardly least, special thanks to the original storytellers, J. M. Barrie and Lewis Carroll. The world would be less magical without *Peter and Wendy* or *Alice's Adventures in Wonderland*.

ABOUT THE AUTHOR

Wendy Spinale is a former character actor for the Disneyland theme park (so she is very familiar with the world of make-believe). She is the author of the Everland trilogy, including *Everland*, *Umberland*, and *Ozland*, as well as the prequel novella, *Lost Boy*.

Wendy lives with her family in the San Francisco Bay Area.